PICTURE PERFECT

OTHER BOOKS BY BEVERLY KING:

Christmas by the Book

PICTURE PERFECT

a novel

BEVERLY KING

Covenant Communications, Inc.

Published by Covenant Communications, Inc.
American Fork, Utah

Printed in the United States of America
First Printing: January 2001

08 07 06 05 04 03 02 01   10 9 8 7 6 5 4 3 2 1

ISBN 1-57734-791-9

In memory of my mother,
my own special Emma,
and for my father,
the handsome sheriff.

CHAPTER 1

The faint rays of December sun couldn't dispel the gloominess of the day or lift Jillian Taylor's spirits. Clutching her coat around her tall, thin figure with one hand, she gripped the handrail tightly with the other and descended from the plane. As she neared the glass door of the Idaho Falls airport, she glimpsed Frank Ross, her father's best friend.

Wondering if he'd even recognize her after all this time, she waved. She made her way inside the airport, and he strode toward her. Tentatively, she reached out her arms for a hug, but his face stopped her cold. Skipping over the pleasantries, he got right to the point. "Give me your claim checks, Jillian, and I'll get your luggage."

Her heart fell at the terseness of his statements, and she flushed. His anger at her for not being with her father when he died had obviously not lessened in the last forty-eight hours since his abrupt phone call. He'd informed her that he had been trying to reach her for two days, her father had died, and the funeral was set for today. Jillian had hoped the hours since their phone conversation would have softened his feelings a little, but from the tone of his voice, it didn't sound like it.

Wary of anything else Frank might say, Jillian quickly dug in her purse, found the three claim tickets, and handed them to him. Then she followed him to the luggage carousel and waited silently for her bags to be delivered.

"There." She pointed at the two tan leather Louis Vuitton suitcases and the canvas garment bag. When she'd bought them eight years before, they'd been expensive but the absolute best. Now although she traveled constantly and they were becoming worn, they still said *money*. Appearances were everything in her present life, now more than ever.

Once in the parking lot Frank hefted the bags into the back of an SUV. It was certainly nothing flashy, but it was a vehicle that Frank probably found convenient for driving from Quail Creek to his law office in Idaho Falls. He held the door for her to get in but remained a silent, implacable study in stoicism.

Jillian was determined that the ninety-minute ride to Quail Creek would not be spent in sullen silence. Besides, she wanted to know more about her father's death. Oh, how she wished she had been with him. The thought sent tears rushing to her eyes.

"What caused Daddy's death?" she asked, biting her bottom lip to control its trembling.

Frank's voice was curt. "He had another heart attack."

"A-Another heart attack?" Jillian clasped her hands together tightly. "You mean he'd had one before? When?"

"His first one was two years ago."

"Two years ago?" Not once had her father ever indicated he was having health problems. How could he have kept something like this a secret? Humiliating as it would have been to admit she was washed up as a model, not even her pride would have kept her away if she'd known. She closed her eyes, attempting to take his words in.

Frank's tone was unforgiving. "He worked too hard. The doctors told him for years to take it easy, but not Jed. He was determined to make the farm pay, and he wouldn't slack off. Tell me, Jillian, what exactly were you doing that was so important you couldn't come back and help your father?"

"I—I—didn't know he needed help," she admitted slowly. What exactly *had* she been doing that was more worthwhile than being with her father when he needed her? The answer was nothing. For the last two years her life had been a succession of parties—rock concerts, theater parties, house parties, yacht parties, the operable word being "parties." Had she been so busy making her dad think she was still successful that she hadn't heard what he'd said to her? She thought back. He had urged her to come home, but he'd never mentioned his health.

Frank's lips curled in disgust. "Did you ever ask him if he needed you? Did you even offer to come back?" He fairly spat the words at her, as if her actions had angered him for a long time and he had finally been given the chance to air his grievances.

"No," Jillian whispered. She hadn't. She was too busy trying to keep her father from finding out that her modeling career was in ruins, and she had no money left. How had she managed to go from having her name on everybody's lips to being mentioned only in the tabloids? Her father had asked her to come home, but she couldn't—wouldn't—until she could return in glory. Any day now, she'd told herself repeatedly. Any day she'd be in demand again. But she'd been wrong. "No," she repeated sadly.

"Just what I thought." Censure hardened his voice.

Closing her eyes, Jillian slumped back in the corner of the seat. Jed Taylor had always seemed so strong, so permanent to her. Even half a world away, he had been the pillar she'd always tied her life to. Now he was gone and she'd never again be able to tell her father how much she loved him. And she'd never even known anything was wrong. How had her relationship with her father deteriorated to the point that she hadn't been able to tell him she was a failure? That she was no longer the same girl who'd left Quail Creek. That she hadn't attended church in years and cared nothing for the beliefs her parents held dear.

Sorrow for her loss and guilt at her neglect washed over her as images of the past filled her mind. She saw herself as a carefree child growing up in Quail Creek on the farm. Then as a young girl, sitting between her parents in church. As a young woman, helping her mother can fruit each summer and admiring their labors, those glistening bottles full of applesauce, peaches, and her favorite of all, pears. In the winter they sat around the kitchen table while her father read them mysteries. They had started with the adventures of Nancy Drew and the Hardy Boys; then over the years they'd graduated to Agatha Christie. Jillian still loved reading mysteries.

She thought of school and Randy, her high school sweetheart, and her other friends. What fun they had had growing up together—hiking and swimming in the summer, skiing in the winter. She'd had a close group of friends and they'd done everything together in high school. They'd been so thrilled for her the night she was crowned Junior Prom Queen, and she'd thought she'd die of happiness.

Not long after that, she'd won the Idaho Falls ZCMI teen advisory board contest. Even now, over ten years later, she could still recall her stunned feeling of disbelief when she was awarded a trip to New York City to appear in an issue of *Seventeen* magazine. To her surprise, she had also been chosen to appear on the cover. By the end of her two weeks in "the City," Quail Creek had faded into the shadow of a distant memory. She hadn't wanted to go home. She needed to be there, where she could become established as a model, and she was set on returning as soon as possible.

At home she begged her parents to let her go back to New York. After months of discussion, they reluctantly agreed, feeling that their daughter was more mature than most sixteen-year-olds and well-founded in the gospel. Her mother telephoned the bishop of the Manhattan ward as well as the director of the modeling agency that *Seventeen* magazine had recommended. When Jillian agreed to their stringent guidelines, they made the decision to let their only daughter move to New York City.

Jillian had lived in a brownstone duplex with the Nelsons, an LDS family the bishop had referred her mother to. Jack Nelson managed a mutual fund for an investment house. Mimi Nelson was personnel director of a bank. They both had high-powered jobs, but they were still very family-oriented. Their four children were all in college, and they welcomed having a teenager with them. She attended church eagerly every Sunday, where she quickly made friends.

Her new school had over two thousand students compared to the one hundred and twenty students at Quail Creek High, but Jillian had exulted in the wide array of interesting classes compared to her old school's limited and basic courses. Nevertheless, she lived for her afternoons, when she had modeling assignments after school.

The next year had been both elating and educational. She worked harder than she'd ever done before, managing to keep her grades up although she worked nearly every afternoon. She missed her parents and spent Christmas and spring vacation with them. The summer after she graduated, she'd had little time to spend in Quail Creek. Her modeling career was taking off, and she wanted to take advantage of the demand for her; Quail Creek seemed an eternity away. Once her mother had gone on a shoot with her to Bali and they'd had a terrific time together. Over the next year, although she and her parents managed barely a half a dozen visits, they talked on the phone frequently, keeping up to date with all the latest happenings.

Then Jillian had received the phone call that changed everything. It was from her father; her mother was ill and not expected to live more than a few months. Jillian had flown home immediately, and the three of them had proceeded to spend an unforgettable summer together. The Taylor family had gone for long, leisurely drives, picnicking and reminiscing about their life together. Although Jillian was only eighteen and had no thought of getting married, her mother had given her an endless supply of marital advice in her usual witty way, knowing she wouldn't be there for that day.

After her mother's death in the fall, Jillian would have stayed home with her father, but he insisted she resume her career since it meant so much to her. She hadn't needed much prodding, and now her heart ached to think how she'd abandoned her father to his own grief.

On her return to New York, Jillian had decided to get her own apartment, her second big mistake after leaving her father alone. She'd made friends with other models whose values weren't the same as hers. She told herself that she could be a good example to them, but she hadn't changed them; she had let them change her.

In no time at all she had left behind most of the things she'd been taught as a girl in Idaho. She'd gone to Paris for more modeling experience, where she'd done her first runway show. Supremely confident of her abilities, she hadn't felt a moment's fear, only excitement at being a part of the couture shows. Her natural exuberance had given her a distinctive flair for runway work. The designers loved her.

This time when she returned to New York, she was a different Jillian than she'd been as a newcomer from Idaho. She met a new "hip" crowd; she liked being with them and the feeling was mutual. She had a knack for getting herself noticed, and at nineteen, she appeared on the cover of *People* magazine. They'd done an article on her, and among other things, told how she had grown up in Idaho, won a trip to New York, and become an internationally recognized model and a familiar face on the New York party scene. According to the article, New Yorkers were enchanted with her Idaho-isms, like "yippy-skippy," "Rave on, White Fang," "sweet treat," and "fetchin',"" which were liberally sprinkled throughout her conversation. After that, the gossip columns inevitably mentioned her name, and people never failed to recognized her. With no one to rein her in, she started to believe her own heady publicity—that her beauty and personality were new and exciting. Of course, it never occurred to her that her time in the spotlight would be so fleeting.

Cocky from her smashing success in Italy, she decided to find a different model agency, one who matched her new image. To her delight she hooked up with Simon Grant, a superficial self-centered man, master of the caustic putdown. Her high-profile life brought her to the attention of a major cosmetic company, and she became their spokeswoman. They created a new perfume named for her: Jillian.

It had seemed that life couldn't get better than this.

Maybe not, but it certainly could get worse. When her popularity began to dim, sales of the perfume plummeted, and before she knew it, the company had canceled her contract and dropped the perfume. Simon dumped her.

Now she was in this sorry place in her life, too broke to even come home for her father's funeral.

Shielding her face from Frank, Jillian angled her body towards the window and took a deep breath to suppress the despair that threatened to engulf her. She'd never felt so alone.

The only thing left was the farm. The farm. Her spirits lifted slightly. Maybe she could expiate her failure to her father by doing something with the property to help others, perhaps start a boys' ranch. Her dad had always had a soft spot for troubled teenage boys. If she could find a manager, he could run the place and have the boys help. Her dad always swore that no one raised on a farm got into trouble. Farm life gave stability.

When the funeral was over, she'd take a few days to think things over. Maybe in the peaceful and calm surroundings of her childhood home, she could figure out a way to resurrect her career. She didn't doubt that she would return to New York, but this time it would not be to the empty life she'd chosen before. She'd learned some hard lessons from her mistakes. Now that was behind her, and she was ready to start fresh.

Even if she could do something useful with the farm, she didn't anticipate staying in Quail Creek more than a few days a year to see how it was running. She'd lived in the small town until she was sixteen, and when she had left, she'd seen a whole new world. She'd seen the Greek Parthenon by moonlight, attended the opera in Italy, explored Mayan ruins in Central America, spent a fabulous week in Bali, and ridden a camel at the Pyramids, all in the name of work. The people in Quail Creek were old friends, but she felt as if she had nothing in common with them anymore.

Still, she thought, it would be nice to see some of the old crowd again. She sighed deeply and rolled her neck around to ease the tension she'd felt for the last several hours. Her movement seemed to act as a reminder to Frank that she was there and that he had more to tell her.

"They're not bringing Jed's body to the ward for the viewing until noon. So I'll run you on home." Frank swung off the highway at the Quail Creek exit. A half mile later she glimpsed the church through the pines, then Myrna's Diner and Ben's Country Store and Service Station. A sudden rush of happiness filled her. It felt good to be home again.

Fifteen minutes later they rounded the hill, and at sight of the family home, Jillian's breath caught as her heart lurched. She hadn't realized how much she'd missed the farm. She blinked back tears. Before Frank could even bring the car to a complete stop, she had the door open. Never had any place looked so good. She shook her head in disbelief. How could she have avoided coming back here all this time?

Quickly sliding out of Frank's car, she walked past the Douglas fir trees and up the snowy path, letting herself savor the permanence of the farm, the house, the feeling that she was truly where she belonged. Maybe that was the answer—to stay in Quail Creek after all—a surprising thought, which she set aside to consider later. Pulling herself away from the beckoning promise of home, she returned to the car to help Frank with her luggage. He unlocked the door to the house and held open the screen.

"What a tragic end to Jed's life. Buried one day, his farm auctioned off the next." He gave a bitter laugh. "I thought surely you'd save it." His eyes looked at her accusingly.

The familiar room spun crazily, and Jillian struggled to grasp the meaning of his words. "Auctioned off?" she repeated numbly.

"Don't try to fool me, Jillian. You must've known your father was on the verge of losing his farm, and with all your money, you never lifted a finger to help him." He narrowed his eyes in disgust. "You were too busy cruising around the world with your friends."

Unexpectedly, her legs turned to jelly and she sank into the nearest chair. This was unbelievable! She couldn't take it in. After all these years, to come home and find everything gone—her dad, the farm, her entire life. Had the suffering he'd felt at losing the family farm and the loneliness of having no close family with him caused his heart attack? She hadn't known a thing about his health problems and certainly not his financial woes. She'd telephoned her father every month, as if to infuse herself with his strength, and he'd never even hinted anything was wrong. Why hadn't he told her? She knew why. She knew exactly why. The wretched, despicable Taylor pride. And she was equally guilty of it.

Her stomach churned and for a minute she thought she was going to be physically ill. Pride had kept her from admitting to her father that she was finished as a model, that she didn't even have enough money to get home. Now her pride had cost her everything. Her father had supported her dreams and subsidized her living expenses in New York until she could pay her own way. But in his time of need, she'd let him down. Regret tightened her throat as she fought back the tears. Nothing she could say would soften Frank's attitude. She was guilty as charged. Lifting her quivering chin, she said, "I'm sorry."

He went on, as if she hadn't spoken. "Breaking your father's heart is a pretty mean business. I wish he'd had other children to care about him."

For a moment a flash of fear crowded out her grief as Jillian absorbed Frank's harsh words without responding. What was she going to do? Even though she hadn't planned to remain in Quail Creek, she'd only borrowed enough money from her friends for a one-way ticket, automatically assuming her father would have left some assets behind. Now she didn't have enough money to leave. She cringed at the foolish thought she'd had of using the farm as a memorial for her father.

However much she hated to further this conversation with Frank, she had to know where she stood. Surely there would be something left so she could start over.

"What will the estate be worth after the auction?" she asked.

"What estate?" Frank snorted. "Your father was so far in debt, his bills will barely be cleared after everything is sold. He was like most farmers; he borrowed when land value was high, and he used everything he owned as collateral, including the household furnishings. When the farm market fell, he couldn't cover his losses. After the auction, it'll all be gone."

Jillian stared at him, stunned. She couldn't speak.

Frank shrugged and turned away. "I expect you won't be hanging around Quail Creek for long," he said over his shoulder as he walked toward the front door.

CHAPTER 2

Jillian's heart stopped, and for a moment she couldn't breathe. She closed her eyes to halt the sudden tears, then after a moment opened them and looked longingly around at the room filled with memories. Her gaze caught the antique breakfront that had been in the family for over a hundred years. Handmade by her mother's great-grandfather out of poplar wood, her mother had dusted it each day, polishing it carefully on Saturday. Every time he was upset, her dad would yank open the drawer that spanned the buffet part. . . . She forced herself to look away and her eyes moved over the worn green recliner and matching sofa, the wooden shelves stuffed haphazardly with books of every description.

"Wait!" she called after him. "Would it be all right if I took something of my mother's?" She heard the pleading note in her voice but didn't seem able to control it.

"Sorry. It's a little late." He sounded anything but sorry. She could see that in his estimation, she was getting exactly what she deserved. Nothing. "The bank has inventoried everything."

She hated to ask. "Don't I get . . . anything?"

"No." His one word was definite and final.

Jillian flinched. Frank's words stung, and without a supreme effort on her part, she would have crumbled. But her pride refused to let her show any sign of weakness. She had hidden her fears for so long that her immediate impulse was to shrug and say something outrageous. In fact, it was right on the tip of her tongue to say flippantly, "Win some, lose some," but she didn't want to increase his animosity towards her.

His lips tightened. "I'll pick you up about 11:30 for the viewing."

"No, thank you," she said quietly. "I can get there myself." Surely either the car or the old truck was still running. Even if she had to walk the entire ten miles to town, she wasn't going with Frank. Although she understood the reason for his anger and knew it masked his grief at her father's death, the past couple of hours in his presence had only emphasized her own loneliness, sorrow, and guilt. Her father would no doubt have wanted her to go with his friend, but she simply couldn't. This day was proving difficult enough without enduring any more of Frank's hostility. She was nearly overcome with the need for a friend in her despair, but she knew that someone as judgmental as Frank could never meet her need.

He shrugged and strode out the front door, leaving her alone with her grief and shock. The second he left she collapsed, falling back limply into the chair, the emotions she'd held so tightly erupting into sobs. The house felt so very empty, and save for the sounds of her weeping, so very quiet. Her father was gone. And she'd never have a chance to tell him she loved him. With tears streaming down her pale cheeks, she gave herself over to the grief. There was no thinking, no planning for the future, just the searing pain of her loss.

At last, the tears ceased. She took a quivery breath and brushed her eyes and cheeks with her fingers. "What am I going do?" she said aloud.

Forcing herself to ignore the memories the house evoked, Jillian pulled herself up wearily from the chair and rummaged through her suitcases for fresh underclothes. She would need to hurry if she wanted to get to the church early enough to spend some time alone with her father and say her final good-byes. In the bathroom she shed her clothes and stepped into the shower, letting the grime of the last two days wash away.

After her shower, she dried herself off and put on her lingerie, then retrieved her make-up case from the living room and set it on the bathroom vanity. She glanced into the mirror reluctantly, knowing what she would see there. Where was America's most beautiful face? Not staring back at her, that was for sure. The face in the mirror was too thin, too gaunt. Dark circles ringed her emerald eyes, and her face appeared drawn. Even her trademark long thick hair seemed dull, evidence of too many late nights, too many house parties.

But all of that was in the past. When she returned to New York—and she was determined that she would—she would approach it all differently this time. Exactly how she would do that, she didn't yet know, nor did she have any idea how she would even get there. She'd get through the funeral first, then she'd figure out what to do next.

Taking out her concealer, she erased the circles and the lines on her face. She carefully applied foundation, added blush and lipstick to give some life to her wan face, and finished off with a smudge of smoky eye shadow and several layers of black and green mascara. Finally, she twisted her silvery-blonde hair into a knot at the back of her head.

She reached for her black woolen dress—a Ralph Lauren—and slipped into it, then pulled on her red cashmere coat, bundling up against the freezing temperatures of Idaho's December weather. The car keys were where her father always kept them, on a nail behind the kitchen door.

Once she left the house, the frigid air blasted right through her coat. Her teeth chattered with the cold as she picked her way between the snow-covered patches of grass to her dad's car. Luckily the cold weather hadn't sapped the battery's life, and after she pumped her foot on the gas a few times, the engine caught. It had been such a long time since she'd driven a car that the steering wheel and gear shift felt awkward.

Leaning forward, she rested her head on her arms, waiting for the motor to warm up. When the engine appeared to be running smoothly, she took her foot off the gas so she could shift. The engine died. But it started again easily enough, and she sighed with relief. As she attempted to ease forward, the car jolted the first few yards; then, with hands tight on the steering wheel and foot steady on the accelerator, Jillian drove out of the yard and down the road.

—m—

At the ward house, with the help of the funeral director, she found her way to the Relief Society room. The building must have been constructed after the summer she'd spent here with her mother. The family never missed a meeting until the very end when her mother was too ill to attend. By this time Jillian's high school friends had scattered, and she had no one to socialize with, which was fine with her. No one was more important than her mother and father. She wanted to spend all her time with them.

Inside the Relief Society room, the polished mahogany casket stood in the alcove on the far wall. It was surrounded by a half dozen large sprays of flowers. At the sight of the flowers, her heart fell. She hadn't even considered the matter of flowers, and she certainly hadn't thought to mention them to Frank. But across the bottom of the casket lay a large arrangement of red roses with a wide ribbon that said "Loving Father" on it. Someone had remembered.

Standing beside the casket, she peered down at her father. Although his weather-beaten face seemed at peace, she felt a great heaviness settle over her. *Oh, Dad . . . I'm so sorry. If only I had . . .* An older man stepped beside her, interrupting her self-recriminations. She thought he seemed vaguely familiar. He held out his hand to shake hers.

"You remember me, don't you, Jillian?" he said. "I'm Bishop Walker. I'm glad you made it here safely, and I want to offer you my deepest regrets for your loss." She nodded, not speaking, as he held a paper out to her. "I wanted you to see the program. It's not too late to make any changes you'd like. When Frank wasn't able to reach you earlier, we went ahead with the arrangements, in case we couldn't find you."

"Thanks." Her voice a near whisper, Jillian took a program from his outstretched hand and started reading it. Starla Peterson, whoever she was, was going to sing "Whispering Hope." She felt a rush of gratitude that Frank had acknowledged her last-minute request for her father's favorite song. She read over the names of the speakers; except for the bishop's name, none of them sounded familiar.

The bishop's face was sympathetic. "Everyone thought so much of your father it was hard to know who to have speak. Frank wanted the stake president, and he agreed to speak. He admired your father greatly. But if you have someone special—" He left the question hanging.

She shook her head. "No, this seems fine." *I just want to be alone with my father.*

As if he understood, the bishop patted her shoulder and moved away. Jillian turned gratefully back to look down at the man who'd done so much for her, who had loved her and believed in her so unconditionally. How could he be gone?

Tears filled her eyes. *I wish I'd been here for you,* she choked back her sobs. *I'm sorry I let you down. I should have come home when you asked me to.* If she'd really tried, she could have found a way. But no, she admitted almost angrily to herself, she hadn't wanted to come until she could come in style, and then it had been too late. Now she'd never see him alive again. All because of her foolish, useless pride. She struggled to hold back her sobs, and her throat burned from the effort.

How will I ever get along without you? Who will believe in me? She stroked his hand tenderly. *What am I going to do now?*

"Jillian?" The sound of her name wrenched her back to the moment, and she realized that her time alone with her father had ended. People had started to arrive and wanted to offer their condolences. With great effort, she composed her features before turning to see who had spoken.

"Randy!" Her sudden delight was unfeigned. Randy Prescott had been her high school boyfriend and one of the nicest boys she'd ever known. He wrapped his arms around her, and she let herself enjoy the comfort of his arms. They'd been great friends, and if she'd stayed in Quail Creek, they would have undoubtedly married.

"Gosh, it's wonderful to see you." He grinned boyishly. Then as if remembering the reason, his face grew somber. "Although I wish it hadn't taken your father's death to get you back."

His arms felt good, and she clung to him a moment longer before releasing herself and giving him a shaky smile.

"I wish it hadn't either," she agreed, her voice unsteady.

"Not that we haven't seen all the pictures of you in magazines, but there's something about having you here in person." His eyes gazed at her admiringly and she allowed herself to enjoy it. Randy's frank, appreciative look was welcome balm to her bruised feelings right now.

A crisp no-nonsense voice cut between them. "I see you made it, Jillian. We were afraid you wouldn't."

Although a small, fragile-looking woman, Randy's mother had a formidable presence. For all her delicate airs, Helen Prescott had exerted a rather tight rein on her son when he and Jillian were dating. Right now she was smiling, but Jillian could find no real warmth in her expression. Nevertheless, she held out her hand.

"Mrs. Prescott, it's good of you to come."

Other ward members gathered to offer their condolences, and Jillian was relieved to move toward them and away from Mrs. Prescott. She thanked them all for their concern, for their friendship toward her father, for being there for him when she had not been.

As she glanced at the next person, her gaze froze and she could feel the blood drain from her face. Luke Prescott, Randy's cousin.

Tall, lean, and tanned in the middle of winter, it was obvious that he spent a great deal of time outdoors. She'd forgotten how handsome he was. More than just handsome. She'd spent the last ten years dealing with handsome men on a daily basis, and Luke's face, beneath thick, dark hair, was simply extraordinary. And he was tall, at least three to four inches taller than her 5'10".

Luke was four years older than his cousin Randy and nothing like him. Jillian had always felt comfortable and secure with Randy, but Luke . . . he'd always intimidated her with his scornful attitude. He had been the one boy in Quail Creek who'd always acted as if she were nothing special, just a run-of-the-mill farm girl.

Now he gave her that familiar mocking smile, his eyes alight with a speculative gleam as if he had swiftly taken her measure and found her sadly wanting. She felt fourteen years old all over again.

"Luke Prescott." She kept her voice calm and deliberate.

"The famous Jillian."

On the surface, his words were cordial enough, but Jillian heard the challenge. Then he held out his hand. Feeling vulnerable, she hesitated before stretching hers out, but to her amazement she found comfort in his warm handshake.

His voice was unexpectedly kind. "I know how hard this is. My father passed away a few years ago. It takes a while to get over the emptiness of losing your only parent."

Jillian nodded slowly. "It's particularly difficult right now because I'd left so much unsaid," she admitted.

"That does make it tough. One consolation though," he said sympathetically, "your father was a good man who will be missed by the entire community."

His kindness made her uncomfortable and she looked away. "Is your wife with you?" she asked, trying to deflect his attention from her. But there were no women close by who looked like his type.

"Oh, I'm still single." His lips twitched humorously and his tone was ironic. This was the Luke she remembered. "You?"

She stared at him. He knew darn well she wasn't. Her marriage was something her dad would never have kept quiet about. Attempting to shrug nonchalantly, she kept her voice cool. "Flitting around the world on modeling assignments doesn't leave time for a husband."

"I can imagine," Luke responded, his tone matching hers. "I'd better move on now so you can speak to everyone. But later on I want you to tell me all about life in the big city."

Jillian stared after him. Sure he did, she thought. She could feel his disdain in every word. Some things never changed and evidently Luke Prescott was one of them.

After everyone had gone into the chapel, leaving behind Jillian, the bishop, and a few close friends, Frank offered the family prayer. His words gave voice to her grief, and after the prayer, she reached over and grasped her dad's hands for the last time. "Good-bye, Dad," she whispered, then the funeral director closed the casket.

—m—

In the chapel, the organist concluded the prelude music as Bishop Walker stepped toward the podium. "Today we have met to honor and to remember our brother, Jedediah Taylor," he said, then explained the program they would follow. The only Mormon funeral Jillian could remember attending was her mother's; she had forgotten what they were like.

After the prayer, the stake president stood. "Few people have made an impact on the world with one singular momentous event," he began, "but numerous individuals have done so through consistent, day-to-day Christlike living. We have lost a giant of a man this week. One who lived a truly Christlike life. The scriptures say, 'Love your neighbor as yourself.' Jed always went out of his way to help others; no one's problem was too large or too small. When people were in need in the community, he made certain they received assistance. I doubt anyone feared asking him for help."

Jillian shook her head sadly. Why had she alone been afraid of asking for help? She bowed her head and looked down, feeling very alone.

"Jed was the epitome of a record keeper. He hunted down membership records and searched diligently to find people whose records he had, but who seemed somehow to be 'lost.' When new clerks were called in other wards, we always referred them to Jed for help.

"Every year he received commendations from the Presiding Bishopric's Office on his outstanding recording of the history of the ward.

"When records became computerized, he learned everything he needed to do. He loved the new technology."

Her father loved computers? When had that happened? Jillian swallowed hard. She'd been so busy trying to cover up her life, she hadn't thought to ask him what was happening in his.

"Jed Taylor had a firm testimony of the gospel and of the plan of salvation. His life was a shining light to others seeking to know the truth."

Jillian had known this; her father had always been quick to speak of his blessings, of his gratitude for the gospel.

"In the premortal world, we dwelled as spirit children with our Father in Heaven. We eagerly anticipated coming to earth and gaining a physical body. Alma tells us that this life is the time to prepare to meet God. We knew that coming here carried risks because we would have our agency, and we would be held accountable for our actions. But we were anxious to prove ourselves, so we might be in our Father's presence for the eternities."

And what had she proved? She was beautiful, reckless, unwise. More like a grasshopper than an ant. Her lips curved into a wry smile, then, hearing her name, she looked up at the speaker.

"I know how hard this will be on you, Jillian, but for your father this is a joyous occasion. For life does not begin at birth or end with death. Though we are sad not to have Jed with us anymore, he has at last been reunited with his beloved Annie and other members of his family who have gone before him."

The words hung in the air around her. Her mother and dad reunited, her grandmothers with them. She'd forgotten that this was one of the teachings of the Church. For the first time in years, she remembered that when she had left Quail Creek after her mother's death, she had resolved to do everything in her power to be with her mother again. But it hadn't been long before that was the farthest thing from her mind. She was kept so busy modeling, showing up at all the right parties and at all the "in" clubs that her resolution slipped right out of her mind in a matter of months. Her mother and father might have a joyous reunion, but Jillian doubted she'd ever be there with them. For the first time in public she couldn't hold the tears back. She barely heard the speaker's final words.

". . . May each of you live your life just a little bit better, in remembrance of how Jed lived his . . . amen."

The organist began to play and soon the sweet tones of the soloist floated through the chapel and swirled around Jillian.

Wait till the darkness is over, wait till the tempest is gone,
Hope for the sunshine tomorrow, after the shower is gone.
Whispering hope . . .

And what of the darkness in her life? Would it ever subside? Jillian reached in her purse and put on her dark glasses. She felt she could not bear for anyone to see her eyes, to know how unbearable it was for her to lose her father in this way. Her mother's death had been painful, but her father's solid presence had shielded her from the loss. Now he was gone, and she was alone.

At the cemetery, while she waited for everyone to arrive, Jillian inspected the family headstone. *Anne and Jedediah Taylor,* then their birth dates and her mother's death date were carved in the rose-colored granite. At the bottom was *Sealed together for eternity in the Idaho Falls Temple.*

She looked around at the crowd of mourners who stood shivering in the cold. Some of the people had made little attempt to mask their hostility toward her. Did they blame her for her father's financial problems, she wondered, or did they resent her apparent modeling success? If only they knew. Her life was nothing to envy, and she had become increasingly and painfully aware of just how empty her life was.

When Frank started to dedicate the grave, panic gripped her, and she felt as if she were suffocating. What was she going to do now? The thought of returning to her acquaintances on the yacht sent waves of nausea curling through her stomach. Who could she turn to? Even God must have given up on her by now.

A gray mist enveloped her. The next moment the ground tilted and her legs wobbled. She reached out blindly to the nearest arm to keep from falling as she felt her knees buckle beneath her.

Strong arms caught her. Looking up, she saw that it was Luke Prescott.

"Take some deep breaths. This will be over in a minute, and then you can sit down."

Through the rough texture of his camel overcoat, she could feel the beating of his heart. He exuded strength and substance, a haven from the tenuousness of her future. The fog around her began to clear and she attempted to stand on her own. But Luke only tightened his hold and she didn't resist. His arms felt wonderful, and for the first time in months—years?—she felt safe.

The thought sent a jolt of alarm through her. Was she crazy? How could she possibly feel safe in Luke Prescott's arms? And of all people to see her weakness, he was absolutely her last choice. She'd never trusted him and she was afraid that sooner or later this episode was sure to come back and haunt her. She stiffened as if to pull away but Luke held her firmly beside him.

At the sound of the final "amen," Bishop Walker announced that a luncheon had been prepared back at the church for those who wanted a chance to visit with Jillian. Releasing her slightly so he could step back and look down at her, he asked quietly, "Will you be all right at the church?"

Though she had tried to free herself of his arms, she now felt bereft of his strength. She would have liked to deny she felt better, but instead said, "I'm fine. I just want to hear what people remember about my father." Who knew where she might be tomorrow? This might be her last chance to talk with his friends.

Still holding Jillian's arm, Luke walked with her to the limousine provided by the mortuary. She'd assumed he'd ride back to the church with the others, but instead he got in beside her, not seeming to notice the faces of Randy Prescott and his mother, who both looked as if they'd like to protest.

"When is the last time you had a decent meal?" he asked abruptly.

The concern in his voice surprised her. "I don't remember."

"Well, you'll have a chance to eat something at the ward." He leaned back against the corner of the seat as the limousine pulled out of the cemetery.

Jillian doubted it. Nerves gripped her throat so tightly, she didn't think she could swallow a bite. She looked through the rearview window as they left the cemetery What a disastrous day. She'd been angrily rebuked by Frank. She'd buried her father. She'd gone from penniless to hopeful prospects then back to penniless again, and it wasn't yet three o'clock in the afternoon. How would she make it through the rest of the day? She wasn't sure; she only knew she had to.

CHAPTER 3

Night was falling as Luke watched Jillian park her car in the farm-yard. She waved briefly, signaling him to go on. She meant the action to be dismissive, but in the car lights she appeared vulnerable and alone. When she entered the house, he accelerated and continued on home. He felt a yearning in the pit of his stomach that he quickly squelched with a burst of anger at himself. Why did he let her disturb him? He knew from his own painful experience with his mother that beautiful women were restless, and he'd never known any to find contentment in a rural community.

He wondered how she could be so cool this afternoon when her father had just passed away. Why didn't she show more emotion? He'd found the experience of losing his own father crushing. His mother had been long gone by then. Not dead like Jillian's mother, but off to seek her fortune with a man who could replace the dull routine of ranch life with excitement. Jillian had always reminded him of his mother—beautiful and shallow. Quail Creek had nothing to offer women like them.

Luke had watched Randy swallow her alluring bait, hook, line, and sinker. After she'd gone to New York to model, Randy had moped around for years, hoping she'd come back permanently. She'd come home several times on short vacations, and she'd spent the entire summer the year her mother had died, but there was no indica-tion she'd ever come back to Quail Creek to stay. Luke had been surprised that she would even take time away from her modeling career to care for her mother. But after Annie Taylor's death, just as he'd expected, Jillian had left almost immediately. She certainly hadn't hung around long to comfort her father.

As far as he could tell, Jillian hadn't changed at all. She was beautiful, picture perfect, and dangerous. He had no doubt he could resist her charm, but looking at the besotted grin on Randy's face, he doubted his cousin could. Luke wasn't about to watch Randy throw himself away on her a second time and ruin his life.

Standing off to the side at the viewing, he'd eyed the number of people entering the room. Jed Taylor had been ward clerk as long as he could remember. A quiet man with great dignity, he was always the first one to offer help when it was needed. The ward members had cared a great deal about him. Luke noticed, though, they weren't overly friendly towards his daughter. They nodded and spoke briefly to her, offering their condolences, then moved into the chapel for the services. The scriptures might say, "Judge not that ye be not judged," but evidently Jed's friends were finding it hard to accept that a pillar of the ward had been neglected by his own daughter.

He'd watched Jillian nod and greet each person, seemingly oblivious to the ward members' antipathy. Except for Randy, none of her old gang was here. Quail Creek was too small to offer any way to make a living if one didn't own property, and they'd all moved on. Frowning slightly, he wondered where her current friends were. He'd heard that Frank Ross had finally located Jillian on a yacht in the Mediterranean. The fact that she'd come alone, with no friends to offer moral support, didn't speak well of her friends. As a matter of common decency, someone should have come back with her. But if her friends were as superficial as she seemed to be, he thought scornfully, they would think nothing of letting a friend travel halfway round the world alone to attend her father's funeral.

As he thought about her, he found it hard to believe her father's death had affected her very deeply. More likely, high living and too many late nights had caused her to faint at the cemetery. And he didn't doubt that being a damsel in distress was one of her ploys. Just the same, she'd appeared fragile and worn out, and for someone as tall as she was, she certainly didn't weigh much. Even with encouragement, she hadn't eaten much at the church afterwards.

Luke clenched his jaw as he turned down the lane to his own ranch house. The entire day had given him an unsettled feeling. Jillian had touched a chord within him, and he found it difficult not to be drawn in by her, even though he interpreted her behavior as the carefully cultivated vulnerability of a woman who no doubt had plenty of practice. He'd once been afraid for Randy, but if he kept having these idiotic soft ideas, he was in danger of becoming her next victim himself.

Parking his car near the split-rail fence at the back of the house, he made his way across the porch and into the kitchen. His closest neighbor, Nancy Jenkins, met him at the door with her coat on. "Sorry to rush out, but Jake just called, and he needs my help. One of the cows is down."

"I'm glad I'm home so you aren't delayed any longer. You'll never know how much I appreciate your help." His warm words expressed his gratitude. "How's Emma doing tonight?" His housekeeper and good friend had had a stroke, and she could no longer take care of herself.

"She's had a pretty good day, and naturally, she's as cheerful as ever. Did you find anyone to come in and take care of her?"

"No. I mentioned it to the bishop again, and he's going to try to find someone. Everyone around here is just like you. They have their own families to care for. We're just too far away from civilization to get anyone willing to stay. What a mess." He shook his head tiredly, then looked at Nancy. "Sorry, I didn't mean to keep you. Thanks again for all your help."

"I wish I could do more. See you tomorrow." She waved as she left.

Closing the door behind her, he hung his coat in the hall closet and went into the living room. He smiled when he saw Emma, propped up by two pillows and dressed in a pink flannel nightgown. Her white hair curled around her head like a halo. She was an angel all right, always ready to show him how much she cared about him. If he'd been choosing a mother, she's exactly who he'd have chosen. But the Lord hadn't seen it like that. His stomach tightened. Emma's frailty worried him. He closed his eyes. *Heavenly Father, please let me find the right person to care for her.*

She lounged on the love seat facing the large picture window. Even at night, she could watch the cars coming in and out or going down the road. This way, she always said, she felt a part of the activity on the ranch.

A smile wreathed her pale face when she saw him. "Did you get Jed Taylor buried?"

"Yes. I think everyone in the county was there. Everybody liked and respected Jed." Too bad he couldn't say the same for his daughter.

"What's the matter, Luke? You seem upset. Did it bring back memories of your father's funeral?"

"Not particularly. That happened years ago." And yet, if he were honest, he'd admit that he still missed his father, not every day perhaps, but his passing had left an emptiness that surfaced every so often. They'd been close; in fact, Emma used to tease him that he was a duplicate of his father. The two looked alike, thought alike, and acted alike.

"Did Jillian get here?" She looked at him with sharp interest.

"Jillian? Why are you so interested in Jillian?" He teased. "You've never even met her."

"Myrna showed me some magazine pictures of her one time when I stopped at the diner. You know how she always keeps tabs on the high school kids. Well, she told me Jillian was about the most popular girl in school, and she was as nice as she was beautiful. Now that's something. I've always said that beauty is as beauty does."

"That's true." Luke didn't want to disillusion Emma, but he doubted if Jillian had ever been known for her niceness. "From what Frank said she arrived in Idaho Falls this morning, and I suppose she'll be leaving right away. There's no reason for her to stay around." Wanting to change the subject, he asked Emma if she'd eaten.

"I'm not hungry. Nancy fixed me a milkshake a little while ago. Do you think Jillian's beautiful?" She watched Luke carefully, seeming to gauge his reply.

"Picture perfect." He couldn't keep the sarcasm out of his voice. Then he shrugged carelessly. "She looks like a model: beautiful and brittle. Nothing underneath the facade."

But as he headed towards the stairs, he wondered if he were being fair. Although he doubted her motives, Jillian had seemed extremely upset after the funeral. But she'd be leaving soon, and there was no point in even thinking about her.

—ɯ—

By the time Jillian entered the house, night had fallen. Going into the living room, she waited for the warmth of the house to envelop her. Although she'd turned the thermostat up, the house seemed cold and empty. Slowly removing her coat, she draped it over a chair. Her head throbbed and her legs felt shaky again, probably from hunger. The food had looked good, but the few bites she'd taken had nauseated her, so she'd spent the time visiting with the neighbors. Their memories of her parents had comforted her as nothing else had. Although she'd noticed a reserve in some of them towards her, they'd reminisced about her father with good humor and respect. On the whole she'd felt welcomed.

She sank into the well-worn leather recliner, her father's favorite chair, and curled up, wishing she had some assurance that everything would be all right, that she wasn't alone. But she was.

Still, she thought Bishop Walker seemed to be a caring person. He'd warmly invited her to visit with him if she felt a need to talk, but she'd declined. She hadn't attended church for years, and she didn't feel comfortable in the bishop's presence. Besides, what could she tell him? She'd deliberately chosen life on the fast track, believing her beauty and her money would last forever. Now, as her life spiraled downward, she realized she'd lost everything that had ever mattered to her, a fall that had culminated with the death of her father.

The bishop couldn't help her. No one could. There was no getting away from the fact that tomorrow morning at ten A.M. sharp, the auctioneer would sound his gavel, and the Taylor family and farm as an entity would be wiped out.

Unable to shake the pervasive feeling of loneliness, Jillian stood up and moved around the room, touching her family's belongings with regret. She lingered over a small Dresden shepherdess, running her fingers across the pale pink bonnet and along the delicate crook of the staff. When she'd been eight, she'd gathered eggs all summer to earn enough money to buy this piece for her mother's birthday. The thrill she'd felt at her mother's delight returned. She set the figurine down. After tomorrow she'd have only her memories.

Soon a new family would be moving in here. When a person looked at the house without the beloved memories of her family, the shabbiness was apparent. But for all its shabbiness, the Taylor home had held more love and more authenticity than any of the decorator-designed houses and apartments she'd lived in and visited during the last few years. Jillian could imagine the scorn of the people with whom she'd been yachting. Her friends would never visit her here. In fact, although she'd been gone only forty-eight hours, she doubted they'd even given her a thought. Someone new would come along and the good times would roll on.

The party life was over for Jillian, and she wasn't sorry. Her body and mind numb with fatigue, she finally gave up and crawled into bed.

—∞—

Hours later she turned over on her side and squinted at the clock, trying to bring the luminous dial into focus. Six A.M. Offhand she couldn't recall the last time she'd had a good night's sleep. But this night had been worse than usual. Not just grief for her father, but worry over her future had kept her mind racing, and just when she'd managed to close her eyes for a few minutes, a series of vivid tormenting dreams kept her from resting. Staying for the auction would give her some closure on this painful episode of her life, but what was she going to do afterwards?

She knew her father would want her to ask Frank for help, but after his harsh words she couldn't let him know the true state of her finances. She couldn't imagine he would loan her money. Still, he would probably take her to Idaho Falls. Jillian grimaced as she envisioned the miserable hour-and-a-half drive. Even worse, with only twenty-seven dollars in her purse, she would probably have a hard time finding a place to stay.

She rolled over onto her back and stretched out slowly. Randy still seemed to think she was wonderful; maybe he would loan her some money. But how could she ask him? He'd been so thrilled with her success, she couldn't admit she was broke. And she couldn't bear to disillusion him. Besides, if there was one thing she'd never done, it was take money from men. She despised women who did. Already she was indebted to the friend who owned the yacht for buying her ticket home, and under no circumstances would she add Randy to the list.

Closing her eyes, she tried to think of a single job she was qualified for outside of modeling, and even then, she thought with grim humor, the last time she'd checked, haggard models weren't "in." But the name "Jillian Taylor" might still have a little glamour out here. Maybe she could find a fashion job in a specialty shop or a department store, if she could get to Idaho Falls or even Salt Lake City.

What if she were to ask Randy to take her to Idaho Falls after the auction? Maybe she could pretend she was catching a flight and have him drop her at the airport. Of course, being the gentleman he was, he'd insist on staying until her flight came. So that was out.

She couldn't concentrate enough to decide how to manage her exit, but something would work out. Anyway she'd leave Quail Creek with a bang. Just like the last time. She'd put on her best dress, her fabulous faux jewelry, and pretend none of this meant anything to her. To be a good model, she had learned how to act—no matter how harsh or hot the weather, no matter what kind of imperious demands the photographers made, no matter what digs and snipes other models might give. She'd had to be good at pretending, at acting as if she were having the time of her life, even if she weren't. And if she was good at anything, it was acting as if she were on top of the world.

She propped herself up and swung her legs onto the floor. No use lying in bed any longer. Who knew when the auctioneer would arrive? She'd better shower and dress.

She'd avoided her parents' bedroom the night before; now she went in to absorb their presence. She stared around the room, carefully taking in the details. It didn't look as if even one knickknack, let alone a piece of furniture, had been moved since her mother had died. Her grandmother had made the patchwork quilt, and against the foot of the bed was her mother's cedar chest.

Wondering what had been saved over the years, Jillian knelt in front of the chest and attempted to open it. But the lid wouldn't budge. She suspected the family pictures were in the chest, along with other items that had little more than sentimental value. Her heart beat faster; maybe she would have a chance to keep something of her family with her after all.

What could she use to force the lock? Her hands shaking, she went through the kitchen drawers and found only a steak knife. Grabbing it, she hurried to the chest again. But the lock wouldn't open. She had to calm down and think clearly. There had to be some way to force the lock. Maybe a narrow piece of lead pipe would work.

Bundling up in the warmest clothes she'd brought, Jillian dashed outside. She caught her breath at the intensity of the cold, and before she reached the outbuildings, she was shivering. But her search was futile. There was no quarter-inch pipe to be found, or anything else small enough to do the job. Discouraged, she returned to the house. She'd think of something else while she got ready for the auction. As soon as she dressed, she'd check the shed again.

There had to be something that would work.

Getting out all of her cosmetics, Jillian didn't spare the eyeliner or shadow. Over the years probably everyone had seen her picture in advertisements for her own perfume or on the cover of magazines. It had started with *Seventeen*, *Vogue*, *Harper's Bazaar* and more and more, until she'd done over fifty covers. Everyone here knew she was a famous model—today she'd look like one. She slipped into her Manolo Blahnik black leather shoes. They'd cost her a fortune—in fact, she thought sadly, about the cost of airfare home. But if a person's shoes weren't expensive, it was a dead giveaway the wearer hadn't any money, and Jillian had been frantic to keep up appearances.

She wore yesterday's black dress, but this time she added strands of oversized pearls and crystal beads. Although they looked fashionable and expensive, they were in fact cheap or she would have pawned them for the money she needed.

It was her pride again, but she couldn't let the people at the sale see her distress over the proceedings. She looked at herself in the full-length mirror. "Well, Jillian Taylor, you look glamorous, famous, and scornful, as if your cold little heart hadn't a care in the world." Just the statement she wanted to make, so no one would suspect her true feelings. She turned from her reflection. She had to get that chest opened.

Slipping on her coat, Jillian started for the shed again. She was about halfway there when a truck drove in. Her heart plummeted as she read *Tom Keane, Auctioneer* on the side. What could she do now that wouldn't draw attention to the fact that she was breaking into the chest?

As soon as the truck stopped, three teenagers in the back began tossing boxes out before unloading a portable platform. An older man climbed out and came towards her. "Miss Taylor?"

"Yes."

"I'm Tom Keane. Sorry about your father and all this." He swept his arm around indicating the farmyard. "We need to set up. Is it okay to start taking the furniture and household items out? My boys need to put the small stuff in boxes—" his tone was apologetic,— "but we'll try to stay out of your way."

Even as her heart warmed at his kindness, the ache of regret penetrated her body. It was too late. She wouldn't get to keep anything of her mother or father. Unable to reply, she led them into the house and watched silently as the boys moved the furniture out piece by piece into the yard. Even before they'd finished, several cars had arrived at the house.

Randy got out of the first one. Jillian watched from the kitchen window while he went around to the other side and helped his mother and a petite brunette out of the car. Jillian couldn't see the second woman clearly, but she seemed young. Randy glanced around the yard and then, walking behind the women, headed for the house. Making sure her smile was in place, Jillian met them at the door.

"Good morning." She carefully kept her voice light. "You're just in time to see the dismantling of the Taylor farm."

Randy gave her a hug. "How are you holding up? I shouldn't have let you come out here alone yesterday. I worried about you all night."

"I'm fine," Jillian reassured him.

Just then the boys came through the kitchen with the sofa. "If we don't want to be trampled, I think we'd better move out into the yard," Randy said. He guided Jillian protectively out the door, leaving the other two to follow. His mother's face wore a decidedly irritated look.

"Jillian, this is Marci Smith, Randy's fiancée," she announced when they were outside. "Marci, Jillian Taylor."

Marci had short, curly brown hair and an innocent, sweet face. She looked like a good Mormon girl, and beside her, Jillian felt old and jaded. Randy had chosen well. His fiancée seemed exactly the right type.

"I'm sorry about your father," Marci said. "I know this must be a hard time for you."

"Thank you. It is." Jillian smiled at her, wondering if Marci was from Quail Creek. Offhand, Jillian didn't remember any Smiths, as common as the name was. Of course, in ten years a lot could change.

When Randy didn't say anything, his mother added, "Marci teaches first grade over at the school. She's just like one of the family."

Jillian turned to reassure Mrs. Prescott, but when the older woman didn't relax her militant stance, Jillian thought better of it. Still, she wanted to say, "Don't worry. I'm not romantically interested in your son." But she knew she couldn't without sounding presumptuous.

As she looked around the yard, her throat tightened. By now most of the furniture was jumbled together by the side of the house. The kitchen table, sofa, and chairs were covered with boxes of dishes and utensils. Jillian turned away, unable to bear the sight of the familiar items that would soon be borne away by whoever was willing to pay the best price. Deciding that she needed her dark glasses as a shield, she excused herself to go back into the house to get her purse. She met the boys as they were bringing out the cedar chest, and her heart lurched.

Only a few more hours to go before this ordeal will be over. Empty, the house looked forlorn and forsaken. Grief clutched at her throat, and she found it hard to breathe. *Do not cry,* she ordered herself sternly. *Do not cry!*

One of the boys had followed her into the bedroom. She pointed to her things. "This is my luggage. Can I leave it here and get it after the auction?"

He nodded. Picking up her purse, she slipped her dark glasses on and left the room, smiling at the boy as if she hadn't a care in the world.

Stepping outside, she saw that Luke had joined the Prescotts, and her pulse quickened. Although dressed in a sheepskin jacket and a Stetson like the other men, he was the first one she noticed in the crowd, and it wasn't just his apparent physical strength that set him apart. No, Luke had an intangible inner strength that gave him a cool self-confidence. A person anyone would want on their side in a fight. Someone people would automatically turn to in time of need.

He'd unexpectedly been her refuge yesterday. Without him, she'd undoubtedly have collapsed at the grave site, but still, she experienced a flutter of anxiety at the sight of him When she'd dated Randy in high school, it seemed as if Luke was always hanging around, quick with a mocking comment at her expense. He made her feel awkward and dumb, and although he used to call her "gorgeous," his tone clearly intimated that he felt she was shallow, absorbed only by her own physical appearance.

Now, years later and to her chagrin, he still had the power to make her awkward and nervous. For all his kindness yesterday, she found it impossible to believe Luke liked her any better than he had then. Maybe she'd be better off standing someplace else during the auction. Behind her dark glasses, her eyes narrowed in determination. No, darn it! For the next couple of hours this was still her farm and she'd stand where she liked. He turned and caught sight of her. Giving him a brilliant smile, she made her way over to join the Prescott family.

"Hello, Jillian." He studied her face for a moment. "Feeling better?"

"Yes. Thanks again. I doubt I'd have made it through yesterday without your help." She placed a grateful hand on his arm and was startled to feel the same rush of sensations she'd had yesterday—a feeling of security and refuge. Comforting feelings, but dangerous. She jerked her hand away. She couldn't let Luke see how a simple touch had affected her. "I hope you're going to bid everything up, so we can make a lot of money today," she said lightly.

"I'm surprised you let it come to this," he said in a low tone, and with that note of censure in his voice, Luke was once again the person she remembered.

She pressed her lips together to control their trembling, not wanting him see her pain at losing the farm and all her family's worldly possessions. Instead she shrugged. "It's just stuff," she lied.

"He who travels lightest, travels fastest?" His disdainful expression tore at her heartstrings.

She pretended indifference. "You know how it is—the life of a jet setter."

All his consolation from yesterday was gone, and Luke stared at her as if she'd just crawled out from under a rock. He turned his head and continued talking to the others.

People kept arriving. They crowded the yard and milled around the outbuildings, sorting through the household items and looking over the machinery. When they caught sight of Jillian, the potential buyers gave her curious glances. Ignoring the heartache and abandonment that gripped her, she stared back imperiously.

"All right, ladies and gentlemen," boomed a voice over the loudspeaker. It was Tom Keane. "It's time to start the auction."

After explaining the rules, he sounded his gavel, then he led the group to the barn, where he began auctioning off the equipment. Over an hour passed before he had all the machinery sold. To Jillian's surprise, it went for thousands of dollars. How much was her father in debt if this wouldn't clear it? Her head started to throb.

When the auctioneer moved back to the yard, Jillian thought she couldn't bear watching as her family's personal possessions were sold off. But as painful as it was, she stood rigidly, bracing herself against the freezing cold morning air and the anguish of seeing her parents' belongings handed over to strangers.

The pain subsided somewhat when the first boxes of kitchen utensils and dishes went for five dollars each. If this was what people were bidding, she would be able to buy at least one of her mother's figurines. But her heart fell when the first figurine, an eighteenth-century woman in a ball gown, went for forty-nine dollars. The next ones sold for less, but even prices of thirty-five and forty dollars were beyond her means. She struggled to remain impassive even as she felt herself slowly succumbing to despair. Finally the auctioneer held up the shepherdess.

"Ten dollars," came from a voice in the crowd.

"Fifteen," Jillian called.

Luke raised her bid. "Twenty."

Darn him! He wasn't going to make her lose the last tie to her mother. Her fingers bit into Luke's arm and she tightened her grip.

"Don't."

His eyes narrowed. "I thought the object was to make money for the bank."

"Not on this item," she said coldly, then released her grasp. She saw something flicker in his eyes as she called out, "Twenty-two dollars."

"I've got twenty-two. Who'll give me twenty-five?" The crowd watched Jillian. She froze, unable to move for fear someone might raise her bid. But no one did. Tom handed the Dresden to one of his sons, who motioned for Jillian to come over. She edged her way through the crowd to the table.

"I'm glad you got this." The boy gave her a shy look.

"Thank you. So am I." She rummaged through her purse, looking for her wallet. She carefully tucked her last five-dollar bill in the coin compartment and counted out the remaining money while the boy jotted down the information on the sales log. Taking the figurine into the house, she wrapped it thoroughly in a brown paper bag from the kitchen, then placed the package in her suitcase.

She returned to the yard just as Tom gaveled the sale of the chest. She waited by the table, hoping whoever bought it would let her have the family pictures. The young woman who came to the front was a stranger.

Jillian hesitated. "I-I wondered if I could have the family pictures?"

"Sure." The woman's voice was filled with the exuberance borne of a good buy. "They're no good to me. How about twenty-five bucks?"

The blood rushed to Jillian's face, and she cringed with embarrassment. "I'm sorry—" The expression on the woman's face said clearly that she thought Jillian was rich and cheap, trying to get something for nothing.

Desperately, Jillian said, "I'll trade you my pearls for them."

Before the woman could reply, Luke stepped up, giving Jillian a penetrating look. "What's the problem?"

"Nothing." The humiliation would be too great if he found out she couldn't come up with twenty-five dollars.

"She wanted the pictures out of the chest." Seeing an opportunity to make some money, the woman had no compunction about telling him.

"How much do you want for them?" He reached for his wallet.

"Twenty-five bucks."

"Sold." He quickly extracted the bills. "Where's the key?"

The woman shrugged, and Jillian said, "I couldn't find it."

"Sounds like a job for a Swiss Army knife." He produced one from his pocket, and with a flick of his wrist, he had the chest opened.

Jillian gasped. Her parent's wedding picture rested on top of a stack of old photos. Without thinking, she grabbed Luke by the arm. "Thank you, Luke. You don't know how much this means to me." Then, embarrassed at revealing her emotions so openly after a morning of doing her best to hide them, she said in a more restrained voice, "Thank you."

His lips curved into a wry half-smile. "Call it a gift."

A gift? To her? She couldn't believe Luke Prescott would give her anything. Taking a deep breath to restore her composure, she released her hold on Luke's arm and turned to look blindly at the pictures. For an instant she had a hard time focusing her thoughts.

"Can I help you with those?" Luke offered.

"No. Thank you." The old photographs were too precious to relinquish to anyone. Slowly picking them up, she cradled the pictures in her arms. At the side of the house, she found an empty box. After placing her priceless bundle inside, she stacked them with her other things. Even if she had to see everything auctioned off, the day was still turning out better than she had hoped. She had the figurine and the pictures.

She rejoined Randy, who greeted her warmly and squeezed her arm. Glancing up, she saw that Luke had an impassive look on his face as he watched her. The rest of the auction passed in a blur until she heard Tom Keane say, "The farm goes to First Federal Bank."

It was over. Now all she had to do was get to Idaho Falls, figure out how she was going to start a new career on five dollars, and live happily ever after.

"What are your plans?" Randy asked.

"I'm taking her into Idaho Falls," Luke said, his tone abrupt.

"No way," Randy interrupted. "She just got here and we've hardly had a chance to say more than hi." He turned to Jillian. "Why don't you stay with us for a few days so we have time to visit?"

She didn't want to stay with them—she could foresee problems—but that would give her time to think of something, to make some plans.

"Do you really mean it? It wouldn't be an imposition?" she asked carefully, not wanting to seem overeager. She glanced at Mrs. Prescott for a confirmation to the invitation. Several emotions flickered across Mrs. Prescott's face. Then evidently afraid of not appearing very charitable, she nodded her assent.

Luke's expression, however, made Jillian uneasy. His earlier compassion had disappeared, and his face had the cynical expression he had often worn in high school.

"Great!" Randy grabbed Jillian's arm and started for the house. "Let's get your things."

Although not nearly as enthused as Randy, Marci nonetheless took Jillian's other arm, and they started for the house. *What a predicament,* Jillian thought ruefully. She didn't want to hurt anyone—she certainly didn't want Randy back—but she was petrified of being put out on the streets. At least she could do one thing. She stopped short, pulling Randy to a halt with her.

"Slow down, Randy. What's your hurry? Marci can't keep up." Jillian gave the girl a friendly glance, attempting to reassure her. Mrs. Prescott and Luke, both looking irritated, said nothing. Luke followed them into the house to help carry her things out to the car.

When everyone was settled in their seats, Luke bent down and spoke only to Jillian. "I'll be seeing you, gorgeous. You can count on it."

His mocking words rang in her ears all the way to the Prescott home, a familiar and disturbing echo of the past.

CHAPTER 4

"Jillian, you're wanted on the phone," Mrs. Prescott said from the kitchen doorway, a grudging note in her voice. Her words startled Jillian, and her pulse raced as once again she relived the last call she had received, Frank's call to the yacht. Who would be calling her here?

With a smile, like that of a welcome guest rather than an ex-girl-friend visiting on sufferance, Jillian thanked the older woman, then stood. Tossing her magazine on the sofa, she followed Mrs. Prescott into the kitchen where the latter had been doing some Christmas baking. Jillian had offered to help but had been turned down flat. After such chilly treatment, she thought hearing from anybody sounded good. Maybe the yacht had come into port and one of the merrymakers had decided to check on Jillian and see how she was doing. But no, how would they find her at the Prescotts'?

She picked up the wall phone receiver. "Hello?"

A deep, husky voice answered, "Hello, Jillian."

It was Luke Prescott, carrying through on his threat, no doubt. Why would he call her? She was immediately suspicious. Although he had been kind to her on Saturday at the auction, he'd quickly reverted to the caustic person she had grown up with. Since he made no effort to hide his condemnation of her, Jillian was willing to bet her last five dollars that whatever he had in mind, it wouldn't be pleasant.

She attempted to speak normally. "Yes?"

"Plan on going to dinner with me tonight," he spoke confidently, as if he knew nothing would keep her from going. "We have to talk."

As Jillian glanced at Mrs. Prescott, who made no effort to disguise her interest, she tried to suppress the rush of excitement that flooded her at Luke's invitation. Even his antipathy was easier to take than another meal with Mrs. Prescott.

"Thanks for asking me," she said pleasantly. "I need to check with Mrs. Prescott to make sure I won't upset her plans." She knew that Randy's mother would be ecstatic that Jillian would be absent, even if it was only for a couple of hours. She'd been here two long days, and while Randy was eager to entertain her, Mrs. Prescott made her dislike of Jillian obvious with every look and word.

"Luke wants me to go to dinner with him." Jillian turned to Mrs. Prescott, her voice deliberately cordial. "Will that upset your dinner plans?"

"Heavens, no. It'll do you good to get out of the house." *And away from my son,* she might well have added.

Jillian relayed the message to Luke and he responded, "I'll pick you up in about an hour."

"It's so gracious of you to ask," she said sweetly. As a matter of fact, a meal spent with Luke, no matter how miserable, couldn't be any worse than one spent under Mrs. Prescott's disapproving scowl.

Luke abruptly hung up and left Jillian holding the phone, the dial tone in her ear. The entire episode made her suspicious. What was he up to? He certainly wasn't interested in her as a woman, that was for sure. At this point she couldn't imagine anything he could do that could make her life any harder. So why was he so insistent she go to dinner with him?

A satisfied expression spread across Mrs. Prescott's face. Although she made it evident that she thought her son was too good for Jillian, she apparently didn't think Luke was.

Grateful for an excuse to go upstairs, Jillian went to her bedroom to get ready, not that she needed much time to decide what to wear. Little by little she'd sold her clothes to "Castoffs," a used clothing shop in New York that handled celebrity clothing. She'd kept only what could be packed in two suitcases and her garment bag. She grimaced. For all practical purposes, at age twenty-six she'd become a bag lady—the only difference being that all her belongings fit into well-worn designer luggage, not shopping bags, and she hadn't yet slept over a heating grate on a street.

Once her money had run out, however, she'd felt just about as welcome in the vacation homes of her friends. She'd stayed with various acquaintances, going from one house party to another these last few years, pretending everything was still the same. She'd had no place to go other than home, and her pride kept her from doing that. She just couldn't admit failure.

She'd paid a high price for her pride—the chance to see her father again.

She flipped through her clothes, hanging in the closet of the spare bedroom. What to wear presented a dilemma. Her dresses were too sophisticated for the truck stop, which was the only eating place in town. She finally settled on a pair of navy polka dot silk pants and a matching knit sweater. Being cruise clothes, they weren't very warm, but they looked casual enough.

Leaving her clothes on the hangers, Jillian carried them down the hall to the bathroom. She would have liked to take a long leisurely bath, soaking in plenty of bath salts, but the spartan bathroom didn't make provisions for anything so luxurious. Long and leisurely were also out since it was the only bathroom in the house, and she was sure to irritate Mrs. Prescott further if she monopolized the room.

So after a strictly utilitarian bath, she donned her clothes and went back to the bedroom to finish getting ready. She brushed her hair and left it down, letting the silvery blond strands float around her shoulders. Stepping away from the dressing table, she scrunched down and then stood on tiptoes, trying to get a good look at herself in the small mirror. What she saw didn't please her. She'd gotten so thin that the pants didn't fit as well as they once had, but—she told herself, counting her blessings—at least she didn't have any bulges. In the modeling world, pounds were lost wages.

Jillian took her coat, a well-worn Canadian wolf jacket, from the closet. Since it had become politically incorrect to wear fur, her coat hadn't been worth anything at Castoffs. But in a small town like Quail Creek, she doubted she'd be harassed by animal rights protesters. Slinging the fur over her arm, she picked up her purse from the bed and went downstairs to wait for Luke.

The back door slammed as Randy came into the kitchen. "Brrrr, it feels good to be inside." Taking off his gloves, he rubbed his hands. "It's zero right now and the forecaster said the temperature could fall to thirty below tonight. I've fed the cattle, so we're all set till morning." He gave Jillian an eager smile. "Want to eat at Myrna's tonight?"

Before she could respond, his mother said firmly, "She's going to dinner with Luke."

Randy looked startled. "Luke?" Then he relaxed. "Oh, he won't mind if I come with you."

"That sounds great!" Maybe to her it did, but she had an idea his presence was the last thing Luke wanted. It would be interesting to see Luke try to get out of taking Randy.

His mother started to say something, but Randy brushed it off and left the room. "I won't be a minute."

Randy had just come back down when Luke arrived. "Jillian tells me you're taking her to dinner. Mind if I come along?"

"Sorry, Randy, not this time." Although Luke sounded affable, his eyes never warmed, and although it wasn't his home, his presence dominated the room. Jillian's lips tightened at his implacable stance. Randy would think there was a romance here when it was only coercion.

Mrs. Prescott looked pleased. "Randy, why don't you invite Marci out here to dinner? I've made fresh apple pie."

Randy looked obstinate. "Not tonight."

Luke shrugged and turned to Jillian, giving her an intimate look that she recognized as being only for Randy's sake. "Are you ready?" When she nodded, he picked up her jacket and helped her into it. Then bidding the others good-bye, they left.

Once outside, the frosty air bit at Jillian's face and legs, going right through the silk of her pants as if her legs were bare. She clutched her jacket tighter and hurried out to the yard, where Luke had parked his pickup truck. His lights illuminated the clouds of exhaust that billowed into the night air. Thank goodness he'd left the motor running. It was bad enough to go with him without freezing to death in the bargain. Unable to control her shivering, she said, "I'd forgotten how cold the weather gets here."

"You mean it's not as warm as the Riviera?" He reached behind her to open the pickup door.

"Not quite," she said dryly, detecting the antagonism in his voice. "There's at least a seventy-degree difference."

"We're lucky there's no wind tonight or the wind-chill factor would make it even colder." Grasping her arm, he boosted her up the step.

While Luke went around the truck to the driver's side, Jillian leaned against the leather seat, unable to relax but savoring the blast of hot air from the heater on her legs. She wasn't surprised to hear country music coming from the radio. For all Luke's sophisticated exterior, underneath he was proving himself to be a country rancher. The music fit his cowboy image: the shearling lamb jacket, jeans, and tooled leather boots. With his looks, she thought he'd be a natural for advertising. A natural magnetism seemed to exude from cowboys, and Luke was no exception. With his macho image, he'd attract both men and women— but not her. She was looking for someone warm and tender.

"Like country music?" He stretched his arm along the back of the seat and looked over his shoulder as he backed the truck around.

"Not particularly." Usually she pretended to like whatever the man she was with liked, but she saw no reason to bother with Luke. She'd make no concession to him, no matter how trivial. "So many of my friends are rock singers, I just never listen to anything else," she said. She didn't add that there was also something about rock music that drove her problems to the back of her mind and made her feel carefree and young.

With a quick turn, they were on the highway. Jillian made no effort to initiate conversation. They weren't friends, and he'd already admitted he had an ulterior motive for insisting she come.

Finally Luke spoke. "So tell me, how did a girl from Quail Creek, Idaho, become a famous model?"

Jillian couldn't imagine that he cared. "Why waste time on small talk? You're not interested in me, and I'm not interested in discussing my life with you."

"In the stories I've read, you never struck me as being particularly reticent about your life." His voice was tinged with scorn.

She clenched her hands. "You're not a reporter, and you can't help my career." In reality, she was worn out with always being "on," always having a clever retort designed to make headlines.

"I don't call 'yippee skippee' scintillating conversation. Did you learn it from the jet set?" His hands firmly gripped the steering wheel, his gaze steady on the dark road ahead.

Jillian looked at him, and her tone dry, she said, "What a short memory you have. That article also said I filled my speech with *Idaho-isms*. Don't you remember everyone said that in high school? With that and every other colloquialism from Quail Creek, I was 'in.' Jaded New Yorkers found me refreshing."

"Sounds like a good career move." He shrugged. "Still, seeing you now, that just doesn't fit."

She stared out the window, suddenly tired. "Of course, it doesn't. That was ten years ago, and believe me, the innocent, naive girl who left Quail Creek to find fame and fortune in the Big Apple is long gone."

"There's nothing like being rich and famous," he drawled.

"There certainly isn't," she agreed, matching his tone. Only now she was no longer rich, and to her regret, notorious defined her better than famous. She'd heard the hostility edging Luke's words and tensed, wondering yet again why he'd insisted she come with him tonight. It was rapidly becoming more and more apparent that he found nothing about her attractive.

Just past the bridge over Quail Creek, the highway widened and they entered the town, which was little more than a "wide spot" in the road. In the dark Jillian could see the lights of maybe a half dozen buildings fronting the highway. Ben's convenience store, Myrna's place, two schools, and a church—none of which gave her much hope for employment.

Luke pulled into the parking lot of the diner. Jillian was surprised to see that there were no other cars, but it was early still and as she remembered, Myrna's usually got busier later in the evening, after high school dances or ball games. She looked forward to seeing Myrna again. She'd come to the funeral but had left immediately afterwards, and Jillian hadn't had a chance to visit with her. As a newly active member in the Church, Myrna had been her Beehive teacher. She loved having a good time as much as the girls did and had quickly become one of the gang.

A string of colored lights outlining each window was the only indication of the Christmas season. Luke and Jillian turned out to be the only diners. He led her to a booth in the back near a picture window, which was wasted at this time of night. Only the headlights of an occasional car pierced the darkness, faintly illuminating the mountain across the highway.

"Hi, Luke, how's it going?" The waitress brought them some water, the menus tucked under her arms.

"As good as can be expected. How're you, Shirley?"

"Can't complain." She handed them each a plastic-covered menu and then hovered over them. "Chicken fried steak's the special tonight."

Chicken fried steak? Why not? She hadn't eaten that since she'd left Quail Creek. She smiled at the waitress. "Sounds good. I'll have it."

Jillian was disappointed that Myrna wasn't there; she didn't even know Shirley. After the waitress left, Jillian looked at Luke and saw that his affability had disappeared as well. A cold reserve now settled on his face, and his blue eyes appeared as frigid as the temperature outside.

"So why did you want me to come tonight?" She stared at him in exasperation.

"We'll discuss it after supper." He removed his jacket and hung it on the chrome rack next to the booth. The food arrived, but with her stomach still tied in knots from the events of the last few days and now Luke's presence, a few bites were all Jillian could manage.

Luke raised his eyebrows. "Not gourmet enough for you?"

"It's delicious, but . . . " She pushed away her plate. The food was good, but after the frugality of her last few meals and the tension that lay heavily between them, she didn't dare risk becoming ill from eating too much.

He looked at the food remaining on her plate. "Dieting to keep your figure?"

She looked at him squarely. "That's one thing I've never had to do."

"You mean you just naturally have that emaciated look?" he asked as he helped himself to another roll. "You'd better eat up; you're losing your looks."

Although seething inwardly, Jillian responded with a saucy smile as if he'd paid her a compliment. "Flatterer. How did you know that's what every woman wants to hear?"

He gave her a pitying look. "I aim to please."

"What a line." Why didn't he just get to the point? "I doubt you've ever gone out of your way to please anyone, unless it fit in precisely with your plans." She continued to smile pleasantly, as if their conversation was all in fun, but on the inside her body trembled wildly.

Luke cleared his plate, then lay down his fork. Gently he picked up her hand and Jillian stiffened, afraid he'd feel her hands trembling. But he didn't appear to as he examined every polished nail. "So soft and white." He turned it over. "Not a callus anywhere. Tell me, has this hand ever done an honest day's work?"

Stung by his action, Jillian pulled her hand away from him. "It depends on how you define honest. If your definition is dirt under the nails and calluses, then modeling doesn't qualify, but then neither does nursing. If you mean long hours, dealing with difficult people, and being dependable, then modeling's as honest as nursing or any other kind of work."

Luke's voice was cold. "You make a lot more money than a nurse. And for what? To look alluring? To sell expensive clothes and perfume to people who already have more money than they can spend in ten lifetimes?" His lips tightened with distaste.

Jillian stared at him without wavering. "Does being a sheep rancher make you an authority, or do you just judge others on principle? Since there doesn't seem to be a point to this evening beyond insulting me, I'm leaving." She slid out of the booth and stood up. Wrapping her coat around her, she headed for the door. She wasn't prolonging this evening a minute longer.

Luke stood up and threw some bills on the table before he followed her. Climbing into the pickup, she huddled against the door, trying to both relax and keep warm enough to control her shaking until the heater started. Her mind raced. Tonight had only served to compound her desperation. She had to discover some way to earn enough money to get back to the city. Maybe Myrna would hire her. Something. Anything.

When they drove into the Prescotts' yard, Jillian wrenched open the door before they'd stopped.

"Wait." He grasped her shoulder before she could slide out of the truck. "When are you leaving town?"

"Maybe never," she shot back. "So that's the mysterious reason you took me to dinner—to warn me off."

"Why not leave tomorrow?" he suggested, his eyes narrowing. The relentlessness of his voice intensified the coldness of the temperature outside. "There's no reason for you to hang around here any longer. I have no intention of letting some dilettante too selfish to save her own father wreck the lives of people I love just because she's at loose ends right now." He released his grip.

Jerking away, Jillian opened the door and fled from the truck. Luke caught her just as she was struggling with the knob on the back door.

"Listen, Jillian. My aunt has done a lot for me and I refuse to stand by and watch while you make her unhappy. If you hang around here messing up Randy's life, I'll make yours so miserable you'll wish you had never come back."

"Just try it," she said, her teeth gritted.

Luke's voice lowered ominously. "Don't play games with me because I haven't even started."

Tearing loose from his hold, Jillian finally got the door opened and slammed it in his face. She blinked back the tears. No wonder Mrs. Prescott had looked so cheerful about her date with Luke; she'd probably known what he had planned to say to her. It was obvious they didn't want her out of here any quicker than she wanted to be gone. But she couldn't go until she had money for a ticket.

She heard the pickup door slam and the gravel fly as Luke roared away. Good riddance! After Luke's warning she was almost tempted to play up to Randy and make both Luke and Mrs. Prescott even more unhappy. But she wouldn't. Neither Randy nor Marci had done anything to hurt her, and they deserved better than that.

"How come you're home so early?" Randy asked, coming out of the living room. "I expected Luke would keep you out till all hours."

Smiling as if she'd just had the time of her life, Jillian said, "Is it still early? Believe me, it seemed like a long evening."

"I'll bet you're the first girl who's ever felt that way. Want to talk for a while?"

They'd spent the last two evenings reminiscing, but she knew she couldn't keep up the pretense that nothing was wrong. Putting her hand over a delicate yawn, she said, "I don't think I can stay awake a minute longer. Do you mind if we talk tomorrow?"

Despite his obvious disappointment, Randy didn't argue. "Not at all." Switching on the hall lights and turning off the kitchen ones, he followed her up the stairs. "We've got a lot of catching up to do, but we'll have all the time we need."

Lying in bed, she felt the guilt of the last two nights start up again. And then the "what-ifs." What if she'd married Randy? She wouldn't be in this mess now. Would she be any happier? Probably not. From the age of twelve she'd dreamed of modeling in New York; to give up that dream would have eaten away at her for the rest of her life. She wondered if Randy thought that discussing the lives they'd each led for the last ten years would bring them to the same point they'd been when they were both sixteen. It wouldn't. She and Randy could never go back. Too much water had flowed over the dam, to borrow a cliché. She'd long since lost the dewy freshness of her youth, but Randy still appeared to possess the same boyish qualities he'd had in high school.

She spent a restless night, and early the next morning, unable to shake the feeling of hopelessness, she slipped out of bed and crept downstairs while the rest of the household still slept. Reluctantly she dialed a familiar number, hating to humiliate herself in this way. She had to talk fast because Randy and his mother could come down any minute, and she didn't want to be overheard.

CHAPTER 5

"Simon Grant's." The receptionist's voice was like honey—smooth, syrupy, exuding success.

"Bonnie, this is Jillian Taylor. May I speak to Simon?" Although she hadn't heard from him in nearly a year, she was desperate for a job, any job.

"Just a minute. I'll see if he's in."

Jillian knew the routine. Simon was in all right, but he only took calls from people who were "hot," and Jillian definitely wasn't. She understood. After all, he was in the business to make money, and ex-clients like Jillian Taylor weren't worth much.

"Sorry, he's tied up on another line. Let me have your number, and he'll call you."

Another version of "Don't call us, we'll call you," but what could she do? Jillian gave her the Prescotts' number then added, "I'm looking for anything right now. My father died and I need to keep busy to get my mind off his death."

"I understand," said Bonnie.

Jillian was sure she did. Undoubtedly, she'd seen right through the ploy. Bonnie had heard them all.

"Jillian, darling. How are you?" To her surprise they were joined on the line by another voice, that of Simon Grant himself.

"A little bored right now, darling." She put a blasé note in her voice, hoping it hid her desperation. "I'm in Idaho and looking for a job so I'll have something to do. Anything available?"

Simon gave a brittle laugh. "Jillian, you know how this business is—you're hot one minute and you're history the next! I doubt I could even get you a showroom job, not that I handle them. With your reputation for being late or not even showing up, no one is going to take a chance on you. You'd better just keep on partying. I haven't had any inquiries for you in at least a year."

"I'd take anything." She hated that pleading tone in her voice.

"I'd heard you were down on your luck, Jillian dearest, but your age is also against you. Unless you're Cindy or Claudia or Christie or even Cheryl, you haven't got a chance. Otherwise, everyone wants fresh, young faces. Most of my models are in their early teens. If I hear of anything, I'll give you a call, but don't hold your breath. *Ciao.*" She heard him tell Bonnie to get her telephone number and he was gone.

A pervasive feeling of bleakness clung to her as she repeated the Prescotts' number. Too bad her first name didn't start with a *C;* she might possibly have found work. And even if by some remote possibility the agency did call her, she wouldn't be here. What would she do now? Go to Idaho Falls and see if she could find a job? Ask Myrna for one? She couldn't stay here. Jillian had no doubt that Luke could make her life wretched if she didn't leave—and she wanted to go. Imposing on the Prescotts wasn't the solution to her problem. She heard their voices from the hall and turned towards the door.

They both looked surprised to see her. Randy looked happy, but his mother's countenance clearly showed she thought Jillian was up to no good. As usual, Jillian pretended not to notice. Instead, putting on a cheerful face, she asked brightly, "Any possibility, Randy, of borrowing your car this morning? I'd like to run into town and pick up a few things."

"Sure," Randy replied, returning her smile. "Feel free to use the car any time you want. If you can wait until this afternoon, I'll even take you."

"I think I'll go this morning," she said, conscious of Mrs. Prescott's resentful stare. With any luck Jillian would have a job by afternoon.

It was nearly nine-thirty by the time she left the Prescott farm and headed for Quail Creek. The Prescotts lived about three miles from town along a curving road that dissected a large tract of government grazing land. Jillian drove straight to the diner and parked the car near the front window, then went in and sat down at the counter. The place was nearly empty, and when she glanced around, Jillian didn't see anyone she recognized.

"Well, as I live and breathe, Jillian Taylor!" Myrna boomed from across the room. "Honey, am I glad to see you!" Tossing her dyed auburn hair out of her eyes, she crossed the room to stand in front of Jillian, her pudgy face beaming. "Golly, it's been a long time. Sorry I couldn't talk to you after your father's funeral, but I had a doctor's appointment in the Falls. Where are you staying? Heard about the farm. What a shame." As she talked, she vigorously polished the black Formica counter.

"At Randy Prescott's."

Myrna gave her a shrewd look. "Renewing old acquaintances?"

Jillian laughed. "Acquaintances only."

Giving the counter one last swipe, Myrna fixed Jillian a cup of hot chocolate and then one for herself. Jillian stirred the drink, thinking that she was in the one place in the world—a Mormon community—where people automatically assumed you drank cocoa rather than coffee.

Myrna seated herself on the stool next to Jillian and gave her a conspiratorial look. "You'd be better off going after Luke, honey. He's not only a pillar of the community, he has the biggest sheep operation in the county, and best of all, he's the one in the family with all the money."

Jillian shuddered. "Not to add a poisonous personality."

Myrna looked surprised at her words. "You're the only woman I've seen who isn't positively drooling over him."

Giving her a look of pure distaste, Jillian said, "That's what happens when you've never been past the city limits of Quail Creek."

Myrna's laughter peeled throughout the diner, causing the few customers to focus their attention on the two of them. "How long you staying, honey?"

Hoping to hide her nervousness, Jillian said lightly, "Actually, I was thinking about moving back."

"You're kidding? What would you want to come back here for?" Myrna's eyes narrowed. "Hey, are you seriously planning on getting back with Randy? He is engaged, you know." She continued before

Jillian could reply, "Honey, Randy's nice, but he's not for you. He wasn't when you were sixteen, and he sure isn't now that you've seen the world. You'd be bored out of your gourd in two weeks."

A flutter of denial ran through Jillian. Boring was lazing around on a yacht or the beach, your only concern the need to look good and make yourself agreeable to the other guests so they'd invite you to their house parties. Parties where no one did anything but make idle chitchat, gossip, flirt, eat, drink, and be merry. Day after day, same old, same old.

Jillian shook her head and smiled. "I was hoping you might have a job for me here."

Myrna shook her head. "Come on, Jillian Taylor slinging hash?" She gave Jillian a penetrating look. "I'm sorry, honey, but the winter season is so slow I've laid off everyone but Shirley. In fact, I've been thinking of closing up entirely and going to Arizona for the winters. I hardly get enough business to make it worth my while to keep the joint open."

Humiliated, Jillian fought to act natural. "That's a shame."

"The only other business is Ben's grocery store, and he has so many kids he don't need to hire anybody else."

So much for that great idea. Disappointment clenched Jillian's body, which felt stiff and unable to move except for the quivering of her lips. She attempted to smile again at Myrna. What could she say? Nothing, short of asking for a loan. But Myrna sounded as if she barely had enough to get her through the next few months, let alone make a loan to anyone else.

Myrna leaned closer and said, "Confidentially, honey, if you want to stay here, go after Luke."

Jillian shook her head vigorously. Go after Luke? What a horrendous thought. Instead she asked, "If I were to get a job in the Falls, do you know anyone who drives in every day that I could ride with?" Just until she got her first paycheck. Then she'd move there.

Myrna thought for a moment, then she nodded. "Frank goes in and I think Gayle Marshall used to go in. You could check with her."

Jillian groaned inwardly. There was nothing like grasping at straws, and this seemed a mighty thin one. While Myrna filled her in on everything that had occurred in the last ten years, Jillian listened, struggling to conceal her distress. Although she was interested in the lives of her former classmates, she found it difficult to concentrate.

Finally, after making her farewells and promising that she'd see Myrna again, Jillian climbed into the car. She waved back as her old friend waved from the café window, then pulled out and started down the road back to the Prescotts'. What should she do now? Obviously there was no work in Quail Creek. She'd driven about a mile when she decided to go on into Idaho Falls. Nothing ventured, nothing gained. Surely some dress shop in Idaho Falls would be hiring for the Christmas season. She could probably stay at Randy's and commute with Gayle Marshall until she got her first paycheck. Her heart beat faster, and for the first time in months, she felt hopeful about her future.

She arrived in Idaho Falls about eleven-thirty and stopped to ask directions to the mall, thinking that would be the best place to start. She decided to begin at ZCMI and nervously made her way to their personnel department. After all, she had once been on their teen board. This was the store that had given Jillian her start as a model.

Hiding her jitters behind an air of confidence, Jillian walked up to the reception desk and cleared her throat before starting to speak.

"E-e-e-e!" The startled woman at the desk let out a yelp. She also dropped the cards she was sorting.

Jillian jumped back. "Sorry!"

"My fault," said the receptionist, disconcerted and distracted. "How can I help you?"

Seeing that they'd both been unnerved for a moment, Jillian felt more at ease. "I'd like to apply for a sales job."

The woman looked apologetic. "I'm sorry. We haven't any openings at present. We've already finished hiring for Christmas. We like to train everyone before Thanksgiving, so we're ready to go the next day. That Friday is always our biggest sales day of the year." She looked closely at Jillian. "You look familiar. Have you applied here before?'

Striving to hide her disappointment, Jillian smiled brightly. "Not in years. I'm Jillian Taylor. You might have seen me in commercials or magazines." *And not the tabloids, I hope.*

The woman looked puzzled for a moment. "Jillian Taylor," she said slowly. "Oh, that Jillian Taylor! That's right. You are from around here, aren't you?"

Jillian nodded, as if pleased at the recognition. "Quail Creek."

"I'm thrilled to meet you. I wish you'd applied two weeks ago; we'd have hired you for sure. But fill out this application." She reached into the bottom drawer and pulled out a form, which she handed to Jillian. "If any of the temporary employees quit, we want you. In fact, the next regular opening is yours. You're just what our fashion department needs. Don't worry, we'll be calling you."

With a deep sigh, Jillian seated herself at the next desk and filled out the papers. The job sounded promising, but she needed something now, not in the future.

By the end of the afternoon, her feet hurt and her head ached. She'd met with similar responses everywhere she'd gone. "Oh! You're not that Jillian Taylor, are you? We'd love to hire you. Just fill out the application, and we'll call you when there's an opening."

Despair filled her as she drove back to Quail Creek. No one wanted her, and she didn't know what to do next. She had just passed Myrna's when suddenly her heart fluttered and she felt lightheaded and weak again. At a campsite turnoff, she pulled off the road and parked. Slumping down in the seat, she made an effort to shake the dizziness.

What was the matter with her? She was having difficulty breathing and her heart was palpitating. What if she were seriously ill? Where could she go? Who would even care? She breathed deeply and slowly in an effort to calm down. She wasn't ill. She was just hungry. That was the problem. She hadn't eaten breakfast today or lunch, and the few bites she'd eaten last night were virtually all she'd had since she'd received the news of her father's death. Hunger, that's all it was. She'd be able to drive in a few minutes. She closed her eyes and attempted to clear her head. She didn't know how long she'd been there when someone rattled the door.

She shot up, her head swimming. Oh, no! It was Luke Prescott, of all people! Why did he have to be the one to see her when she had a problem. He'd caught her dizzy and fainting at the funeral and now this. Like a bad penny, he always seemed to turn up.

"Go away!"

"Open the door." He rattled the handle again.

She shook her head. "Just go away!" Before she understood his intentions, he circled the car and tried the passenger door. Drat! She hadn't noticed it wasn't locked.

"What are you doing?" he demanded, sliding in beside her.

"I felt dizzy. I stopped. I pulled off the road. Now I'm just waiting until my head clears. I'm perfectly all right, so go on home. " His persistence exacerbated her headache. Why couldn't he just leave her alone?

His eyes narrowed accusingly. "Why don't you just stop dieting and eat normally like other people? But you wouldn't dare, would you? Your face and figure are money in the bank."

Her head still reeling, Jillian tried to glare at him. "No kidding!"

"But what are you going to do when your assets run out?" He gave her a grim look. "You'd better start looking for a man who can keep you in the way you've become accustomed before you lose those flashy looks of yours. Just remember one thing—that man isn't Randy."

"Oh, no," she said slowly, closing her eyes and leaning her head back against the headrest. "Much better to go after *you,* since according to Myrna you have the money in the family."

His voice turned to ice. "You're wasting your time. Shallow women are a dime a dozen."

She opened her eyes and looked at him. "Not ones who have been the toast of seven continents."

His eyes seemed to bore through her. "I'm not interested."

Dizziness swept over Jillian again. As her eyes closed, she glimpsed concern on Luke's face. He leaned across her and unlocked the door. Then he pulled her over to the passenger side. "I'll drive you home."

"Please don't bother." It was an effort to even speak. "I can do it." After she'd rested a little longer.

"I have my doubts, and I'd hate to have something happen to Randy's car." He climbed out, slamming the door, and returned to the driver's side where he slipped behind the steering wheel.

Barely aware of the trip home, Jillian roused herself only when Luke gently lifted her in his arms and carried her to the house. His arms felt so warm and comforting, it was hard to remember he was the enemy. He placed her carefully on the living room couch.

Mrs. Prescott fluttered around, undoubtedly scared to death she might be stuck with her unwelcome house guest even longer. "What's the matter with her?"

"Probably nothing that a few square meals wouldn't cure," Luke said, as if reassuring his aunt that Jillian's fragile condition was purely temporary.

Unable to gather enough energy to speak, Jillian closed her eyes, ignoring them both.

Mrs. Prescott gasped. "She hasn't fainted, has she?"

Jillian heard Luke's voice as if from a distance. "I don't know what's the matter."

That couldn't be concern she heard in his voice, she thought vaguely. She felt strong fingers pick up one of her hands and massage it, as if trying to infuse her with his strength.

"Open your eyes, Jillian," he commanded.

She felt perverse enough to keep her eyes shut deliberately, but in reality her eyelids were so heavy she couldn't open them. She didn't even try. The darkness was closing in and she let it surround her with its comforting warmth.

—⁓—

When she awoke, Luke was gone and Randy's mother was sitting in the chair across from her, watching.

"Here, let me fix you some herbal tea. Randy's taken Luke to get his truck. When they get back, we'll have supper." She left the room.

Not tea! It was Jillian's least favorite drink. But she didn't protest. With great effort, she swung her feet off the couch and attempted to sit up, but waves of dizziness forced her to sink back against the cushions. She knew neither Mrs. Prescott nor Luke would believe this wasn't an act. When Helen Prescott returned with a steaming pot of tea, Jillian slowly rose to a sitting position. As she poured herself a cup, the scent of peppermint wafted up.

She stirred the tea for a few moments enjoying the fragrance before looking directly at Mrs. Prescott. She lacked the strength to speak in more than a soft whisper. "Luke told me to leave town last night. I'm sure he wasn't speaking for himself alone."

The older woman had the grace to look uncomfortable. "He's only concerned about the family, and you know you don't want to stay around here. Why make Randy think you do?"

"You're wrong. I would like to stay." She added a heaping teaspoon of sugar to the tea and slowly stirred it. "But not because of Randy. I needed a friend, and it was good of you to let me stay."

Mrs. Prescott wasn't reassured. "But you don't love Randy. You walked away and probably never gave him another thought. But for years I've watched him looking eagerly through magazines for pictures of you, and he even reads those cheap newspapers at the checkout stand, trying to find news of you." Her voice trembled. "I won't see him heartbroken again. Can't you see that no matter what you do, it'll ruin his life?" Jillian could see that Randy's mother was near tears.

"I wouldn't do anything to hurt him," she said honestly. "Randy's a good friend and he deserves to be happy."

As if Jillian hadn't spoken, Mrs. Prescott continued, "You'd never be content to stay here. Besides, Randy's not rich enough to give you the things you want."

"Believe me, my wants have become simpler," Jillian said dryly. Once, at the height of her career, she could never have imagined returning to Quail Creek to live. But she'd always considered Quail Creek a cozy little community where people cared about each other, an image that had been shattered when she'd actually come here and felt the resentment towards her. They'd cared about her father, and she'd automatically thought they'd feel that way about her. In the last few days, she'd realized that people here not only didn't care about her, they were threatened by her. Seeing this, she was on her guard, and nothing would convince her to lower her defenses. She would just put on her best self-confident pose and act as if she wasn't bothered in the least that the town had judged her and found her lacking.

Putting down the spoon, she lifted the cup to her lips and shuddered as the first sip went down. Medicinal or not, she couldn't stand the taste.

Mrs. Prescott continued to eye her. "You're fooling yourself, Jillian, if you think you could be happy here." Her voice was cold and sharp. "A rancher puts in long, hard hours and needs a wife who knows what hard work is. Cooking, gardening, canning fruit become old pretty fast."

Feeling disliked and unwanted, Jillian felt the woman's words cut through her like a knife. She'd known this conversation wouldn't be easy, but she'd had no idea it would leave her feeling so raw.

"And Marci wouldn't get tired of hard work?" Jillian said, with a casual lift of her eyebrows. It was obvious that Randy's mother had endowed his fiancée with every possible virtue.

Ignoring the jab, Mrs. Prescott let her eyes drift over Jillian's thin, listless form. "You need a well-to-do husband. Look at you. You're their type."

Maybe so, but the rich men she knew hadn't wanted to marry her. Flirt with her, be seen with her, have an affair with her, yes. Marry her, no. When she'd been at the height of her popularity, she'd turned down a dozen marriage proposals. She was too young and having too much fun to settle down. Now she thought it would be nice to have someone who cared about her, but . . .

Helen Prescott sniffed. "Even Luke is more your type."

"Surely you jest!" Jillian set her cup down. "Marrying Luke would be a fate worse than death!"

"Probably not, but you'll never have a chance to find out." Luke stood in the kitchen doorway.

"That's a relief," Jillian said with asperity as she watched him cross the room.

He patted his aunt's shoulder. "Don't worry, Aunt Helen. Jillian's not interested in Randy." He gave Jillian a quelling glance. "Don't try me."

A shiver ran through her. Luke was in earnest, and he was a powerful adversary. He had determination stamped all over him, and she recognized how ruthless he would be if anyone threatened his family.

At that moment, Randy came through the doorway and gazed around the room, looking perplexed. "What's going on?"

"Your mother and Luke are—" she began, but Luke waved an impatient hand toward her.

"Nothing," he effectively cut her off.

Randy didn't waste any time on analyzing undercurrents. "Then could you help me out?" he asked Luke. "One of the cows is having problems calving, and I could use your help."

"Sure." With a final look at Jillian, he followed Randy out. Jillian knew Luke wasn't finished with her. Like an avenging god, he was going to see that she received just retribution.

When the outside door banged shut, Helen Prescott stood and stared down at Jillian. "What about the Church?" she demanded.

"What about the Church?" The sudden change of subject bewildered Jillian.

"Are you active? Do you even want to go to the temple?" Mrs. Prescott demanded.

Jillian stiffened. She never thought about the Church anymore. It simply wasn't a part of her life. She'd given it more consideration during her father's funeral than she had in years. She remained silent.

"I thought not," Mrs. Prescott sniffed. "Randy's been on a mission to Argentina and the gospel means a lot to him. Marci wants to be married in the temple." She paused. "I'm sorry, Jillian, but you're forcing me to say this: you're not welcome in this house any longer. One day Randy will inherit this ranch, but right now it belongs to me and you're leaving immediately. I won't have his life ruined."

Jillian's stomach knotted and waves of nausea swept over her. For a moment she thought she was going to be sick. Randy's mother must really be afraid of her if she'd go this far. Jillian stood up shakily. What could she say that would alleviate the older woman's fears? Hadn't she heard a word Jillian had said?

Refusing to appear as forlorn as she felt, Jillian flashed her most sincere model's smile. "You win, Mrs. Prescott, but as in all good westerns, you will give me twenty-four hours to leave town, won't you?" She'd come up with something. She had to.

Randy's mother looked suspiciously at Jillian. "All right, but not a minute longer."

"Of course not. Isn't that when the sheriff and his posse take matters into their own hands? Believe me, I want to avoid another showdown."

Without waiting for anything further from Mrs. Prescott, Jillian climbed the stairs to her room, unable to calm the nervous tremors that bombarded her stomach. She didn't want any supper; the mere thought of food gagged her.

Closing the door firmly behind her, she went straight to the bed and huddled under the comforter in an attempt to ease her anxiety. What could she do? There were no jobs in Quail Creek, and none immediately available in Idaho Falls. She had no place to live. She had five dollars to her name. She might try calling the yacht, but her "friends" could be anywhere in the Mediterranean by now since they'd had no definite itinerary.

This wasn't the time for pride. The only thing she could think of was to ask Randy for a loan. She groaned. If Mrs. Prescott also controlled the purse strings, Jillian could foresee problems. Randy would probably insist she stay with them. She gave a bitter laugh. That in itself ought to make his mother eager to give her the money. Who did she know around here that would possibly give her a loan? Frank Ross would set her bags on the highway and say, "Start thumbing." Myrna was out. Her mind whirled. Surely there was someone she could ask for a loan. She lay there, frantically searching for any possible solution. She couldn't get a grip on her thoughts. They seemed to slide right out of her mind, and she couldn't think clearly enough to stop them. Who around here cared about her? Or was there anyone generous enough to help her out?

The bishop! He had said he was there if she needed to talk to someone. For the first time in years, she prayed.

Please, God, let the bishop help me.

CHAPTER 6

Slowly Jillian pulled the church door open. If Randy hadn't been right behind her, she would have turned and run. Suddenly she was terrified of talking to the bishop. When she'd called him, he'd asked her to come to his office at the ward. She thought she'd be able to ask for money to leave on, but as the time of the appointment drew closer, her throat had begun to tighten. She didn't know if she would even be able to get any words out. The once proud Jillian Taylor forced to beg for money in order to exist. What a humiliating predicament.

Since her fainting spell earlier, Randy had insisted on driving her to the meeting. She could scarcely tell him now to never mind and to take her back to his place. His mother would hardly welcome her, and she only had about twenty hours left of the twenty-four before she had to be out of town! She tried to swallow to steady herself, but the lump in her throat was so enormous she found it impossible. She hoped she would be able to speak when the time came.

"The bishop's office is this way." Taking her arm, Randy guided her down the hall to the right. Jillian had to force herself not to hang back.

The door to Bishop Walker's office was open. When he looked up, he stood and motioned for her to come in. "Good evening, Jillian. Randy. Is it cold enough for you?" His manner was genial and brisk.

"And then some." Randy grabbed the doorknob. "I'll wait out here until you're finished." Pulling the door closed, he left.

"Sit down, Jillian. I'm glad you decided to come in and visit with me. I've been concerned about you ever since your father's funeral. How are you doing?"

As she tried to answer his question, Jillian's lips trembled and her words sounded weak and quivery to her ears. "At this point, not so good."

Bishop Walker nodded. "I was afraid of that. Let's see." His brow furrowed as if trying to remember. "How long have you been gone from Quail Creek?"

"About ten years. I left when I was sixteen."

"Knowing your dad, I'm surprised he let you go when you were so young."

"My folks didn't want me to go, but I'd won the ZCMI Teenage Fashion Board award in Idaho Falls and had represented this area in modeling for the Back-to-School issue of *Seventeen* magazine. I won a trip to New York." Her voice became wistful. "I loved New York, and I couldn't wait to go back and model full time. Finally, I wore my parents down and they spoke to the bishop of the Manhattan ward. He recommended an LDS family for me to live with, and they met with the head of the modeling agency. Finally they allowed me to go, and my mother went with me to get me settled."

"I understand better now." He gave her an encouraging look. "Are you still modeling?"

Jillian hesitated. She wanted to say yes, but she had the feeling that the bishop would know she wasn't being honest. "No. Not too often."

A shadow of concern crossed his face. "Then how are you managing to live? Do you have savings?"

Guilt like a flame of fire curled through her. She couldn't confess her lifestyle to the bishop. Over the last several years her life had been anything but religious. What would the bishop think of her? She couldn't dishonor her family by telling him the truth. What should she do? She closed her eyes and sat silently, unable to speak.

The bishop broke the silence. "Jillian, I don't know what has happened, but I think you need to talk. I can tell how burdened you are by your life. In Matthew the Savior says, 'Come unto me, all ye that labour and are heavy laden, and I will give you rest.' Don't be afraid. I'm here to listen."

Tears burned as they poured out of her eyes, and for a few minutes all she could do was sob. The bishop handed her some tissues, and she mopped up the ravages of the tears. Taking several deep breaths, she started to speak. Unable to meet the bishop's eyes, she looked around the room instead as she spoke, her words tremulous and halting.

"I haven't modeled regularly in three or four years. After my early success, I'm ashamed to admit I started acting like a diva. I was demanding and undependable at shoots. Sometimes I'd be late; other times I wouldn't even show up. I didn't save anything because I was living high and spending everything I made. I was the 'belle of the ball' in New York, and I thought I'd always be in demand as a model or a spokeswoman.

"But after too many late nights, my life began to show in my face. That along with my reputation for being unreliable made me unemployable. No one wanted to use me anymore. Two years ago I hit rock bottom. I couldn't pay my rent, so I sold my furniture, took my clothes to a consignment shop, and became a perennial house guest." She tried to smile, but the muscles of her face wouldn't respond. "I've been going from party to party, making myself charming and fun to be around so others will invite me to be their house guest. Every few months I get small residuals from commercials, but not enough to live on. I use that money to replenish my wardrobe." Hesitantly, she met the bishop's eyes. "I always used to sneer at hanger-ons and now I'm one myself." A sob punctuated the end of her sentence.

"Why didn't you tell your father and come home?" he said gently.

"I was too ashamed. I'd left in glory, and I wanted to come home the same way. I couldn't let people know I'd failed, that I was washed up."

Jillian found that the words came more easily now. "I'd say pride was a failing of the Taylor family. My father never let me know he was sick or had lost the farm. And I never told him that I couldn't find work as a model. If I'd only put aside my vanity and told him the truth, I could have come home and helped him more. I feel so guilty. So far my life has amounted to a big fat zero. I'm broke, Bishop. I don't even have enough money to get back to New York."

She was quiet now, hoping he would offer her some financial help without her having to ask outright. She felt as if she were groveling as it was. She gazed down at his desk, feeling painfully vulnerable. What a horrible feeling. It felt as if the bishop could see right through her, as if she hadn't a secret left.

Bishop Walker folded his hands and contemplated Jillian for a few minutes. "I don't suppose you're active in the Church?" His voice was mild and nonjudgmental.

"No." She swallowed, embarrassed. "I haven't really gone to church since the first few years I was in New York, when I lived with the Nelsons."

"Why did you leave them?"

"I left to come home to take care of my mother before she died. Then when I went back to New York, I was eighteen and tired of their restrictions. I felt I was old enough to manage my own life. Once I got my own apartment, to be honest, I stayed out so late on Saturday nights that I could never get up in time for church. Every week, I told myself I'd go the next week. But I never did. And finally, I just quit thinking about it."

She sounded like a real winner, she thought in disgust. And although he didn't show it, she thought the bishop was probably equally disgusted with her. Hearing herself speak, she shook her head in disbelief at her naivete and downright stupidity.

He reached across the desk for his scriptures and opening them, he said, "The Lord is talking to the Israelites here, but the promise is given to us as well. 'Cease to do evil,' He says. 'Learn to do well,' which means to do good works. 'Seek judgment,' which is justice. 'Judge the fatherless, plead for the widow.' Then He says, 'Come now, and let us reason together. . . . Though your sins be as scarlet, they shall be as white as snow; though they be red like crimson, they shall be as wool. If ye be willing and obedient, ye shall eat the good of the land.'"

The bishop closed the book and met Jillian's eyes. "The Lord loves you no matter what you have done, Jillian, and He's anxious to forgive you." He paused, seeming to ponder what to say next. Finally he spoke again, "As a bishop I could buy you a ticket for New York. I'm sure you could find a job there, even if it weren't modeling. But I feel impressed that the Lord wants you to stay here."

"Stay here?" Jillian could hardly believe her ears. "Mrs. Prescott has given me twenty-four hours to leave town!" Now why did she tell him that? She hadn't planned to mention Randy's mother at all. She cringed. What if Randy had heard her shriek his mother's name?

The bishop looked amused, but he didn't comment on Jillian's outburst. "You've told me how guilty you feel for neglecting your dad and how, so far, your life has added up to 'a big fat zero.' I'm going to suggest a way in which you can follow the instructions in Isaiah. The Lord says to do good works, to plead for the widow. We have a sister in our ward who has had several strokes. She is unable to care for herself. Her husband has passed away, and at the present time, she is staying with her former employer, who loves her as any son would love his mother. But he can't find anyone to care for her and take care of the house for him.

"If you took this job, you would be doing good works for a widow who is in need, you would earn a small salary along with board and room, and the Lord has promised you that your sins, whatever they are, will be as white as snow and like wool."

Jillian mulled over his words. This would give her a chance to help others, maybe assuage part of her guilt, and earn some money in the bargain. She certainly didn't have anyone who gave two pins about her and would wonder where she was. But she didn't know if the Lord could forgive her or if He really wanted her here. But she really didn't have any other options.

"I'm interested," she admitted, "but I'll warn you, I haven't had much experience nursing people or taking care of a house."

"Love will help make up for the lack of skill, and Emma is easy to love, I promise you." He reached for his telephone. "If you only have twenty-four hours to leave town—" his face softened and his eyes twinkled, "—I guess you'll want to start tomorrow."

Relief inundated Jillian and she agreed. "Thank you, Bishop." She would be out of the Prescotts' home and someplace where people would welcome her and be grateful for her presence.

"Let me call Luke. You'll be lifting a burden from his shoulders."

"Luke Prescott?" She prayed there were other Lukes in town.

"Yes." He smiled at her as he dialed the phone. "I think you'll find Luke easy to work for. He's actually a very caring, compassionate man. I'm sure he will do what he can to help you out."

Caring? Compassionate? Were they thinking of the same man?

She reached over and pressed the receiver back down in its cradle. "Bishop," she warned him, "Luke has a very low opinion of me. I can't believe he'd go for this idea."

He smiled gently at her. "I think he will." He patted her hand gently and picked up the phone again. He keyed in a number, listened for a moment, then hung up. "The line's busy. I'll try again in a minute."

When the line continued to give a busy signal for the next fifteen minutes, the bishop stood up. "I hate to keep Randy waiting any longer, so why don't you go on home? I'll have Luke call you to make the arrangements."

"All right. And thanks again." Jillian slipped into her jacket and left the office, joining Randy in the hall. Despite the fear of working for Luke, she had an overwhelming feeling of relief. At last—a job, a home, money. At this point she couldn't ask for anything more.

They were at the front door of the church before Randy started probing. "What did you find out?"

Before she could answer him, he opened the door, and a blast of arctic air hit her. She gasped, causing the words to come out in little puffs. "The bishop . . . says . . . Luke needs someone . . . to care for a-a-a . . ." The frigid air must have frozen her brain. Of all things, she couldn't think of the woman's name.

"Emma?" Randy's voice rang in disbelief.

"Yes." She stuck her hands in her pockets and gripped the sides of her body with her elbows, attempting to stop shaking from the cold.

They hurried to the car and he opened the door. "You can't do that." His words were firm and decisive.

She slid in and waited while he settled himself. After he started the motor, she replied, "What do you mean, I can't do that?" She had doubts herself about her ability to do the work, but she didn't like hearing Randy doubt her as well.

He immediately jumped to her defense. "I think they'd be lucky to get you, but keeping house and nursing isn't something I can imagine you ever wanting to do."

She hadn't, but a desperate sailor is glad for any port in a storm. "Your mother does it," she pointed out to him.

"That's different," he objected.

It sure was, Jillian thought. His mother knew how.

"She's never done anything else," Randy continued. "Somehow I just can't see you washing dishes, mopping floors, cooking meals, that kind of thing. You look above that kind of work."

Well, as she'd quickly found out—she wasn't.

Suddenly needles of fear punctuated her relief. She'd never known anyone who'd had a stroke. A couple of times on TV she'd seen actors portraying stroke victims, but that meant nothing. Were they always paralyzed? Did it always affect their speech? If this woman was stricken that way, how could Jillian ever care for her?

"Just how bad was Emma's stroke?" she asked slowly.

"I don't really know, only that she's pretty much homebound. I don't think I've seen her at church in about a month."

Jillian started to worry. Why had she ever agreed to the bishop's outrageous suggestion? What if bedpans were necessary? She couldn't handle that. Then she caught herself. Yes, she could. She had no choice. She needed money, and she really did yearn to have her sins become white as wool, and to find relief from the burden of her bad choices. She could do that through service, according to the bishop.

"Then again, since you don't mind, the more I consider it, the more I think it will be just great having you here. I didn't want you to go anyway, and now you're not. That's fantastic." He started to sound more cheerful.

Oh, great, Jillian sighed wearily. Just when she was starting to feel terrified, Randy had begun thinking it would be fantastic. Then there was Luke, who mostly definitely would not think it was fantastic. He'd probably be furious, especially if he heard what Randy thought.

Lost in her own thoughts, Jillian merely nodded. Smiling to himself, Randy drove toward home, silently planning her future in Quail Creek.

—⁓—

"Jillian Taylor?!" The force of Luke's words hurdled through the phone line. "Bishop, do you know what you're suggesting? I'd lay odds she hasn't a clue how to do anything as mundane as nursing or housework."

The bishop seemed unperturbed. "Sorry, Luke. It's against Church policy to gamble." But the smile in his voice didn't allay Luke's fears.

"Do you even know her?" He made a great effort not to let the bishop see the anger his suggestion had aroused in him. He gripped the phone tighter. "I don't think she has good enough judgment that I'd be comfortable leaving Emma alone with her."

"I think you're underestimating her ability. Desire is one of the most important aspects of this job, and no one has more desire to take care of Emma or to do it successfully than Jillian. Face it, Luke, you haven't been able to find anyone from Idaho Falls who will brave the remoteness of your ranch, and no one around here is available. I feel Jillian will work out just fine. Give her a two-week trial and see how she does."

"Okay," Luke said grudgingly, "but not a minute longer." His tone changed to resignation. "I just hope Emma and I survive the two weeks."

The bishop laughed. "I haven't a doubt you will. Now call Jillian and make the arrangements. She's ready to start tomorrow."

Shaking his head, Luke slowly walked into the living room where Emma lay on the sofa. "That was the bishop. What do you think about Jillian Taylor giving us a hand for a while?"

Emma perked right up. "Fabulous. Now you can quit hovering about the house, and she can tell me all about her modeling career. I've never been anyplace bigger than Salt Lake." Her eyes twinkled as she grinned at him. "Having her here will be very educational."

"For whom, I wonder." He returned to the kitchen to call Jillian.

—∞—

After a brisk message from Luke, telling her he would be by to pick her up about eleven, Jillian had gone to bed to spend a restless night, worrying how she would cope with managing Luke's household.

This morning she still had the jitters, but she prayed everything would work out. It had to. She couldn't allow herself to consider the alternatives. A visibly relieved Mrs. Prescott bustled around getting breakfast, showing her guest considerably more warmth since learning of her imminent departure. Even so, Jillian felt uncomfortable. Unable to sit and wait quietly, she kept pulling back the curtains and peering out the window, watching for Luke's truck. Just as the clock pointed to eleven, Luke pulled up in the driveway. Before he could make it up the steps, she flung open the front door.

"I'll get my bags and be right down."

"Let me give you a hand." He followed her upstairs.

"Thanks for the help. It's over here." Jillian pointed out the two suitcases by the closet. "I'll take my garment bag."

"Just a minute," he said, closing the bedroom door and leaning against it. "Before we leave, we need to get a few things straight." His eyes narrowed as he stared steadily at her, his gaze burned through her. "Why are you taking this job?"

Feeling on the defensive, she gritted her teeth. "I need money in order to leave."

"You mean to tell me that the fabulous Jillian Taylor, the toast of seven continents, is broke?"

Her face burned as she nodded.

"I thought as much when you would have haggled over twenty-five dollars at the auction." He frowned at her. "That's preposterous. How could anyone run through as much money as you've made?"

"Quite easily, in fact," she said. *It's easy to spend money in New York City, especially when you're young and foolish and think you're a golden girl whom the gods will always favor.*

"Have you learned anything worthwhile? Can you cook? Clean?" He gave her a piercing look. "Do you know anything about nursing an elderly woman?"

His tone told her that if she admitted to any weaknesses, Luke might well refuse to hire her after all. "I grew up on a farm, didn't I?" She kept her voice light. "Doesn't farm living produce competent women?" What a lie! Her growing up years were another lifetime ago, and offhand the last time she could recall cleaning or cooking was years ago, when her mother was ill. And her mother was the only one she'd ever nursed. But if she wanted a place to live and enough money to return to New York, she'd learn. She had an idea that this might be the hardest money she'd ever earned and Luke the most difficult employer she'd ever worked for. Her stomach knotted again.

Giving her a skeptical look, he picked up her suitcases and opened the door.

What a turn her life had taken. A week ago she was the toast of the tabloids, now the hired woman. But, she admitted to herself, this was much, much better.

CHAPTER 7

Surreptitiously, Jillian studied Luke's profile as they traveled to his ranch. The bishop might have thought Luke would be easy to work for, but something about his manner seemed at odds with the bishop's assessment. At the same time, she thought, not everyone would hire someone to care for his housekeeper. Even so, his unyielding jaw and the glacial blue of his eyes made it plain he didn't suffer fools gladly. Somewhere in the recesses of her mind, she felt he placed her in that category. But she'd prove him wrong.

She shivered as she remembered all too clearly his mocking words. Here was someone used to having his own way, and he held her immediate future in his hands. She would need to watch what she said. No more caustic comments, or else. Or else she might find herself out on the streets.

She'd felt only relief leaving the Prescotts', and she knew the feeling was mutual, at least for Mrs. Prescott. However tough the next few months might be, Jillian was certain she'd be far happier at Luke's than at Randy's. Mrs. Prescott had made little effort to suppress her delight at no longer having Jillian as a house guest.

When they finally turned off the highway, Jillian spotted a log structure about a quarter of a mile away; behind it stood several outbuildings. Unlike her family's farm with its house and barn and a few sheds, this appeared to be a small community at the edge of the foothills. Even Randy's farm hadn't been this size.

A split-rail fence enclosed the area between the county road and a house. Surely it must be a pasture; they couldn't have that much lawn. What if her job included mowing the grass? Good grief, what a dumb thought. It was the middle of winter. She'd be long gone by the time the lawn needed to be mowed.

Trees stretched along the lane to the ranch, their stark black branches outlined against the harsh gray sky. When she caught a closer view of the house, her heart fell. This was no farmer's dwelling. It appeared more like a lodge than a cabin. In fact, she'd spent time at a friend's hunting lodge in Canada that hadn't seemed much larger than this. Talk about "a man's home being his castle," Luke's family must have taken this concept literally. Overwhelmed at the immensity of the house, she shook her head in disbelief, at the same time trying to stifle her dismay. What had she gotten herself into? An impressive porch swept across the front from the left wing to the right one. A large bay window surrounded by fieldstone formed a cupola at the right corner.

When she had envisioned keeping the house clean, she'd never even considered what size it might be. Why hadn't she realized that anything involving Luke Prescott would never be ordinary? After all, Myrna had said he was wealthy. At the time Jillian had considered it an exaggeration, but seeing this place, she was rapidly becoming convinced that it might have been an understatement.

Luke pulled into the driveway at the rear of the house and parked. Jillian could see that the fence ended here, beside the house, just beneath a towering fir tree.

"We're here," he announced unnecessarily.

Another porch extended along the rear of the house with varnished timber pillars holding up the roof. Did this house ever end? And what would the inside be like?

Across the way were more buildings, several corrals, and some large tin-roofed sheds. "I didn't expect all these buildings," she said, looking around.

"When you run 12,000 sheep, it takes quite a few." He pointed to a long, low, grimy-white cinder block building. "That's the bunkhouse. We usually have about fifteen men working here, and they live over there."

"Do they cook for themselves?" Apprehension filled her voice. Maybe she could fix meals for Luke and Emma given her lack of kitchen skills, but cook for fifteen men?

He gave her a knowing smile. "Relax. They have their own cook."

"That's a relief." Although Jillian attempted to give a dramatic sigh, she was afraid it sounded woefully heartfelt.

Luke opened the door and got out. "No time like the present to go in and meet Emma."

Fighting her nervousness, Jillian climbed out of the truck holding her garment bag while Luke removed her cases from the pickup bed. Expertly juggling her bags, he led the way up the stairs to the porch, wiped his feet on the doormat, and nudged the door open, holding it for her. "Welcome to your home away from home."

Although surprised at the light tone of his voice, Jillian crossed her fingers anyway. "I'm sure I'll enjoy it. Lead the way."

The warm homey smells of freshly baked bread took the edge off Jillian's nerves as she stepped into the ranch kitchen. Yellow pine cabinets and tiled floor reminded her that for all the hunting lodge grandeur of the outside, this was still a rancher's home and a working ranch kitchen.

Standing at the island in the center of the room, a short brunette ladled soup into yellow and blue oversized mugs. Before Luke could say anything, she greeted them warmly, "You must be Jillian. I'm Nancy Jenkins, your next-door neighbor—if you consider five miles to be next door. We're certainly glad you could come and stay with Emma."

At these words Jillian glanced at Luke, who was setting her bags down by the dining room door, and was surprised to see that his expression didn't contradict Nancy's statement.

Attempting to shake off her jitters, she smiled back at the woman. "I'm looking forward to it." She paused, wordless. What else could she say in the face of such friendliness? "It's nice to meet my neighbors so soon."

"Go on in. Emma's eager to see you. I'll finish dishing up lunch." Nancy began buttering a slice of the warm bread.

Jillian tensed again. She hoped Emma liked her. She'd loved staying with her grandparents when she was a child, and she'd always had a soft spot in her heart for the elderly because of them. She followed Luke through the kitchen doorway into the dining room. To her right, French doors opened to the veranda and a long harvest table divided the area.

On the other side of the room she saw a frail white-haired woman, her neck glowing with strand after strand of pearls, sitting on a black leather love seat in front of a mammoth stone fireplace. To the left an open stairway curved up to a balcony.

When Emma spied them, her face lit up, and she looked at Jillian expectantly. "You're Jillian. I'm so glad you've come to stay with us." She held out a thin hand ablaze with bright red fingernails. "I promise I won't be any work for you."

Her words touched Jillian. Someone was glad to see her! Other than Myrna and Randy, no one in Quail Creek had been this gracious to her. Usually with her friends, they kissed the air around each cheek along with a light hug and that sufficed. But she could sense that Emma was real. She longed to bask in the warmth of someone's love. Without warning, an unexpected tenderness permeated Jillian's entire being. She placed her bag on an overstuffed chair and gently took the elderly woman's hand in her own.

"Don't worry about making work for me." Jillian patted her hand reassuringly. "Don't you know, Emma? From now on you're the center of my universe. I'm just happy to be here."

Emma placed her other hand over Jillian's and squeezed. "Oh, my dear, you don't want an old woman to be the center of your universe, but I'm thrilled you'd say so. We're going to get along famously."

"Yes, we are." Jillian nodded in agreement, then glanced at Luke, giving him a genuine smile for the first time. "Now where should I put my things? I don't want to waste any more time before Emma and I get further acquainted." She picked up the garment bag again.

Beneath the balcony, against the rear wall, stood a doorway. Luke led her over to the door and motioned her through it into a short T-shaped hallway. Pointing to the left, he said, "Emma's room is opposite yours. The bathroom is in between, and—" he pointed to the other side, "—this one is yours. That way you can help her if she needs anything during the night."

The size of the room amazed Jillian, and she hardly heard his words. *This much space for the hired help?* The room was enormous; in fact, it was more like a master bedroom. Dominating the area was an immense log fence bed covered with a plump red and white quilt. An armoire with faded blue paint stood in one corner next to a bay window. In front of the window, a sofa faced a window seat, and alongside the bed was a whitewashed night stand.

She could see distant mountains through the top panes of the bay windows while matching red and white curtains covered the bottom ones. Next to the bed a cheery red and blue rag rug accented the shiny wood floor.

"Is there a closet or should I use the armoire?" she asked.

"The armoire has a television in it, so you might find it a little crowded." He opened a door, and Jillian found herself staring into a huge walk-in closet.

As she stood there bemused, Luke left the room, saying, "I'll get your suitcases and you can settle in."

Glad for a respite from Luke's company, Jillian hung her garment bag in the closet, then sank onto the red sofa. Her apprehension over caring for Emma had vanished; she knew her charge would be a delight.

With worry for her future no longer a burden on her senses, she could allow herself to feel the emotions she had suppressed since her father's funeral. Now, for the first time since the day of the auction, a feeling of loneliness invaded her. Even Emma with all her kindness couldn't assuage it. Staying with the Prescotts, she had been too concerned about what she was going to do next to allow herself to feel the full weight of her loss. Her parents were both gone and she had no one. She couldn't curb the trembling inside or the feeling of total abandonment. She had no anchor.

"Nancy has lunch ready." Luke came through her door and neatly deposited the cases at the foot of the bed. "You can settle in after we eat."

She followed him back to the dining room where Nancy was putting silverware on the table. Wanting to appear capable and willing, but feeling awkward, Jillian said, "Can I help?"

Nancy's quick glance was grateful. "Sure. Would you bring in the food?"

In the kitchen Jillian found a plate of hot bread and three mugs of homemade vegetable soup. "Who isn't eating or is my counting off?" she asked when Nancy joined her in the kitchen.

"I'm on my way home," Nancy said, "leaving everything in your competent hands."

Panic coursed down Jillian's spine. She'd wanted to look capable, but not so capable that she was left with everything to do when she didn't know how to do it. She smiled weakly. "I wish I had your confidence in me."

"Emma's an angel and Luke isn't hard to please," she assured Jillian.

Jillian found those last words hard to believe. In her experience Luke appeared extremely difficult to please, and she wished people would quit telling her otherwise.

"For dessert there's chocolate cake and ice cream. Emma's favorite." She patted Jillian's shoulder. "You'll do just fine. Don't worry."

Jillian carefully picked up two mugs and started for the dining room, Nancy following behind her carrying the other mug and plate. Luke had seated Emma on the side and himself at the end of the table, which left the spot across from Emma for Jillian. Nancy placed the bread in the center of the table, set the mug in front of Emma, and gave her a quick hug.

"Good-bye, sweetie," she said. "I'll see you later, Luke." Then she disappeared into the kitchen and out the back door.

Jillian sat down. Gazing around the table, her eyes paused on Emma. The approval from the elderly lady warmed her soul the way nothing else had this week, deflecting part of the loneliness of a moment ago. She didn't know what it was about Emma, but she had felt an immediate connection to her.

When her eyes met Luke's, he gave her a measured look. "We have the blessing first."

"Of course." She didn't expect anything else.

He bowed his head. "Our Father in Heaven, we acknowledge the many blessings thou has bestowed upon us. Most especially today we are grateful that Jillian is with us so that Emma might have companionship. We ask thee to bless Jillian that she will be guided to do what is best in caring for Emma and this household. We're also thankful for this food, and we ask a blessing on it that we might receive nourishment and strength to our minds and our bodies. We thank thee for all thou has done for us. We ask these favors and blessings in the name of thy beloved son, Jesus Christ. Amen."

Luke's words surprised her. She hadn't felt he was thankful that he was stuck with her at all, but he certainly wouldn't lie to God. The deep resonance of his voice had an honesty in it that she found moving. After swallowing several times, she finally felt the lump in her throat dissolve. "My favorite—soup and hot bread on a cold day," she managed to say.

"Mine, too." Daintily, Emma lifted a spoonful of the soup to her mouth. She ate several spoonfuls, then lay her spoon on her bread plate and waited for Jillian and Luke to finish.

After they'd finished eating, Jillian carried the dishes into the kitchen and looked in the cupboards for some saucers or bowls for the ice cream and cake. Then she cut the chocolate cake and slid it onto the dishes. Finding two half gallons of Baskin Robbins pecan praline ice cream in the freezer, she decided that either Emma or Luke was obviously addicted to it. She dished up healthy portions and stood back, eyeing the dessert plates. This part of the job was turning out to be easier than she'd expected. Literally a piece of cake. She smiled to herself.

Carefully carrying the dishes into the other room, she placed them in front of Emma and Luke. "So which one of you is the pecan praline aficionado?" she asked.

Emma's laugh was delightful. "I'm afraid I'm guilty."

Jillian noticed that she ate all of her ice cream and cake.

Luke helped her clear the table and carry the dishes to the kitchen. "There's the dishwasher," he said, with a quick motion of his hand. He looked at her pointedly. "You do know how to operate one, don't you?"

"Of course." But her parents hadn't had one, and in New York she always ate out. She opened the door and saw that the appliance was nearly full. She loaded the lunch dishes, then finding a dishcloth on the sink, she wiped the counters off.

Luke watched her for a few moments. "It looks as if you can handle the kitchen. I need to check with my foreman, then I'll be back, and we can go over your duties." Luke grabbed his jacket from the closet by the door and left.

Watching his back, Jillian shrugged. She couldn't imagine what could be so difficult about running a dishwasher. She found a bottle of detergent under the sink and filled the cup in the door of the dish-washer. It didn't look like enough soap, so she squirted some more on the inside of the door before closing and locking it shut. Turning the dial to on, she glanced proudly around the clean kitchen. So far, so good. She'd show Luke how efficient she was.

She returned to the living room and found Emma sitting in front of the fire, looking at a magazine. When the elderly woman looked up and saw Jillian, she patted the spot next to her. "Sit right here. I'm dying to hear all about your fabulous life."

Jillian brushed aside her statement and smiled. "I'd much rather hear about you. I'm sure your life's been more meaningful than mine."

"Maybe more meaningful," Emma's eyes twinkled as she laughed, "but certainly not more interesting. What were you doing just before you came home?"

"Sailing along the Greek isles on Baron von Fredrickson's yacht."

"A yacht! Tell me all about it."

Jillian didn't think Emma would be interested in the decadent lifestyle on board the ship so she started with the size. "Well, it was large—280 feet long."

"Oh my!" Emma's eyes widened. "That's about the size of a foot-ball field!"

"Just about," Jillian agreed. "It had eight guest suites and a master suite. They all had mirrored ceilings, which always encouraged me to go to bed looking good since I was reflected all around the room." She laughed. "Since all the wood was white Chinese-lacquer, the entire place had a lovely glow about it. The walls were plain old beige suede, but Thai wall hangings covered the portholes and gave the illusion of large windows. And beside each bed was a control panel for the television, radio, and the drapes."

Emma's excitement enchanted Jillian. It was so much more fun than the blasé, world-weary attitude of the actual guests.

"You mean you had TV out there?" she asked, amazed. "We don't get good reception here and we're not out in the middle of the ocean."

"To be honest, I doubt if anyone spent much time watching TV, and I have no idea how the reception was, but it would have undoubtedly been the best that money could buy!"

Emma shook her head in wonderment.

Jillian was having fun now, and for Emma's benefit, she adopted the tone of a storyteller. "The dining room had a large white lacquered table. It was surrounded by white leather swivel chairs, and it seated eighteen people. The meals were served by young men in white uniform. The lights from the ceiling cast this marvelous, soft pink glow, and it made everyone's skin look radiant, even when it was dry or sunburned."

Enthusiasm for the extravagant details lit Emma's face. "What did the Baron do for a living to be able to afford such luxury?" she asked curiously.

Jillian didn't really know. "I think he inherited his money," she said lightly, "and from my observation, his profession was playboy of the western world." Thank goodness his credo seemed to be "easy come, easy go." And he'd provided liberally for his guests.

"Tell me more," Emma demanded.

"Each suite had its own bathroom, and mine had a miniature waterfall along the side of a large marble tub. And listen to this: the toilet was a rectangle box out of lapis lazuli. Have you ever heard of such a thing? When you lifted the gold handle on the lid, there was a hole just like in an old outhouse, though not nearly as primitive."

Emma's eyes were enormous as if trying to picture these peculiar but luxurious bathrooms. Jillian laughed softly. "And the walls of the bath were marble with lots of mirrors," she added.

"What did you do all day?" Emma asked next.

"We spent the days on the beach or shopping." Mostly Jillian had just looked. "Sometimes we stayed on deck during the day and sometimes in the evening. The weather was spectacular. The main salon served as the living room, and everything was—"

She heard the back door open and Luke's shout, "What's this?" A brief silence. Then, "Oh, no! Jillian, you didn't!"

By this time Jillian had reached the kitchen doorway. "Didn't what?" She glanced down. There were suds everywhere and more seeping out the sides of the dishwasher. "What happened?"

"What did you use for soap?" Luke demanded to know.

"I just filled the cup from the green bottle," Jillian explained, bewildered.

"That's what I thought," Luke grumbled as he moved the dial to the end of the rinse cycle. "You don't use detergent in the dishwasher. You use dishwasher soap. It's the one in the box."

All hope of proving her efficiency to Luke vanished. Her heart sank. "Where's the mop?" she asked with a sigh.

"In the closet over there." He glanced at her polka-dot silk pants and said, "I think you'd better let me do it. Those are hardly scrubbing up clothes."

"I made this mess, I'll clean it up." Her voice was determined and Luke shrugged in agreement. Tiptoeing cautiously through the warm soapy water, she could feel it sloshing over her feet and instep. Then, just as she dared to breathe a sigh of relief, she slipped. Trying to catch herself, she reached out and clutched the closet door handle, which opened with a jerk and banged her on the head. Fortunately, Luke caught her before she could slip any farther.

"Are you all right?" he asked. His voice sounded concerned and his arms felt solid and dependable.

"If seeing stars is all right, I'm fine and dandy." She strove to keep her tone light. No need for him to know how hard the door had whacked her. She straightened and pulled away. "Now for the mop." She found one at the back of the closet along with assorted brooms and a vacuum cleaner.

To her relief the suds had stopped trickling from the dishwasher, and she started mopping. When the mop was soaked, she wrung it out over the porch railing, then she mopped some more. Luke stood watching for a few minutes, but she waved him off, saying she could handle the job. She moved back and forth from the kitchen to the porch again and again while her head throbbed.

Finally she finished. After taking a moment to wash her hands, she rejoined Emma and dropped with a loud sigh onto an overstuffed chair.

"Well, I managed to make a mess," she announced, "and I want to know why detergent bottles aren't labeled DO NOT USE IN DISHWASHER, UNDER PENALTY OF MESS!"

Emma laughed. "My dear, I've done that very same thing more than once. The first time I didn't know any better, like you. Then another time I was out of dishwasher soap, and I thought a smidgen of liquid detergent would be okay. It wasn't."

"Try a cup full and some extra squirts besides for good measure." Jillian shook her head, which caused the throbbing in her head to intensify. "Anyway, I've learned a valuable lesson: no detergent in the dishwasher. I hope everything I learn won't be this much work, or Luke will never believe I can handle this job." She leaned back against the chair, sending a jolt of pain through her head and causing her to sit up suddenly. Gingerly she touched her fingers to her head.

"What's wrong?" Emma asked, concerned.

"Nothing really," Jillian brushed aside the older woman's fears. "In my ineptitude, I bumped into the closet door. I have a small bump. Nothing serious." She leaned back against the chair, albeit gently this time, to reassure Emma she was all right.

"Are you sure? Maybe you should put ice on it."

Jillian waved off Emma's suggestion. "No, I'm fine." Her head ached, but she didn't want Luke to come in and think she'd injured herself on top of everything else. From now on she was determined that no matter what, everything would be perfect.

Apparently sensing that Jillian would resist any further coddling, Emma tried a different approach. "Why don't you make grilled cheese sandwiches for supper? Luke loves them, and he'll forget all about the dishwasher disaster. Besides, they're easy to fix. I'm sure we have pickles and chips. Of course," Emma's easy laugh punctuated her sentence, "for dessert we can have chocolate cake and pecan praline ice cream."

Jillian gave Emma a conspiratorial smile. "That sounds like a winner. I'll do it!"

"Now, if you can help me to the bathroom and bed for a nap, I'll leave you alone."

Jillian brought the wheelchair to the side of the love seat and lifted the elderly woman into it. After she'd tucked Emma in bed and covered her with an afghan, she returned to the living room and sank wearily into the nearest chair. What a day. She'd been here only three hours, and already she felt as if she'd put in a full day at hard labor.

Just as she felt herself starting to nod off, Jillian heard the back door open and sat up abruptly. What now?

"Ready to go over your responsibilities?" Luke asked, standing at the kitchen doorway.

"Sure." She eased carefully out of the chair, making sure she didn't add further stress to her aching body, and joined Luke at the dining room table.

He pulled out a chair for her, and then seated himself across from her. "Mostly you're responsible for caring for Emma. She gets up about eight, and you need to help her bathe and get dressed. She has some exercises she does three times a day. The physical therapist left instructions. Sometimes she needs to be reminded. Breakfast is your responsibility. There will be just Emma and you."

Was he trying to avoid her. "What about you?"

"I eat early and fix it myself."

"Whew." She glanced up at Luke. "Then I'll have no worries."

He gave her a half smile before continuing. "Emma, you might have noticed, eats hardly anything at all. She likes Instant Breakfast made with hot milk and marshmallows on top. Sometimes a scoop of ice cream. She has this everyday. Once in a while she might want a pancake. I'm in and out during the morning, but I'll eat lunch and dinner with you. Fix whatever she wants, or whatever you want if she doesn't have a preference. Her medicine is in her bathroom and she takes it morning and night.

"The housework will include mopping the kitchen," he gave her a mocking glance, "although after today, I doubt it will need it for a while. You'll also make Emma's bed and clean the entire house, including the bathrooms. But you don't have to do these things daily because your main job is to keep Emma company." Luke gave her a penetrating look. "Don't forget—you've got two weeks to prove you're capable of managing this household. Emma's taken to you, but that won't be enough to save your job if you mess up."

Jillian nodded her head soberly, but she felt like rebelling already. She wanted to ask who he'd get if she didn't stay. After all, if there'd been a chance of hiring anyone else, he would never have hired her. Then again, he could always fire her and continue to struggle on as he had been. She probably needed this job more than he needed her. But she said nothing.

He pushed back his chair and stood up, looking at his watch. "It's nearly two now and we eat between five and six. So as long as Emma's napping, you're free until she wakes up." He paused, as if thinking of what he might have forgotten, and Jillian decided to speak up.

"I promise to do the best job possible. I can see that spending time with her won't take any effort at all."

Luke looked at her skeptically, as if he questioned her ability either to recognize Emma's worth or to take care of her. "Any questions?" His expression seemed to dare her to ask anything

Jillian just had one. "At the risk of sounding mercenary, when do I get paid?"

"You? Mercenary?" He rolled his eyes. "Every Saturday."

CHAPTER 8

Every Saturday! That sounded fantastic. Seven days and she'd be *rich*. At this point in her life anything over five dollars was rich. Jillian heaved a huge sigh of relief. Already the load on her shoulders seemed lighter. What a reprieve to be away from Mrs. Prescott and to have Luke out of sight for an hour or so. She returned to her new room anxious for the opportunity to get settled in.

She ignored the temptation to lie down for a while on the inviting bed, and instead put her suitcase on the sofa. After a week crammed in bags, her clothes needed to air out. She shook the wrinkles out of each garment before hanging it in the closet. When she finished, she gazed at the remnants of her once plentiful wardrobe. How foolish she'd been to spend her money on things of such little worth, but those had been the golden days of her youth when she'd thought the good times would roll on and on and on. She could always put something away later.

She shook her head in disbelief at her lack of foresight. She received payment every time one of her commercials played on television anywhere in the world, but at this point her residuals barely trickled in. She shut the closet door. Now for the rest of her belongings, which would fit easily into one of the drawers at the base of the armoire.

Now for the important stuff. Jillian sorted through the pile of family photographs Luke had bought for her. Or to be honest, ransomed for her. Opening the gray folder on top, she discovered her parents' wedding picture, taken in front of the Idaho Falls Temple. Her mother's long straight hair parted in the middle was a dead giveaway that this was a seventies wedding. The coronet of white flowers on her head even made her look like a flower child, although Jillian knew that lifestyle had never interested her mother. She smiled at her father's long sideburns. Her parents both looked so young. She placed the picture on her night stand where she could easily see it.

Choosing one of her baby pictures, several pictures of her grandparents, and a family picture taken when she was eight, she set them strategically around the room so that her family surrounded her.

Then she carefully removed the final object—her mother's figurine. After considering each spot in the room, she finally decided it would go on the top of the armoire. It would be out of harm's way where it couldn't be accidentally knocked over, and best of all, it would be in clear sight.

With that task finished, Jillian put the suitcases and the garment bag at the back of the closet. Sitting down on the side of the bed, she swung her feet up and lay back against the pillows. The pain in her head had dulled slightly, and she thought she could make it through the rest of the evening. Snuggling under the quilt, she let her mind drift to thoughts of belonging, of love, and of her family.

—◊—

"Jillian!"

Her eyes snapped open as she awoke with a start. It was Emma calling her. Ignoring her headache, Jillian jumped to her feet and hurried across the hall to her bedroom.

She stood in the doorway and looked into the room. "Are you all right?"

"Oh yes, my dear," Emma said with a deprecating flutter of her hands. "I hate to be a bother, but I'm stuck here until I'm rescued. Could you help me to my wheelchair?"

"I'm not a knight in shining armor, but I think I can help a damsel in distress." Jillian hurried to the bed and gently raised the elderly lady to a sitting position, at the same time moving Emma's legs so they hung off the side of the bed.

"Ready for the wheelchair?"

"Yes, and then with some assistance to the bathroom, I'll be all set until bed time."

Jillian helped Emma off the bed and into her wheelchair, then wheeled her into the other room. She looked around at Emma's bedroom. It was bigger than hers. The Prescotts evidently didn't believe in stinting. This room had pale blue carpeting, a dark mahogany poster bed with a matching chest and two blue and rose floral easy chairs.

She turned to look at Emma when she came out; in the interim Jillian could see that she'd applied fresh makeup.

"Let me show you what's in the kitchen cupboards. That way you'll know where we store everything and what you've got to work with."

"Sounds like a good idea." She pushed Emma's wheelchair through the living room into the kitchen.

Opening the first cupboard door, Jillian found a jar of peanut butter, several jars of jam, and numerous boxes of mixes. "You've got everything from soup to nut bread," she laughed. Then she spied half a dozen boxes of chocolate cake. "Oh, Emma, you're something else!"

Emma looked up at the cupboard to see what Jillian was looking at, then chuckled. "Well, you know what's closest to my heart."

"Is it just chocolate cake or anything as long as it's chocolate?" Jillian asked, wanting to know.

Emma's tone was definite. "Chocolate!"

"That's what I thought." Emma's unabashed enthusiasm amused Jillian.

"The cheese and meat are in the meat keeper in the refrigerator, and the bread is in the container next to the dishwasher," Emma said, then pointed to a cupboard on the far wall. "The chips are in there."

Opening a few more cupboards, Jillian found rows and rows of canned goods. "There's certainly a lot of food here. Do you usually get snowed in?"

"Oh no. You're just looking at our year's supply," Emma casually informed her.

Her words surprised Jillian, who looked at Emma blankly. "Why would anyone want a year's supply of food?"

"The Church wants us to have it in case of an emergency."

"They do?" Bewilderment filled her voice before she remembered her parents talking about it when she was growing up. But even so they weren't exactly in "the wilds." The grocery store was only twenty or so miles away. "If you don't mind my asking, what kinds of emergencies do you get out here?"

Emma's dimples showed when she smiled. "None, really. Oh, a few times we've been caught short between shopping trips, but nothing major."

"I'd think you'd give up."

"If nothing else, we've been obedient to the Lord."

Obedient to the Lord. The words echoed through her mind and Jillian was silent, thinking. It had been a long time since she'd even thought about the concept of obedience. It was a topic for a church talk or a lesson. But keeping the ten commandments was one thing and storing a year's supply of food was something totally different. She couldn't conceive God caring about such mundane things.

Emma glanced at the dainty watch on her arm. "It's getting close to dinner time. Maybe you'd better get started."

Jillian took the cheese and bread out. What did she do next? As inconceivable as it seemed, she'd never grilled cheese sandwiches in her life.

At her hesitation, Emma spoke up. "Butter two slices of bread and put the buttered sides together. Then put some butter in the pan and turn it on low. Put a piece of bread in the pan, buttered side down. Put a slice of cheese on it and then the other piece of bread, buttered side up. Turn it over after a few minutes. Simple as can be."

Jillian listened carefully. "You're right. Even I ought to be able to prepare them."

Following Emma's directions she had them made in no time at all. She found a large frying pan in the stove drawer that suited her purpose fine. Substituting margarine for butter, she set the pan on the stove.

"What should I do about these dishes in the dishwasher?"

"I think if you just start them over again this time without any soap, they'll wash up fine."

"I hope so," she grinned at Emma. "Mopping up the kitchen twice in one day is two times too many."

She opened the cupboard above the sink and found some plates. "Shall I use these?"

"Sure. You'll find the silverware in the first drawer."

She took the silverware to the dining room and set the table. The table lacked color. What she needed was something to liven it up. But what? If she were nearer Idaho Falls, she'd spend the last of her money on flowers. "I wish we were close to a florist and I'd order some flowers."

Emma looked thoughtful. "There are pyracantha bushes all around the house. Cut some branches of that. With its red berries, it'll look Christmasy and Decembery, all-in-one. Under the sink is a large milk glass vase you can put them in."

Snatching some kitchen shears that were hanging by the counter, Jillian dashed out without her coat, hoping to make it a quick trip. Enthusiasm bubbled up in her when she saw the bushes, but quickly subsided when she grabbed the first one and felt the thorns bite into her fingers. This didn't deter her, but after that she handled the branches more carefully. Finally she had a half dozen or so, and she carried them cautiously into the house.

Laying her load on the counter, she examined her hand. Other than stinging a little, it seemed okay. The perils of farm life!

Poking the branches into the vase, she sought Emma's approval. "What do you think?"

"Very festive. Just the thing to brighten up the table."

Looking at the arrangement critically, she thought that it was probably too large for their end of the table. She'd better set it in the middle or they'd spend dinner dodging the pyracantha in order to see each other. Not that she minded not seeing Luke, but she was afraid it would be Emma who was hidden by the greenery.

Jillian was setting cups of hot chocolate at each place when she heard Luke come in and greet Emma.

"Dinner ready?"

"Just about. Jillian's having grilled cheese sandwiches just for you."

Luke raised his eyebrows at those words, and Jillian pretended to ignore him. Meanwhile, Emma plowed right on, paying no attention to the reactions on their faces. "Let's go in the living room while she finishes up."

Luke nodded agreeably and pushed the wheelchair into the other room.

"Isn't the pyracantha lovely? Jillian thought we needed some decorations, and so I suggested this."

Nervous that she'd keep Luke waiting too long, Jillian melted the margarine and then turned up the heat to hurry the sandwiches along. She put some chips in a bowl and opened some sweet pickles. Taking a fork from the silverware drawer, she dug a few pickles from the bottle and put them in a smaller bowl.

Just then she smelled something burning. She turned away from the counter, but before she could move, the fire alarm went off. For a moment she stood frozen to the spot as smoke streamed out from around the edge of the frying pan lid. She reached for the pan and just in time remembered to grab a hot pad to wrap around the handle before pulling the pan off the burner. The sound of the smoke alarm was deafening and Jillian, desperate to get it turned off, looked around the room for some kind of switch.

Just then Luke ducked through the doorway. "What's on fire?" he hollered over the clanging of the alarm.

"Just supper," she shouted back. "How do you turn the darn thing off?"

He flung the back door open. "Take the pan outside." Snatching up the pan, she darted for the door and put the crispy, black, well-done sandwiches, pan included, on the porch railing. Luke fanned the door a couple of times and the noise ceased. Never had silence sounded so good to Jillian.

Slipping past Luke into the kitchen, Jillian set about cutting some more bread and cheese. As far as she could tell, her cooking skill, or lack thereof, had also ruined the skillet.

Luke glanced at the stove. "I suggest you cook your next batch on low. Although my grandmother always said that burnt toast would make my hair curly, at this stage of the game, I prefer it just like it is."

Jillian could see no humor in his statement. At this rate she'd never make it through two weeks; she'd be lucky to make it through the weekend. At least Emma liked her. Feelings of dejection swamped her as she made fresh sandwiches. She just had to succeed. *Dear God, don't let me fail again,* she prayed, and then immediately scorned her thoughts. Why would God listen to her after all these years? The answer to that was no, nada, never. She'd burned her bridges behind her, and she was in this horrible fix alone.

She found a smaller pan and started all over again. Turning the stove to low, she added margarine and then the sandwiches. This time she never took her eyes off the food. She swore this dinner would be perfect if she had to make the sandwiches over and over again until they ran out of bread and cheese. Of course, then she could be faulted for being wasteful. Oh, well, she sighed, win some, lose some, and so far she was losing more often than not.

Finally, she took the golden brown sandwiches out of the pan and put them on the plates. Cheese oozed out the sides and to her inexperienced eyes they looked perfect.

"Ready at last," she said to the other two as she set the plates down and went back for the chips and pickles. Emma's eyes sparkled. "They look good enough to eat, don't they?" she nodded at Luke.

"They do," he agreed.

As soon as Luke had offered the blessing, they began eating. Jillian was beginning to relax when she took a swallow of the cocoa. Oh, no, practically stone cold. She set her cup down abruptly. "Let me warm up your cocoa."

"I think it would be easier, if I warmed up every one's. *I know* I know how to use the microwave."

Ignoring Luke's sarcasm, Jillian smiled sweetly. "Why, thank you." As soon as he was out of the room, she let out her breath. Until that moment she'd had no idea she was even holding it.

Luke returned with steaming mugs of hot chocolate, and Emma raved on about how good the sandwiches were until Jillian was embarrassed. Nevertheless, for all her compliments she ate only a few bites. Instead, she sipped her cocoa genteelly, smiling at Luke and Jillian. Nobody said much.

When Jillian cleared the table, she saw that Emma had left almost half of her cocoa, but later she ate every bit of her cake and ice cream. She wouldn't starve to death, Jillian acknowledged, but her diet was anything but nutritious.

They watched the news, *Lawrence Welk,* and *Antique Roadshow* before Emma announced she was ready for bed. Luke had gone upstairs right after the news, so Jillian tucked her in, turned out the lights, and went into her own room, where she collapsed on her bed. What a day! Her head ached from the bump and her back hurt. She'd done everything wrong except drop Emma, and if Emma had weighed more, she'd probably have managed that as well.

She'd had been here eight hours, and it seemed more like twenty-eight hours. Another day like today and her polka dot pants would be shot. Silk definitely wasn't practical for cooking, or mopping, or burning cheese sandwiches. She sniffed her sweater and found it still smelled faintly of burnt toast.

What would she wear tomorrow? Did Emma go to church on Sunday? She didn't think she herself was up to going, but Luke hadn't mentioned her having Sunday off, and she for one wasn't going to bring up the subject. She was in enough hot water as it was. If tomorrow was anything like today, she'd never last two weeks.

She undressed and slipped into bed, thinking how wonderful the bed felt. Although her day had been disastrous, her head ached, her back hurt, and Luke considered her inept, she felt an inner peace she couldn't remember feeling for a long, long time—no doubt the result of Emma's warm acceptance.

Just wait, Luke Prescott, she vowed. *You're going to have the world's best housekeeper. So there!*

—∞—

Luke flipped on the lights at the top of the stairs. The living room looked dark, so evidently Jillian and Emma were in bed. He always checked the house at night before retiring. First the fireplace and then the doors. Living so far off the highway, they were undoubtedly safe with the house unlocked, but his dad had always locked up and when he passed away, Luke had carried on the tradition. After he made sure Emma was all right, he turned the thermostat down.

One day he expected to find Emma gone. He didn't know what his reaction would be. He'd found the pain of losing his dad nearly overwhelming although he'd shrugged it off publicly. Though Emma wasn't related by blood, he couldn't fathom life without her.

He found it intriguing that Emma had taken an instant liking to Jillian, which was good, although why was beyond him. He considered Jillian Taylor a glamorous lightweight. Interested in one thing: M-o-n-e-y. He grimaced, remembering her only question: when would she get paid? But he wanted Emma to be happy, and she seemed thrilled to have Jillian taking care of her. Of course, they'd be lucky if she didn't flood them out, poison them with her cooking, or burn the house down. For all her talk of growing up on a farm, he'd bet her mother had done all the cooking and cleaning before Jillian had gone to New York. It was enough to have someone to care for Emma, he supposed, but a good cook would have been nice, too.

Still, no matter what Jillian said or did, he didn't trust her, he didn't like her, and he planned on holding her to a two-week trial period.

CHAPTER 9

"Hello." Luke didn't hide his surprise at finding Jillian unloading the dishwasher. "I'm amazed to find you up already. After the demands of yesterday, I thought you'd sleep in." Luke closed the door noiselessly behind him.

Jillian was startled by his cordiality and she matched her tone to his. "I was afraid I'd miss you, and I needed to find what's expected on Sunday. Does Emma go to church?"

He shook his head. "Rarely. After her last stroke, she hasn't had the strength. Making the drive and sitting through even one meeting takes a lot out of her. Usually she watches the tabernacle choir and other religious programs on TV."

"That sounds easy enough," Jillian said, sighing with relief. She didn't want to face the bishop, Mrs. Prescott, or for that matter, even sit through three hours of church. It had been years since she'd attended her meetings, and she didn't welcome the thought now. Right now she didn't feel she could feign interest in a church she hardly knew anymore. He gave her a quizzical look which caused her a momentary pang. Did he know something he wasn't telling her?

Opening the refrigerator door, he pointed to the meat keeper. "Here's a beef roast. Emma can tell you how to do it for dinner." He said dryly, "I think you'll find it easier to fix than toasted cheese sandwiches."

"And don't forget to add running the dishwasher!" She smiled, determined to be cheerful so he would never guess how his words panicked her. What if something else did go wrong?

"Make yourself comfortable until Emma wakes up." She followed him out of the kitchen. While he went on upstairs, she returned to her room and stretched out on the sofa that faced the window. No need to mess up the bed again. At least she knew what Luke expected for lunch. He was right about one thing, roast beef did sound simpler than toasted cheese sandwiches, but she still felt edgy. Worry over what was expected for today had prompted her early morning visit to the kitchen. Now she'd try to relax until Emma woke up.

Lying on the sofa, Jillian gazed at her family portrait. The picture had been taken the day she was baptized. Sitting up, she reached for the picture and studied it. The young blond girl in the picture appeared thrilled as she looked into the camera. Her smile lit up her entire face. Had she really been so happy that day? She couldn't remember. She had only vague memories of that day eighteen long years ago. Her most vivid memories were of her parents and how loved they made her feel. She would give anything to have them back again. She closed her eyes, and tears squeezed out from under her lashes and ran down her cheeks.

When she awoke, it was after eight. She listened a moment to see if she could hear anything from Emma's room, but the only sound was that of footsteps on the stairs and then the quiet closing of the back door.

Tiptoeing across the hall, she silently opened the door a crack. Emma appeared to be sleeping, so Jillian went into the living room and made herself comfortable on the couch. A fashion magazine lay on the lamp table. Emma's? Do eighty-year-olds read fashion magazines? Do they polish their nails fire engine red? Jillian grinned. Emma did.

"Jillian, are you there?"

Tossing the magazine aside, Jillian rose to her feet and hurried into the next room.

"Good morning! Did you sleep well?"

Emma's face gleamed, reminding Jillian of a small child who had just awakened, happy to greet the day. "Yes, and I'm ready to get up."

Jillian helped her to a sitting position. "Do you take a bath or a shower?"

"There's a stool in the shower for me to sit on. You'll find my underclothes in the second drawer of the dresser, and on Sundays, I always wear one of my good dresses. Today I feel like blue."

Helping someone shower and dress sounded easy enough, but an hour later Jillian felt as if she'd had a strenuous workout. Her clothes were damp from the shower, wisps of hair dangled in her eyes, and her blouse was no longer tucked in her pants. Evidently she wasn't lifting Emma right because her back also ached.

But dressed and ready for the day, Emma looked beautiful in a blue dress with the strands of pearls entwined around her neck, makeup perfectly in place, and hair fluffed into a silver halo around her face.

Once in the kitchen, Emma directed her to the Instant Breakfast and told her how to prepare it—hot with marshmallows. Jillian had cold cereal. They sat at the dining room table where Emma sipped her drink, ate the marshmallows, and watched Jillian eat.

"You are very beautiful." This came from the elderly lady as a comment. "I can see where you would be a good model. But do you need to be so thin?"

She'd lost weight, Jillian knew, the result of worry and stress since her return to Quail Creek. But she kept her tone light as she teased, "Why, Emma, haven't you ever heard, 'You can't be too rich or too thin'?"

"No, I never have," Emma admitted. "But you are too thin. You need to gain weight."

"I'm not a whit thinner than you are," Jillian pointed out. "But let's make a deal. I'll eat more if you'll eat more." She was glad Emma had given her the opportunity to address her eating habits, which concerned her greatly.

"I'm just never hungry." Emma's blue eyes looked at Jillian mildly.

"Neither am I," Jillian challenged. "So we're starting off dead even."

Emma nodded in agreement although she didn't look convinced. "All right, my dear, if that's the only way to get some fat on you, I'll try."

Jillian patted her hand. "I've eaten all my cereal. How about finishing your drink? Shall I warm it for you?"

"No. It's okay." She lifted the mug and took a long swallow. Then another. And another. Setting down her mug, she made a face and shuddered. "I don't know whether or not I can do this."

She looked so miserable that Jillian felt guilty. Getting up from the table, she went around to Emma and patted her shoulder. "I don't want to make you sick. Maybe you could start with just a few more bites each time."

Emma's lips curled into a smile. "That sounds easier. My stomach rebels at food. But since Luke's doesn't, we'd better get the roast on."

Jillian pushed her wheelchair into the kitchen, and Emma didn't hesitate to give directions. "Set the oven at 350 degrees. In that cupboard there's a pan it will fit in."

Jillian found the pan and the meat and set them on the counter. "Now what?"

"In the fridge are some carrots and potatoes."

Jillian added them to the other items. "Next?"

"Put the roast in the pan, peel the potatoes and carrots, and place them around it. In the cupboard with all the other mixes is some onion soup. Sprinkle it over the top. Put the lid on and set it in the oven. You're all set!"

"Luke was right." Jillian laughed at the simplicity involved in a major meal. "This is simpler than grilled cheese sandwiches."

When everything was safely in the oven, Jillian cleared the table and placed the dishes in the dishwasher. Then, after making themselves comfortable in the overstuffed chairs, Jillian turned on the television just in time for the Tabernacle Choir.

As the program started, she attempted to ease her aching back by nestling against the cushions. But she found only a few moments of relief before the pain started again. Thank goodness her head didn't hurt this morning. She'd never contemplated when she started this job that she'd get so banged up. What could be more harmless than carrying for a kindly old woman? Little had she known!

"*Jerusalem . . . Jerusalem . . .*" The choir voices soared into the room. She watched Emma, who was totally absorbed by the music. What a wonderful woman she was. She seemed so contented with her life. Jillian wished she could be as satisfied with her own. But, frankly, she'd rather be anyplace than here with two weeks to prove herself. At this moment, yachting with breakfast in bed everyday sounded wonderful. No mopping floors, no backaches from lifting, her every need attended to instead of attending to someone else's. She'd never fully appreciated maid service before; she'd just taken it for granted. She grimaced as she scrunched deeper in the pillows. She never would again—not that there was any likelihood of her being in that position in the future.

"*. . . Peace on earth, good will to men.*"

The choir was silent and the speaker began. "At this time of year when we celebrate the Savior's birth, we seek his peace in our lives. Except for life itself, there is nothing we cherish more than peace. But how can we find it? Peace does not come from superficial gifts. The scriptures tell us not to spend our money on things of little worth, but to seek after the gifts of the spirit. Shakespeare reminded us to our own selves be true, and Emerson said, "Nothing can bring you peace but the triumph of principles." No man is at peace who has been untrue to himself by breaking the principles of right. His accusing conscience won't let him. . . .""

As she listened to the speaker, Jillian agreed that she had been untrue to herself. But it wasn't her conscience that accused her. She had been miserable because she'd been broke, not because of her conscience.

". . . Peace comes by obedience to law, and it is that message that Jesus would have us proclaim among men. May we all find peace, not just this season but always."

As her mind drifted over the last few years, she realized that she'd been swamped with feelings of restiveness for some time now. Somewhere along the road to and from success, she'd realized she was missing something. Only now, sitting here with Emma, did she understand what it was. The house exuded peace, and she longed to be filled with it.

"*Where can I turn for peace? Where is my solace when other sources cease to make me whole?*" The majestic tones of the organ accompanied the voices and the magnificent sound resonated through the living room. If it was necessary to go to church, this was the way to do it—in a soft chair and listening to beautiful music.

"Wasn't that a superb program?" Emma said when it was over. "I love the choir. Now change the channel to eleven for sacrament meeting."

Sacrament meeting? On TV? Doubts that this would be as pleasant filled Jillian's mind. She was right. Neither the music nor the speakers were as polished, but their sincerity was obvious, even to her.

"You can just tell what a wonderful man that bishop is from his warmth," Emma said at the conclusion of the program. "All bishops should be like him."

Jillian murmured a quiet assent, although personally, she preferred Bishop Walker. "Is there more?"

Emma looked at the clock. "Oh, yes, now comes the BYU devotional."

Jillian winced. She hadn't minded the choir, but an hour and a half of preaching was a little much. Still, she was getting paid for watching television, and as one of the speakers had reminded them, "Count your blessings." So things could be worse. She could be unemployed and on the streets.

As a comfortable position continued to elude her, she straightened out her legs and placed a small pillow behind her lower back. Emma appeared spellbound by the speaker, but Jillian was more interested in examining her earlier thoughts. Peace. She would never have thought it as valuable as a successful career, money in the bank, and good times. But now . . . the thought of peace was enormously appealing.

In the two days she'd known Emma, the woman's peace of mind had been apparent. Jillian knew the older woman was a widow and that her husband had died some years ago; she'd had several strokes, and she was now unable to care for herself. She couldn't even go from one room to the next without assistance. Even so, serenity enveloped Emma, discernible to everyone who came in contact with her.

The only other person she'd ever known with this same aura had been her mother, that summer she'd passed away. Annie Taylor had suffered greatly from the insidious cancer that had taken her life, but she'd had an air of contentment that had comforted Jillian. How had she been able to find peace? Her mother had known that she wouldn't be getting better and that she was leaving behind a husband and daughter who would hardly know how to get along without her. At the time, Jillian hadn't questioned her mother's good spirits; she'd just been happy to see that her mother was comfortable and at peace.

Jillian's thoughts wandered to other memories of her childhood. As a girl she'd adored her father and in her eyes he could do no wrong. Until she'd discovered modeling, she'd wanted nothing more than to be just like her own mother. The three of them had been closer than any other family Jillian had ever known. How had their relationships changed so much that she had avoided her father for years, all to protect her pride? Why had she left home against her parents' wishes in the first place? How could she have been so selfish? She had lost something intangible and irreplaceable when she had left home. She'd been famous, but she'd left behind the only people who had truly cared about her.

Feeling a lump in her throat, she took a deep breath and slowly released it. What was all this introspection doing for her beyond making her gloomy and sad? At last the speaker concluded, much to her relief. Jillian prayed that two hours of religion was enough for Emma, since it had been more than enough for her.

Emma gave a contented sigh. "Now we can hear this wonderful woman organist. She plays the great organs in cathedrals all over the world."

Jillian decided it was definitely time to check on the roast. "Why don't you sit here and enjoy yourself while I set the table and finish getting lunch? I'll be able to hear it from the kitchen."

Emma looked up and smiled as Jillian made her escape.

In the drawer she found some red place mats, which had probably been chosen by Emma, and put them on the table. She moved the pyracantha from the center of the table to the end, then she set out the plates and silver. She filled some glasses with ice cubes and water, making her way leisurely back and forth from the kitchen to the dining room.

When she thought she'd dawdled enough, she checked the roast beef. The smell was incredible and the meat looked as if it were falling apart, so she hoped it would be tender. Just as she slid it back into the oven, Luke walked through the back door.

His sudden appearance startled her and she felt herself flush as their eyes met. No matter how aggravating he could be, he was very handsome, dressed as he was in his Sunday clothes. His white shirt emphasized his tanned face and dark hair, and in his suit he looked as well dressed as any man she had dated in the past several years.

"Perfect timing," she attempted to speak casually. "Dinner's ready."

He looked amused. "No fire alarms have gone off?"

She was insulted. "No!"

"Any floods yet?"

"Absolutely not!"

His mouth curled up in a captivating grin, and Jillian's stomach turned somersaults.

"How's Emma?" he asked.

"She seems fine," Jillian was glad to report. "Cheerful as always." Jillian pulled the roasting pan out of the oven and set it on the stove as Luke continued on into the living room. She heard him greet Emma, then go upstairs. A few minutes later, he came back downstairs and assisted Emma into her wheel chair and to the table, where Jillian could see that he'd changed from his suit into a more casual shirt and slacks.

When the blessing was over, Luke served Emma a small portion of meat and a few vegetables. Jillian wondered how much of that she would eat. Then Luke turned to Jillian with a quizzical expression on his face. "The bishop asked me how you were doing so far."

Her heart leaped to her throat and for a moment she thought she would choke. Oh, great, now he'd had a chance to tell the bishop she wasn't working out. She responded as nonchalantly as she could, the muscles in her face quivering. "I hoped you stressed how efficient I am," she said, attempting to meet his eyes fearlessly.

"Certainly. Not everyone could manage a flood and a fire in one day." He helped himself to a fork full of potatoes and began eating.

Jillian tried to swallow the gasp of horror that rose to her lips. "Did you really tell him that?" she said faintly.

Emma reassured Jillian. "No, Luke wouldn't say anything like that. He's always very positive."

At those words Jillian rolled her eyes. How had he managed to fool everyone?

"I'm sure he only told him what a wonderful addition you are to our home. Not only beautiful, but caring, and such a big help to Luke." Emma smiled at them both and Luke returned her smile.

Jillian watched him with narrowed eyes, doubtful that he could say anything positive about her to anyone, let alone the person who had coerced him into hiring her. She eyed Luke, challenging him to tell them what he'd actually said. He merely continued eating.

She gave up.

Luke chewed and swallowed. "By the way, Randy seemed to think you would be at church this morning. Any idea how he got that idea?"

"No." She didn't elaborate. She glanced over at Emma, whose eyes gleamed as she ate the last bite on her plate.

"Okay, Jillian, can I have dessert?"

Jillian pretended to examine Emma's plate closely, then gave her approval. "Not only dessert, but you can be a charter member of the Clean Plates Club." Afterwards she helped Emma lie down for her nap.

When she cleaned up the kitchen this time, she was careful to use dishwasher soap.

The day passed slowly, probably because she was on tenterhooks, not knowing exactly what was expected of her. While Emma napped, Luke spent the time upstairs. He came down once, just wondering if everything was all right, which made her even more uncomfortable. She felt as if he expected her to be doing more, but when she asked him he only shrugged.

That night, when she finally crawled into bed, it was a relief to know that she'd made it through Day Two. She hadn't dropped Emma and the house was still intact. A long soak in the tub had eased her back pain, and she was beginning to think she might make it through the first week after all.

CHAPTER 10

Although he hadn't told the bishop of Jillian's mishaps in the kitchen, Luke was not enthusiastic about her presence at the ranch. He left the house early Monday, as usual, to work with his men. When he returned to the house later Monday morning, he found her energetically sweeping the kitchen floor, dressed in a flowery costume that looked utterly out of place.

"Are those the only clothes you have?" He looked at her critically. "Maybe it's the red and yellow flowers, but they seem a little too frivolous for a cold December day in Idaho."

"You're wrong," she said, leaning against the broom handle and smiling at him. "They're *exactly* what one needs on a cold, overcast December day in Idaho. Emma finds them very cheery and so do I."

Luke rolled his eyes at this explanation. "I guess I'm more practical than Emma, but I think you need something sturdier, like Levis. I've got some things to pick up at Ben's Store in a little while. You'd better come with me and get some real work clothes," he suggested.

"That's a wonderful idea, Luke," she drawled, still smiling, "with only one small problem. What do I use for money?"

"You can charge it against your two weeks' pay."

"Do I hear the hint of a suggestion that I'd ought not to count on more than two weeks' pay?" Jillian asked, her eyebrows raised.

He shrugged. He refused to acknowledge at this point that she probably had the job permanently, as far as Emma was concerned anyway.

To his annoyance, Jillian didn't let up. "And after I've gone a whole day without burning down the house or flooding you out. Really, Luke, what more can you ask?"

"A lot." He scowled. "Don't you take anything seriously?"

Refusing to let his irritation change her good spirits, she raised her eyebrows and made a *moue* at him. As she finished her sweeping, she asked, "Who's going to watch Emma?"

Luke watched her as she dug at one corner of the kitchen with the broom. He would never tell her but she did, indeed, brighten up the kitchen in her colorful outfit. "If she feels well enough, she can come along. If she doesn't, tell me your size and I'll buy the things for you. I'll see what she wants to do." He ducked into the other room.

As he dropped down on one knee in front of Emma, all he could do was worry. Despite all her jewelry and make-up, Emma seemed frailer every time he looked at her. He cradled her pale delicate hand in his large tanned one, noticing how even her hand seemed lighter, more fragile than ever. His heart sank but he tried to sound upbeat as he asked, "Feel like riding into town? Jillian needs to pick up a few things, but I can get them for her if you'd rather stay home."

"I'd love the ride, but I'll stay in the car." She glanced down at the duster she wore. "Of course, even if I only sit in the car, I should change clothes. I need something a little dressier."

He lifted her into the wheelchair as Jillian joined them. Before he could say anything she whisked Emma down the hall, asking, "What do you want to wear?"

"Something red."

Red, of course. Luke smiled. Some things never changed. He wished he could count on the status quo for a few other things, like Emma's good health.

He wanted Emma's trip to be comfortable and the three of them needed more room than the pickup provided, so Luke brought his car instead of his pickup to the back door. The harsh December wind stung his cheeks and he left the motor running for a while to warm up the car. When the car felt toasty warm, he entered the house, wanting to make sure Jillian had dressed Emma warmly enough. He wasn't taking any chances.

When he saw Jillian in her wolf jacket, he grimaced. Trust Jillian to wear just the right thing for a shopping trip to a country store. Tall, blonde, and wearing fur. One thing for sure, she'd never get lost in a crowd.

Jillian leaned over Emma, helping her into her heavy winter coat. Emma wiggled her hand through the sleeve. "Look, Luke, it's perfect." She held her hand up. "My fingernails just match my pants."

"You're color-coordinated." Jillian drew Emma's other arm through the opening before snuggling the coat around her face and body. She then tied a red wool scarf around Emma's head.

Jillian's affectionate way of helping Emma gratified Luke. She treated Emma like her best friend, which also surprised him. Luke settled the older woman in the front seat, and Jillian slid into the back.

"Don't forget your seatbelt," he said over his shoulder.

"Depend on you, Luke, to offer unnecessary advice. I'm already fastening it," she said in the long-suffering voice of a parent trying to be patient with a small child.

Luke dismissed her words. No one would ever convince him that Jillian was a seatbelt person. With her long blonde hair flouncing around her face and the careless confidence of her stride, she was the type who'd drive a snappy red convertible Mercedes at top speed, leaving the undone seatbelt to blow in the wind.

As they drove along, Emma enthusiastically commented on the scenery and the neighbors who lived along the road. She sparkled just like her old self, and he thought with some relief that she wasn't as weak as he had thought. With her remarks and Jillian's rejoinders, the miles sped by.

Luke parked at the side of the faded green cinderblock building, out of the way of anyone who wanted to buy gasoline out front. Ben had the only gas station within a sixty-mile radius, so his store was usually pretty busy. A string of gaudily colored lights flashed across the top of a large window, and a few fir trees leaned against the wall of the store. That had to be Ben's way of reminding people about the Christmas season. Luke's father had never liked Christmas, and following his example, Luke had adopted the same habit of never making any to-do over the holiday. The season brought back too many memories of his mother and her desertion of her husband and son.

"Now you two take your time," Emma directed them. "I'll just sit here and watch the people."

"What people?" Jillian said, looking around the vacant parking area. "Even Myrna's looks empty."

"Oh, there's sure to be more people anytime." Her eyes twinkled. "After all, this is a thriving metropolis."

Luke left the motor running to keep the car warm, and the two entered the store.

"Hi, Sally, how's it going?" He smiled at the middle-aged woman behind the counter.

"Just fine." Her eyes sparkled with good humor. "Anything I can help you with?"

"No. I need some bolts and screws for a feeder, and I'll just check your bins." He motioned towards Jillian. "Jillian's looking for work clothes, so she might need help." He made his way over to the hardware section, ostensibly searching through the bolts, but in reality, he was keeping a close eye on Jillian, curious as to how she'd react to the lack of selection.

Sally led her across the room to where several racks of clothes, and tables stacked with merchandise crowded the wall. "Honestly, I can't imagine you'll find anything you want in this stuff. We mostly just have things people need in a pinch. They go into the Falls if they want style."

Jillian gave the woman a reassuring smile. "Style's the last thing I'm worried about." She held up a pair of Levis to her body. "I just need something serviceable." She glanced at Luke and said wryly, "For mopping floors, making toasted cheese sandwiches—you get the idea."

Understanding filled Sally's face; she immediately saw Jillian's problem. "The sizes will probably be a problem since most of us aren't as tall and thin as you." She rolled her eyes, patting her own well-rounded hips. "I heard you're taking care of Emma."

"Yes, I am," Jillian answered as she set aside the first pair of pants and checked the size tags on the others. "She's waiting in the car for us."

The cashier's face lit up. "I'll run out and say hello." She grabbed a handful of Hershey bars and hurried out to the car.

The minute the door swung shut, Jillian said, "I must say, Ben's would never be confused with Saks Fifth Avenue."

"Oh really? Why?" He continued sorting through the bins.

She didn't seem to notice his acerbic tone. "Well, for starters, there are no gourmet foods."

"Ben's or Saks?"

"Saks!" Her voice exploded with laughter at the incongruity of her answer. "But they did have clothes in my size."

"Can't you find anything you like?" Why didn't that surprise him?

"I just can't find anything that fits. But let me try these," she said, adopting a more positive tone. "They may have to do."

She took a pair into a small curtained-off space in the corner and then came out with them on, clutching a handful of material at the waist to keep them from falling down. Looking at her reflection in the narrow mirror, she gave a cynical smile.

"If you don't mind pants two or three inches too big around the waist, these aren't too bad." Still holding the pants up with one hand, she struck a modeling pose. "And on the runway, modeling the latest in domestic house wear, we have the . . ."

"The toast of seven continents, Miss Jillian Taylor."

Jillian turned around elegantly and gave him a pouty look over her shoulder. "Why, yes." She made the words sound like a come-on. Then she laughed and Luke realized she'd been poking fun at herself.

She glanced down. "All I need is a belt, and I'll be in business. Best of all, I have one at home already, so I won't have to spend any of my hard-earned money on it." She returned to the dressing room and came out a minute later. Picking up a couple of more pairs of pants, she moved over toward the tables holding stacks of folded shirts.

Luke found his bolts and took them over to the counter. Leaning back against it, he watched while she picked out a red plaid flannel shirt, a black sweatshirt, a couple of white T-shirts, and a top to some men's long johns that she found after rummaging through the stuff on the sale table. Surely she wasn't getting those? She was. He folded his arms across his chest, watching her. What next?

She moved over to the shoes and tried on some hefty walking shoes.

He raised his eyebrows. "I don't believe it. Jillian Taylor in heavy-duty shoes."

"I know." She shuddered dramatically. "They look atrocious, but serviceable is the operative word since sandals aren't exactly winter wear." She picked up a large economy-sized package of socks. "Emma would be pleased to know that I now have 'my year's supply.'"

Luke stepped out of the way as she approached the counter and dropped her armload of clothes on it.

"Now what else do I want?" Her eyes lit on the jars of candy and hurried over to them. "I'd forgotten how many varieties of penny candy there are. Filled Christmas candy! I have to have some. Christmas isn't Christmas without it!" She grabbed a brown bag and filled it, then reached for a couple more sacks. When they were chock-full, she put them on the counter with the rest of her things.

Luke watched as she went to the magazine rack and leafed through the magazines, then added a *Today's Home* to her stack of purchases.

"A home magazine, not fashion?" He shook his head. "I don't believe it."

"It has a lot of Christmas ideas in it."

The suggestion that she might be thinking of decorating his house really shook him and he stiffened. Striving to keep his voice matter-of-fact, he said, "We don't really do a lot for Christmas."

"So?" She stared at him, then she looked away from him, deliberately considering the rest of the store one last time. "Now, what else do I want?"

Luke looked over her pile of merchandise on the counter. "Isn't that enough?"

She watched him and pursed her lips in thought. "Probably."

"I hope it's not more than your two weeks' salary," he warned.

"It doesn't matter." With a sassy look at him, she tossed her head, causing the long blonde strands to curl around her face. "You're not getting rid of me that soon."

Luke caught his breath. She was beautiful, he'd give her that. Then he scowled as she gave him an impertinent grin and flounced out to the car. When all was said and done, he reminded himself, she was just a shallow, heartless flirt used to getting her own way.

—⚶—

When Jillian arrived at the car, she found Emma with her hands full of Hershey bars. Sally was saying good-bye.

"Thanks for the candy," Emma called after Sally as she returned to the store.

Jillian slid into the backseat. "Does everyone in town know how much you love chocolate, Emma?"

"Just about. Which makes it handy," she chuckled. "I don't have to buy candy myself; other people give it to me. In fact, I can't wait another minute. Want to share?"

"Sure. I see you have extra." In fact, she counted seven.

Emma handed her a bar and then unwrapped one for herself, dividing all the squares before she began eating them one by one.

Jillian had just taken her first bite when Emma spoke up. "I wish we could get a Christmas tree this year. Luke's just like his father and thinks they're too much bother. When my husband was alive, we always went all out, but when I moved in with Luke and his dad a few years ago, I had to curtail my enthusiasm. But Christmas is my favorite holiday and my theory is," her tinkling laugh punctuated her sentence, "too much isn't enough.

"Let's get one then." Jillian opened the car door and strode over to the trees. "Tell me which one to get," she called to Emma. She straightened each tree, shook it, and held it for Emma to judge. Finally she settled on the fourth one. Jillian pulled the tag off and raced back into the store where Sally was putting the last item in a plastic bag.

"I'm just in time," Jillian said, panting slightly. "I want one of those Christmas trees. Here's the tag; just add it to my bill."

Luke looked alarmed. "Wait a minute—"

But she didn't let Luke finish. She turned to Sally. "Where are the Christmas tree lights?"

Sally retrieved them from a cardboard box under the store window. "One enough?" she asked.

"Make it three." Jillian's tone was decisive. "If there's one thing a tree needs, it's plenty of lights."

Luke's face darkened but he didn't say anything as he reached for his wallet. He didn't want to make a scene, and he could tell from the determined look on Jillian's face that she wasn't about to back down.

Picking up several bags, she headed for the car, and he followed her with the rest of the packages.

"Which tree did you buy?"

"Emma wants the fourth one." Jillian opened the car door and slid the sacks over onto the floor behind the driver's seat. Luke added his to the others before he unlocked the trunk of the car and took out some rope. He put the tree in the trunk, looped the rope around the hook, and fastened it down.

They'd only gone a mile or so when Emma nodded off. Luke's mind was occupied with thoughts of Jillian's Christmas tree purchase, and he said nothing, preferring the silence. Jillian Taylor hadn't a docile bone in her body, and if he weren't careful, she'd be running roughshod over him. He gritted his teeth, refusing to even consider the possibility.

In the backseat, Jillian slumped tiredly against the gray leather seat, imagining ways she might trim the tree. The magazine she'd purchased had some beautifully decorated ones and—she hoped—plenty of directions for duplicating them. She hadn't decorated a tree since she was a kid. As a family they'd always had such a good time at Christmas. Her mother did tons of baking, loading down all their friends and neighbors with homemade treats. As she remembered, it hadn't seemed too difficult.

Memories of the yearly trip to the hills with her father to find a tree flooded her mind, and her eyes started to sting with unshed tears. With Christmas right around the corner, she couldn't help thinking just how much she missed her father and just how alone she was now. During her early years in New York, she'd been so busy and absorbed in her life, she'd never even considered the day would come when she'd be all by herself. She had thought that fame and recognition were as good as love, and that having fun times with people meant they were friends who cared about each other. With her father gone, she felt the weight of being alone, a feeling that intensified as she looked at the rigid set of Luke's shoulders and remembered his look in the store when she'd bought the Christmas tree.

Images of her father's life here in Quail Creek without her mother suddenly filled her mind. She had gone back to New York without a twinge of guilt at leaving him alone. After all, he'd insisted she go. She shook her head in disbelief at her thoughtlessness. No, not thoughtlessness; it had been selfishness. While she spent the holidays at a round of Christmas parties and New Year celebrations, he spent them by himself. Feeling at last her father's loneliness with both his wife and daughter gone, Jillian took a ragged breath as she struggled to hold back her tears. Her whole body shook at the realization of how badly she had hurt her father. How could she have been so selfish? So full of pride at her narrow, meaningless life? She wished she could see her parents again, tell them how foolish she'd been. But they were gone and there was no going back. She had to look ahead.

As she felt the car turn into the lane, she opened her eyes. Remembering Luke's reaction to the Christmas tree, Jillian scowled through her tears. She needed to keep in mind the reason for her presence here—Emma needed her. No matter what, she was determined to stay focused on that thought. She might have forsaken her father, but she'd fight to make Emma happy. And Emma wanted Christmas with all the trimmings.

"Here we are," Luke broke the silence, pulling to a stop near the back porch. He gave Emma an affectionate look, as she awakened with a start, her eyelashes fanning her cheeks.

Tender feelings welled up in Jillian again. "Let her rest for a few minutes while I take my stuff in. When she's completely awake, I'll help her inside." She avoided Luke's eyes while she poked around for her packages.

"Where do you want me to put the tree?" He appeared resigned to the fact that they were having a tree.

"The living room will be fine for now. Ultimately it's Emma's decision." Loaded down with her purchases, she struggled up the steps and into the house. Why had she found it necessary to bring everything in one trip? She dumped it all on her bed and hurried out to help Emma inside.

She smiled down at the elderly lady who was still blinking her eyes awake. "Are you ready?" At her nod, Jillian buttoned Emma's coat and helped her up the porch steps to the wheelchair.

"Don't forget my Hersheys." Emma pointed to the seat where five bars lay.

"Never!" Jillian assured her. "I know what's important here, and it isn't worth my life to leave them behind."

Her eyes twinkling, Emma took the candy from Jillian. "I like people who have their priorities straight!"

In the living room Jillian took Emma's coat and hung it in the bedroom closet. "I'll heat some of the soup Nancy made the other day, then we'll eat. Would you rather sit in your wheelchair or on the sofa?"

"The wheelchair's fine." Emma smoothed out the wrinkles in her dress as she made herself comfortable.

Jillian hurried to the kitchen to heat the soup. While it was warming on the stove, she sliced some bread and toasted it. Moving quickly around the kitchen, she congratulated herself on how handy she was becoming. She could now heat soup and toast bread at the same time. In no time at all, she had the table set and the soup mugs filled. Luke entered at just the right moment, and they all sat down.

After the blessing, Emma asked, "Where's the tree?"

"It needed a stand so I haven't brought it in yet. I thought we might have an old one in the basement, and we did." Luke glanced at Jillian. "I also found some old decorations you might be able to use. I never realized how much junk we've got down there. One of these days we need to clean it out."

He broke off a piece of toast and dipped it in his hot soup before saying, "After we eat, I'll set up the tree."

"Great!" Jillian met Emma's grin. "We only have two weeks to get ready."

Emma turned to Luke. "Do you think for once we could invite Randy and Helen over here Christmas Day instead of going there? I know it's your family tradition, but I get tired just thinking about it."

Luke raised his eyebrows. "Christmas here instead of over there? Don't tell me you've forgotten what a good cook Helen is."

"Jillian can fix a dinner every bit as good as Helen's." Emma's eyes sparkled as she looked at Jillian. "Isn't that right?"

Jillian's heart nearly stopped. She didn't want to admit any weaknesses in front of Luke, but on the other hand . . . "I-I certainly wouldn't put myself in Mrs. Prescott's category, but I'd be happy to make Christmas dinner for everyone." The last was an out-and-out lie, but she did want to make Emma happy. If this was what it took, she'd do it. Exactly how she'd do it was another question completely.

Emma beamed. "I knew it! What about it, Luke?"

Conflicting emotions crossed his face, with skepticism emerging as the final winner. "I guess if we don't have toasted cheese sandwiches, and if someone else does the dishes, you'll get along fine," he said, with an appraising look at Jillian.

"Cheap shot!" Jillian looked amused.

His eyes glinted. "We'll see."

Emma put down her spoon and watched while her two companions finished eating. "Any cake and ice cream left, by chance?"

Jillian smiled at her. Emma was as predictable as the morning sun. "Coming right up," she promised, gathering the dishes to take to the kitchen. She returned a few minutes later with their dessert.

This Emma devoured with relish. "Nap time," she said, slowly laying her napkin on the table. "It's discouraging, but rest is what I do best."

Luke helped her into the wheelchair, and Jillian took her into the bedroom. After she had Emma situated comfortably in bed, she returned to the dining table. Luke looked up at her.

"I've been thinking about what Emma said," he began. "What if I asked Helen to fix the meal here instead. That way Emma wouldn't have to go out and—" his eyes narrowed, "—we could still have a fantastic meal."

Jillian didn't like the message she was hearing, but she decided to keep things light. "How do you know that among my many attributes I'm not a Cordon Bleu chef?" she said, returning to her seat.

"Are you?" Luke asked, with an ironic lift of an eyebrow.

Jillian lifted her chin. "No, but I'm certain I can manage Christmas dinner for five. Or six. I suppose Marci will come."

"Look, I told you I prefer not to celebrate Christmas, but the part of it I do enjoy is Helen's dinners. I don't mind having dinner here because I honestly think that Emma is too weak to spend hours away from home. But don't let any false pride keep you from admitting you can't cook well enough to fix Christmas dinner by yourself."

Jillian didn't like the determined set of his voice or his all-too-apparent disbelief in her abilities. Leaning across the table, she met Luke's steely gaze with one of her own. "I've already said I'm not in Mrs. Prescott's league when it comes to cooking, but I can manage." If it killed her, she'd manage.

Luke didn't like losing and Jillian heard it in his voice. "All right. It's all yours, but I'm warning you—" he emphasized the next words, "—don't ruin Christmas dinner." He stood up and started toward the door.

"Don't worry," she retorted in an irritated tone that equaled his. Standing up with a huff, she cleared away the rest of the dishes, loaded them in the dishwasher, and straightened up the kitchen. No matter what Myrna and the others thought, she for one, would hate to be married to Luke. He was too obstinate.

When she had finished, she returned to her bedroom to put away her new things, all except for the long john top and the jeans. Changing her clothes, she tightened the belt through the loops of her new pants and looked into the mirror. What a difference three days could make. In these clothes and with the lines of exhaustion and stress in her face, no one would even think of taking her for a celebrity. She looked exactly like what she was—a housekeeper. Picking up her magazine, she headed for the living room.

The tree stood in front of the bay windows. Even without decorations it looked majestic. Luke was kneeling in front of it, adding water to the base. "It's all set. Now as soon as Emma tells me exactly where she wants it, you can start decorating. Since I only found a few decorations, that shouldn't take long."

"That's good." Jillian made her voice enthusiastic. She didn't want to disabuse him of the notion any earlier than she had to, but she expected it would take a lot longer than that to decorate the tree. She was planning on loads of decorations. She glanced at the old-fashioned tree on the front of the magazine. Cookie angels and big bows adorned it. She flipped the magazine open.

The phone rang and Luke disappeared into the kitchen to answer it. He stuck his head around the door a moment later. "It's for you."

She wondered at the frosty tone in his voice. "Who is it?" she asked. Who knew she was even here?

He shrugged, his eyes unreadable. She rose from the couch, and he stepped aside as she approached the door, but she felt his eyes upon her. As she entered the kitchen, the thought occurred to her it might be Simon Grant calling her back at last. She'd given the agency Randy's number, and if Simon wanted to reach her, Randy or his mother would have given him this number. The thought made her heart soar momentarily. To be able to tell Luke she didn't need this job, that she was wanted in New York, left her breathless.

She realized she was shaking in anticipation. She placed both hands on the kitchen counter and took a deep breath to calm herself, then looked up abruptly as the scent of the freshly cut pine tree filled her nostrils. Christmas. Emma. How could she have forgotten?

She tried to slow her racing thoughts, tried to think. What would she do? Even if Luke felt her presence here was a desperate and uninspired last choice, she knew Emma needed her.

The phone lay on the counter top, waiting for her. What would she say? She didn't know. She had an impulse to simply hang up the phone, to turn around, and go into Emma, just to be near her and feel her remarkable spirit.

Nerves made her voice tentative and she tried to keep her voice from shaking as she spoke. "Hello? This is Jillian Taylor."

CHAPTER 11

"Jillian!" The familiar voice was completely unexpected.

It was Randy. The sound of his voice shocked her as disappointment raged through her body. Clearly she would have no decisions to make. She was still stuck here.

"How's it going?" he asked. "Missed you at church yesterday. I thought sure I'd see you there. What happened? I asked Luke but he just shrugged it off." Randy talked on, oblivious of Jillian's silence.

Her mouth was so dry, she didn't think she could speak, and she felt a moment's gratitude for the reprieve.

"Jillian? Are you all right? If you're sick, I can come over—" Randy sounded worried and Jillian knew if she didn't speak quickly, he'd be over in no time.

"I'm here to take care of Emma, remember? She didn't feel like going to church, so we stayed home."

"Oh." His disappointment was evident in that one word. "I wanted to talk to you."

"We watched the Tabernacle Choir and the BYU channel. I'm sure it was as good as any meeting at the ward." *And a whole lot easier to sit through,* she wanted to add.

"Probably. The other reason I called was to find out what days you have off. I thought we might have dinner in Idaho Falls. In fact, we could make a day of it."

"It sounds like fun," she said pleasantly, "but I don't think I have a day off. Luke hasn't mentioned it." She didn't enjoy the thought of asking Luke about time off. He already considered her a money grubber, and after only three days if she even mentioned a day off, she could imagine his reaction. Besides Randy was engaged to Marci. Jillian hardly knew her but she would never consider hurting her, or for that matter, stirring up the wrath of Luke and Mrs. Prescott.

"Luke doesn't expect you to work seven days a week," Randy said reasonably.

"Probably not," she agreed, "but until he informs me differently, I don't want to broach the subject."

Randy conceded that she probably had a point, but he wanted to take her to lunch when she did have some time off. "There's not much to do on the farm right now, and I can get away anytime," he assured her. "You just tell me when."

A few minutes later Jillian hung up. The thought of returning to the excitement of New York had sent a rush of adrenalin through her, and then hearing Randy's voice had left her limp. She sagged back down into the living room chair. Did she really want to go anywhere with Randy? No, she didn't, and she most certainly didn't want to lead him on. She picked up her magazine.

Luke glanced questioningly at her, but she made no effort to respond. After a few minutes he left the living room. She was glad to see him go. Right now she needed a few minutes by herself without his daunting presence. Making herself more comfortable, she continued looking at *Today's Home*.

She skipped the columnists and got right to the main part of the magazine. "Countdown to Christmas" was written in old English letters with an ivy motif, which embellished the first page. An advent calendar provided the background. Elated by the pictures, Jillian thought she'd found just what she needed to get ready for Christmas. After only two days in Emma's company, Jillian wanted to do whatever she could to make the holidays extra special for her, but when she read further, she saw that the calendar started five weeks before Christmas. She certainly wouldn't have time to follow all their directions. She was already three weeks late in starting.

She scanned the first section, "Gifts from the Garden." The enterprising writer suggested forcing paperwhites and amaryllis bulbs to enhance the traditional Christmas colors of red and green, something Jillian had no interest in doing. Other suggestions included collecting gourds, squashes, artichokes, and pomegranates, which could then be dried for decorative arrangements. She could cross that off.

She skipped down to "Gifts from Your Pantry." *Gather up your odd-sized bottles and make flavored vinegars,* she read. Several recipes followed, along with some inviting pictures of the finished product. That wasn't for her, either. Besides with her talent for catastrophe, she'd probably poison everybody.

Finally she came to the day after Thanksgiving. Play Christmas music while you write out your Christmas card list. That would be simple enough since she wasn't sending any. She glanced down the page to December twelfth. *Clean your house thoroughly so it will be a sparkling backdrop when you start decorating.*

Now that was a downer. Cleaning wasn't her forte. She thought of herself more as artistic. But deciding to get into the spirit of things, she took a hard look at the furniture and grimaced. She could write her name in the dust on each piece without any difficulty. *I guess no one could accuse me of focusing on the fine points,* she thought wryly.

The dust cloths and furniture oil were probably in the kitchen closet. If she wanted a sparkling backdrop, she'd better get started.

Eager anticipation of turning this regulation living room into a Christmas wonderland lifted her spirits. She peered into the cleaning closet where the vacuum was stored. If Emma weren't napping, she'd get started with the vacuuming. But that could wait until tomorrow. She'd do it first thing. Looking around, she shook her head in dismay. The size of the house made the job appalling. Whoever planned this house obviously never planned on cleaning it.

When she finished dusting, she appraised her work. The editors were right—polishing the furniture did make the room sparkle. She took a deep breath, savoring the lemon scent of the oil mixed with the fresh pine of the Christmas tree.

What to do next?

She flipped the page to the second week of Christmas. *Decorate your tree.* Several trees were pictured, but the one with sugar cookie angels looked the easiest, especially since the ingredients could undoubtedly be found in the kitchen. The directions even included a pattern for the angels, so she was all set. She glanced at the clock. One-thirty. She had plenty of time to do it today.

But making the cookies turned out to be harder than Jillian had expected. Rolling the dough evenly so she didn't have browned spots on the angels took a skill it turned out she didn't possess.

"Jillian!"

That must be Emma, ready to get up, she thought. Wiping her floury hands on a paper towel, she hurried into the bedroom.

"What's that tantalizing smell, darling girl?" Emma's smile along with her words lifted Jillian's spirits. "It's wonderful."

"Cookies for our tree," Jillian answered, enjoying the look of pleasure on Emma's face. "I've made one dozen and have another three dozen to go. After we've baked them all, we'll frost them." She helped Emma into the wheelchair and straightened the bedspread before taking her into the living room. "Then as soon as you tell Luke where you want the tree, we can start decorating."

Emma spied the tree. "It's perfect just where it is! People will be able to see the lights from the road, and we can enjoy it, too. I'll frost while you finish baking the cookies because I can't wait to start. After my nap I'm ready to tackle anything."

"Why don't you supervise while I do the work?" Jillian suggested instead, knowing that Emma's strength wouldn't last long.

"Okay," she said agreeably, her eyes twinkling. "I like that division of labor."

After making four batches of cookies, Jillian had forty-eight large angels plus a backache, tired feet, and flour everywhere. Under Emma's helpful tutelage, Jillian frosted the cookies next.

Just as she brought out the lights and started to assemble them on the living room floor, Luke returned. The cold from the frigid air clung to him, causing both Emma and Jillian to gasp and shiver.

"Did you make all these cookies?" He rubbed his hands together, blowing on them as he entered. "Whatever for?"

"To decorate the tree. You're just in time, Luke." Emma pointed to the tree. "Putting the lights on is a man's job."

After his reluctance at celebrating Christmas, Jillian fully expected him to demur. To her surprise, his mouth quirked into an engaging grin as he said, "I should have stayed outdoors longer."

As he unraveled the lights and wove them down each branch, Jillian stared in disbelief. She hardly recognized this warm, friendly stranger who joked and talked as they worked. When they ran out of lights before they ran out of tree, he remembered that there were more lights stored in the basement. "If not, we can get more from Ben's tomorrow," he said, almost cheerfully.

Jillian stood bemused as he hurried down the stairs. What had gotten into him? What had happened to the arrogant person she knew in high school? Or at Mrs. Prescott's, for that matter? She was still pondering on this mystery when he returned some minutes later, gingerly holding a dusty paper bag that contained three more boxes of lights.

"This ought to do it," Luke said, stringing the lights on the lower branches just as carefully as he'd done the top ones. It turned out that they had enough to finish the tree, even though the top ones were small and twinkly, and the bottom ones were nearly three times that size. When he plugged them in, their warm glow filled the entire corner of the room.

Emma clapped. "Marvelous! I'm getting into the Christmas spirit already."

"You knew what you were doing, Emma, when you assigned the lights to Luke. He has a real knack for decorating."

"That I do," he grinned at Jillian. "But the rest is up to you." Although his words were lightly spoken, his eyes were steely, warning her that while Emma might get him to help, Jillian would not find him as cooperative.

"I've got just the thing we need now," Emma's enthusiastic voice drew their attention back to her. "On the top shelf in my closet, Jillian, there's some white yarn. If you'll get it, we can use it to tie the angels on."

With the yarn and a cookie sheet full of angels, Jillian started on the tree. True to his word, Luke left the tree decorating to Jillian. But he remained with them, chatting with Emma and reading a little.

When she finally crept into bed at 10:30, her body felt as if she'd spent a day at digging ditches, but she lay there smiling as a feeling of satisfaction filled her. The tree glowed, imbuing the room with a special spirit. Emma seemed happier and even Luke was a different person—one she found very appealing. The next day she planned to go through the box of decorations he'd brought upstairs and see what else they had. She punched her pillow, trying to get more comfortable, then turned over on her side.

—⁓—

Jillian awoke the next morning with the same happy sense of anticipation. Anxious to get started, she threw back the covers and dressed hurriedly. After breakfast she settled Emma in front of the tree with a magazine while she dragged the vacuum out of the closet. Most of the first floor was plank with area rugs, so the job moved quickly. But not upstairs. She hadn't been up here before and she looked around with interest. A beige Berber rug covered the floor of the wide hall that divided the rooms. Upon opening the doors, she found Luke's office, three smaller bedrooms, a bathroom, and a large master bedroom at the end of the hall. The smaller rooms looked as if they hadn't been used in ages, and they all had the regulation lodgepole pine beds like her room, with either red or blue rag rugs and matching curtains. Someone had obviously gotten into a decorating rut, though probably not Luke. She couldn't imagine his taste running to rag rugs.

She was right. Except for a few patches of bare wood, three large, dark blue and cream Persian rugs hid the floor. A king-sized lodgepole pine bed with a brown furry throw dominated his quarters. Along the left wall, two mahogany leather chairs sat in front of a television. She shook her head in disbelief at the volumes filling a massive bookcase on the right side of the room. Never would she have taken Luke for a reader. He seemed such a hearty outdoors type that if she'd thought about it she would have guessed he disdained books. Curious about his reading interests, she moved closer to the shelves to look at the titles. They were mostly church books and American history books. She didn't see any novels, so evidently he didn't go for the light stuff. She quickly vacuumed all the rugs. Already she'd spent too much time looking around his room, and she knew Luke would accuse her of an ulterior motive if he ever found out.

Putting the vacuum in the closet downstairs, she discovered a dust mop. If she'd realized it was there when she'd first looked, she would have taken it with her and saved herself a trip. Next time she'd get organized and take everything with her the first time. She found some clean dust rags and returned upstairs.

Finally when she'd dusted the floors in the living room, she was ready for a break. A job she'd imagined would take a few minutes had consumed over an hour.

"Come on over here and sit down for a bit. You're just in time to watch the BYU devotionals."

Emma's warm and inviting voice made Jillian feel as if the older woman truly wanted her here. Although the idea of more church didn't really appeal to her, the thought of a rest did, so she sat down next to Emma.

"How long is this?" she asked. "I don't think Luke expects me to sit around all the time. Maybe just a fifteen-minute break a couple times a day."

"It's only an hour. If I don't mind, why should he?" Emma patted her hand.

Jillian doubted the two things were synonymous. "I'll tell you what—I'll sit with you and watch for fifteen minutes, and then I'll unwrap the ornaments Luke brought up."

Emma nodded in agreement, her eyes fastened on the television. Jillian let the words roll over her, the low rumble of voices soothing her. She'd gone from no religion in her life to religion every time she turned around. She knew Emma believed in the Church. Her parents had believed it with all their hearts. Once she had, but now she didn't know. It seemed easy enough for people here to go to church; what else was there to do? But once she left. . .

Looking up at the clock, Jillian smiled at Emma as she released her hand. She picked up the sack of decorations sitting beside the tree and took it to the table. Inside she found about a half a dozen bedraggled ornaments.

"Emma, are these someone's favorite childhood ornaments?" she called.

Emma looked up. "Heavens, no. I think we brought them with us when we moved here, and that was over twenty years ago. They certainly look the worse for wear. Toss them out! But there are several boxes of nice ones in the basement. After this is over, go on down and look for them."

Throwing the dilapidated decorations into the kitchen garbage, Jillian decided to go downstairs and find the others. The basement was unfinished and appeared to be used primarily for storage. By shifting the boxes around, she managed to find four marked Xmas. She lugged them upstairs one at a time. They were dusty, and she felt as if she needed another shower by the time she'd finished. She washed her arms thoroughly in the kitchen sink and dusted off her shirt and pants before putting the first box on the counter. The box contained village shops and people, each one wrapped carefully in newspaper. Jillian's heart beat faster and she eagerly opened the others. Two of the boxes held more of the village, and in the last box she found several colorful ball ornaments on top of more newspaper-wrapped items.

She picked up one of the houses and hurried in to see Emma. "Look! There are three boxes of a Christmas village."

Emma looked delighted. "How darling! I don't remember seeing them before so they're probably Luke's. He won't care if you use them. Where should we put them?"

Jillian looked around. Along the outside wall of the dining room was a massive pine sideboard that would hold them. The fireplace mantle or the coffee table were two other possibilities. All of them offered a great deal of space.

Jillian looked at Emma indecisively. "What do you think? The sideboard, the mantle, or the coffee table?"

"Either the mantle or the table," Emma suggested. "That way they'll be in plain view all the time."

Jillian dusted off the village and carried it to the coffee table, where she carefully arranged the houses, shops, trees, benches and all the small pieces. When she'd finished, she stood back and admired it, thrilled with how festive the house was beginning to look.

"The other box had some ball ornaments and something in the bottom that I haven't taken out yet," she told Emma, wondering if she might use those as well.

"Those are mine. Why don't you add the white and silver balls to the tree? The others are too garish." Emma squinted her eyes. "If I remember right, there are some snowmen in the bottom."

"I'd better get lunch ready, then we can check out the other box."

It was easy enough to warm up Sunday's leftovers, and she soon had everything ready and waiting for Luke's arrival.

He walked in, the cold air still clinging to him, and sniffed. "Something smells good!"

"It does, doesn't it?" His pleasant mood made her happier. "It's Sunday's roast. We're having leftovers." When he was like this, she found him one of the most attractive men she'd ever known.

Luke went to the living room to get Emma and a moment later, Jillian heard an outraged yell. "What have you done?" Dashing out of the kitchen, she stopped short in the living room at the sight of his face.

"Depend on you to snoop around the basement," he said in a cutting tone, his expression fierce. "If I'd wanted those things up here, I'd have brought them up." Before Jillian could say a word, he went on, "I know where those boxes were. You must have been snooping around in the basement, looking through everything, in order to find them."

Jillian could feel the color drain out of her face. Why was he so upset at the sight of the little village? It made no sense to her. "I'm sorry," she said at last. "I didn't mean to get into your private things. I'll put it away." Although her knees trembled at Luke's unexpected attack, she moved towards the coffee table.

Emma spoke up, her voice hushed and soothing. "It's my fault, Luke. Jillian would never had brought up those boxes if I hadn't told her to go down and look for some old ornaments of mine. I've never seen the village before, but I might have known it had a special meaning for you. We'll take it all down immediately. This is a season for joy, and I certainly don't want anyone miserable over a thoughtless act of mine."

Luke breathed deeply and some of the tenseness left his shoulders. "I'm sorry, Emma. I overreacted. My mother gave that to me the Christmas she left; I haven't seen it since. But don't bother about it now. Leave it out." His face looked bleak and his voice remained harsh. "I guess it's about time I grew up and got over it." He turned abruptly and went upstairs.

Her body trembling, Jillian sank into the nearest chair. In the short time she'd been here, she'd never seen Emma look so solemn. "I know I have a lot of faults, but I'd never snoop through Luke's things," Jillian said in defense of herself, although it was Luke, not Emma, whose judgment she feared.

"I know you wouldn't, darling," Emma said gently, though her voice was troubled. "Luke's mother wounded him badly when she left his father and him. I thought he'd gotten over it. He never talks about her leaving, but I should have known his feelings about her were still so tender."

"I thought she died. I didn't know she'd abandoned them." No wonder he'd reacted so violently.

Not long after, Luke came downstairs for lunch, acting as if nothing had happened. Emma and Luke kept up a running conversation as they ate, but Jillian could only sit there, still bruised from Luke's condemnation. She didn't know why. Heavens, in the modeling business it seemed as if there had been a tirade every session by someone or other. She'd simply ignored them. But the anger in his eyes and voice had cut her to the core.

Without a word in her direction, Luke finished his lunch and went upstairs to his office. Numb, Jillian cleared away the dishes, then returned to the living room to unpack the last box, hoping it held no unhappy surprises for anyone.

Emma was right. The bottom half contained snowmen. Jillian thought they were darling, and since they were Emma's, she couldn't imagine that Luke would have any problem with them. She put eight silver and white balls on the empty branches of the tree and scattered the snowmen along the mantelpiece.

"It's looking good." Satisfaction filled Emma's voice.

Jillian looked around the room appraisingly. The tree and mantel looked wonderful, but the rest of the room was still bare. She shook her head at Emma. "If your motto is 'Too much is not enough,' we still have a ways to go."

Taking the empty boxes back downstairs, Jillian returned hopefully to her *Today's Home* magazine, looking for more ideas. With a little luck, she would also be able to forget the burning accusation in Luke's eyes.

—⁂—

Luke went upstairs to his office, he found himself unable to concentrate on the paperwork. For a person who took pride in self-control, he had really lost it today. The intensity of his reaction after all these years had even shocked him. How could something that had happened to him so long ago resurrect such anger or such pain?

He and his father had always worked on the ranch together. The summer he turned twelve, he and his dad had even herded a band of sheep for a week. Their usual sheepherders were from South America, but his dad wanted him to experience what they did. He'd enjoyed every minute of it. His father could do anything and Luke admired him more than any other person he knew.

He'd loved his mother, too. His lips twisted sardonically at the thought of her. He'd never seen anyone as beautiful as she was. His first memories of her were of her singing to him. In fact, she used to sing a lot, she'd been so happy all the time. He remembered helping her do spring cleaning and weeding her vegetable garden with her. He liked helping his dad better, but she could make even drudgery fun.

The Christmas holidays before his mother left had been wonderful. She'd gotten the village for him and had displayed it on the coffee table. She'd done everything she could to make the season memorable by decorating the entire house and putting up a tree that must have been nine feet tall. Although he was twelve and considered himself too old for kid things, he'd secretly loved it all.

In between Christmas and New Year's, he and his dad had gone cross-country skiing nearly everyday. They'd also gone winter camping with Luke's scout troop. His mother had wanted to go into the Falls and see the lights, but his dad hadn't been interested. Since Luke had wanted to be with his father, she'd gone alone. In fact, she'd left the house nearly every afternoon that week.

On New Year's Day, he had awakened to find his father alone and his mother gone. His dad's jaw was set, and he hadn't said much. Just that his mother wanted to be where she could enjoy the bright lights. She found ranch life dull.

Luke couldn't understand it. How could his mother just leave? He couldn't understand how his mother could have ever loved him, if she could abandon her son so easily. Now, as a grown man, Luke still felt the same way. Sandra Prescott wanted a more glamorous life, and she'd simply taken it, letting no one stand in her way, especially not a twelve-year-old boy. Her commitments to her family hadn't meant a thing, and he knew now her temple covenants hadn't either.

That was the last time he and his dad had made a big deal over Christmas. From then on, they hadn't bothered with a tree or presents; his Aunt Helen always invited them to eat with them. Since she was such a good cook, dinner at her house had been no hardship.

Luke had always felt that Jillian had an allure just like his mother's. On the surface she might appear dutiful to Emma—as she had to her mother—but look how she had failed her father. Luke feared that ultimately Jillian would abandon Emma in the same way, when something better came along. To borrow a phrase his father had often used, Jillian was "all horn and no motor." She made him edgy and he didn't trust her.

He picked up his phone to call his aunt. The sooner she became aware of the change in their Christmas plans the better. The meal would probably be a disaster, but he would honor Emma's wishes to spend Christmas at home.

His aunt picked up at the first ring. "Hello." Even her voice portrayed her resoluteness.

"Aunt Helen, it's Luke—"

"Luke, am I glad you called. We have a big problem. Marci told me Randy was having doubts about getting married. Can you believe it?"

Luke could believe it all right. He thought the trouble lay right in his own household.

"I blame Jillian," his aunt continued, her voice beginning to rise. "Randy was perfectly happy and contented being engaged to Marci until that hussy showed up. I don't know why Frank had to locate her. She'd ignored her father for years. Why come back for his funeral? That woman hasn't a decent, caring bone in her body—"

"Helen—" the decisiveness in Luke's voice stopped his aunt abruptly, "—Jillian loved her father deeply. It's not for us to judge why she stayed away while Jed was alive." His words surprised even himself. The last thing he thought he'd ever do was defend Jillian Taylor. He himself had criticized her for paying her father so little attention, but he hadn't realized what a bitter and unforgiving attitude that was until he heard it from Helen's lips.

She ignored him as she ignored anyone who disagreed with her. "But, Luke, you've got to get rid of her. She can't be this close to Randy. Who knows what foolish mistake Randy might make with her around?"

"Randy is a grownup," he reminded his aunt. "He has to make his own mistakes. Neither you nor I can run his life." Not that he hadn't interfered enough times at her behest, but now he could feel his patience evaporating. "Besides, Emma is the reason Jillian is here. Have you forgotten there is no one else to look after her?"

"She can't be the only one available. You just need to keep looking." Her sobs resounded through the receiver. "She's wrecking our family!"

Luke waited for his aunt to calm down. "Since I couldn't find anyone else to care for Emma, I consider Jillian an answer to prayer," he said pointedly, although he would never have considered Jillian a likely possibility without the bishop's intervention. "Emma loves her, and I wouldn't get anyone else even if someone were available." Listening to himself, he could hardly believe what he was saying, but it was true. He didn't know how much longer he'd have Emma, and he'd do anything to make her happy.

The sound of Helen's sobs continued through the phone, but Luke thought they seemed to have subsided somewhat. He could imagine her reaction when she learned the reason for his call. He plunged ahead to get it over with.

"Emma isn't feeling strong enough to go out on Christmas Day, so we thought we'd have dinner here." He paused, waiting for her to absorb this unexpected change in their holiday traditions.

His aunt gave a strangled cry. "You know Emma's not able to cook, and that leaves Jillian! I'll bet she's never cooked Christmas dinner in her life. You expect me to eat badly prepared food and throw my son into the lion's den all in one?" Her voice quivered with outrage. "Please spare me."

"Emma really wants you to come," he said, knowing how much Helen loved Emma. "I'll make a deal with you, all right? If you'll come, I'll keep Randy and Jillian apart."

Helen sniffed. "I'll come, then, if you promise. I'd better bring my ham, and no one makes bread and pie crust as good as mine. I do want this to be a good meal so I'll bring the pies and rolls, too."

She sounded more like herself now, for which Luke was grateful.

"If you want me to bring anything else, just let me know. But remember you promised," she reminded him forcefully. "No Randy and Jillian sneaking off together."

When they finally hung up, Luke sighed. Now he had yet another reason to dread Christmas.

CHAPTER 12

"I spoke to Aunt Helen, and she agreed to come here for Christmas."

Jillian had been concentrating on her magazine, and she hadn't heard Luke come downstairs. His words startled her and she looked up to see Luke smiling at her. Given the state of his mood an hour ago, she found this change near miraculous.

"She wants to bring a ham, rolls, and pies," he added. "No one makes pie crust like she does, so she didn't get any argument from me. But she's willing to leave the rest of the meal in your eager hands."

"Gee, thanks," Jillian said, trying not to roll her eyes. She turned to Emma. "We'll have to get busy."

"Make a list of what you want," Luke invited them both. "I'm going into Idaho Falls tomorrow for supplies for the workers' commissary. I can pick up the groceries at the same time." The tension seemed to leave him as he looked around the living room, and his voice was more subdued as he said, "If you need anything else to decorate with, add that to the list."

Jillian stared at him. "Will the real Luke Prescott please stand up?" she said dryly. She found it hard to believe how tractable he appeared, given his earlier outburst.

"I like the way the house is looking," he admitted slowly, as if he were strangling on the words.

Emma caught Jillian's eye and grinned. "Good," Jillian said, waving her magazine at him. "I'm getting lots more ideas from this magazine."

Suddenly he didn't look quite so agreeable, but she didn't let that stop her. "I'll get you a list."

"And see if that magazine has some new recipes for the menu," Emma spoke up. "I get tired of the same old thing."

Luke looked at her as if he couldn't believe his ears. "What's wrong with turkey and dressing?"

"But we have that every year," Emma pointed out. "This year let's do something different."

Luke looked at the two women and shrugged helplessly. "All right, if that's what you want."

She nodded. "I do."

Jillian had to give Luke credit. Where Emma was concerned, he willingly went to great lengths to make her happy. She thought it would be nice to have someone as considerate of her happiness. But she didn't think that person lived in Quail Creek.

—⟋⟍—

It was bedtime before Jillian and Emma had their list ready for Luke. They had poured over the magazine and considered several menus before Emma decided they should have Beef Wellington for Christmas dinner. She'd never tasted it, but she thought it sounded good, and she had no doubt that Jillian was perfectly capable of making it. Jillian herself wasn't as sure, but she dutifully listed the ingredients. She'd try for Emma's sake. To her surprise, but not Emma's, Luke bought them everything on their list.

Two days later, while Emma was resting, Jillian decided it was time to do something with the hard candy she'd bought at Ben's while shopping for her new clothes. Her magazine suggested making Christmas trees out of the hard candy, and she planned to use them to decorate the sideboard.

Jillian gathered all her materials in the kitchen, along with the candy and the hot glue gun Luke had bought for her. She'd put it on her shopping list, though she hadn't expected him to actually buy it for her, and though she'd never used one before, she thought she could handle it. The night before, she had stapled some cardboard rounds into cones, which ranged in size, since she hadn't found any two pieces of cardboard alike. Now she was ready.

Once again, she studied the directions carefully. It sounded simple enough. *Using a glue gun, attach hard Christmas candy to the cardboard. Glue them close enough together that no part of the base shows through.*

She plugged the glue gun into the outlet, and while she waited for it to heat, she poured the candy out onto the kitchen counter. Selecting the first piece, she glued it to the bottom edge of the largest cone. That was simple enough, she decided. She took another piece and glued it to the cone, and another, until it was completely covered.

She stepped back to admire her handiwork. "Spectacular, if I do say so myself. Now for the next one."

From the amount of candy she had left, she doubted she had enough for more than three trees. Since they'd look better if the heights were staggered, she picked up one of the smaller cones this time.

She glued on the first row without incident and was very pleased with herself. But as she started to glue on the next piece of candy, it slipped and the hot glue hit her finger instead of the candy.

"Ou-w-w-w-w-w-w!"

The pain was excruciating. Dropping the glue gun, she ran to the sink and stuck her finger under the cold water, but the burning didn't stop. She flung open the freezer door and grabbed for some ice, anything to stop the fiery torment. But even ice offered no relief. How could such a small burn hurt this badly? What else could she do? She leaned against the counter holding the ice to her finger, moaning softly to herself.

Hearing someone at the back door, she glanced up. It was Luke.

"What's wrong?" he asked, seeing that she was holding a melting ice cube in her hands.

"I burned myself," she said, trying to laugh at herself for yet another mishap, but her voice sounded wobbly even to her. "I got some hot glue on my finger. I don't mean to be such a baby, but it really hurts."

The look he gave her was unfathomable, and she had no doubt that was exactly what he thought she was acting like. "We should have some burn ointment in the First Aid kit that will deaden the pain," he said, opening the closet and pulling out a white tin box with the emblem of the Red Cross. "Here it is."

He took out a large tube and reached for Jillian's hand. Taking the half-melted ice cube, he tossed it into the sink, then gently examined her fingers. He squeezed some ointment from the tube and dabbed it on the burn, then lightly stroked it over the reddened flesh where she had burned herself.

At his touch the throbbing pain of her burned finger seemed to diminish, and Jillian watched him curiously. In the last few days she'd seen so many different facets to Luke she hadn't known existed—the charming Luke who decorated the tree, the furious Luke who had scorched her with a look, and now this tender Luke whose gentle touch caused a pleasant ripple of feeling through her. Without any conscious volition, she looked up into his eyes and allowed herself to be drawn into them, feeling as if she were swimming in their dark blue depths. As his eyes traced the features of her face, she sensed the same uneasiness in him. Finally she forced herself to look at her burned finger, which he still held firmly but gently in his hands. His very touch generated a surprising awareness in her of how much he attracted her.

She spoke, breaking the spell between them. "Thanks. That was great timing."

Slowly he released her hand. "I think you've done enough for today. I'll unplug the glue gun. You go in and sit down."

She gave him a faint smile. "You won't get any argument from me." Still feeling weak-kneed, she made herself comfortable in a chair near the fireplace, sitting back and closing her eyes.

A few minutes later Luke joined her. "You've got this place looking great for Emma. What's next?"

As he reclined in the overstuffed chair across from her, her awareness of him as an attractive man persisted. She tried to sound matter-of-fact. "I wish we had some evergreen branches for the stair railing. Is there any place nearby where you could get some?"

The corners of his mouth turned upward and his eyes twinkled. "Have you looked out the window lately?" he teased lightly. "We're surrounded by a national forest." He paused for a minute, thinking. "Maybe we could get Nancy to come over for an hour tomorrow and visit with Emma while we get some." He nodded. "I think you need a break, even if it's only a small one like getting fir boughs."

"It'll be fun. Brisk country air, beautiful mountains, the scent of pine trees, some vigorous exercise . . ."

"Don't get too carried away." Luke's tone was dry. "We can drive right up to the spot."

Luke was right. Jillian had gotten carried away, as she learned the following day. The mountains were beautiful, which Jillian already knew from looking out her bedroom windows, and the air was brisk all right. But she'd never have managed without her fur jacket, and she got more exercise going upstairs to clean the bedrooms. Even so, she reveled in the wonderful scent of the woods. The aroma of their Christmas tree seemed pitiful compared to this. And the trees themselves looked green and fresh and pure.

Most of all, she liked being with Luke. The delightful way one side of his mouth curled up and his eyes flashed when he found something Jillian said humorous sent curls of pleasant sensations spiraling through her body. So she spent her time trying to make him laugh and to her joy often succeeding. She couldn't remember when she'd had such a wonderful time.

When they'd finished decorating the stairway, the intersecting aromas of cranberry candles, fresh greens, and fudge permeated the house. She'd made chocolate fudge for Emma from a recipe she found for No-Fail Fudge, and true to its name, it hadn't. Emma devoured most of it in an afternoon and begged Jillian to make more, so she did.

Each day Emma's pleasure became more evident. Luke appeared to be on his best behavior, and Jillian could feel the Christmas spirit in abundance. For the first time in years, she felt as if she belonged, and from time to time she wondered if she ever wanted to leave this place. Could she have changed that much in only a few days? Right now New York sounded okay, but not as good as it had a week ago. Would she really want to stay here permanently? Was it Quail Creek and Emma?

Or was it Luke?

If he'd treated her this well in high school, instead of mocking her all the time, she doubted she'd have ever left. A kind Luke was an attractive Luke. He'd been well liked in high school, she remembered. His senior year he'd been student body president, which had intimidated her, since she and Randy were merely freshmen. The senior girls all seemed to be crazy about him, though she could never figure out why. Now she knew. She was also just as intimidated by him now as she'd been then. Now he had the power to break her heart if she let him, and she knew she could not let that happen. Broken hearts in high school were one thing; but at this point in her life, she knew it would be more than she could bear.

—⁓—

Emma continued to insist that Jillian watch the BYU devotionals with her each day. At first it had taken real effort to sit through them quietly, but by the end of the week, Jillian had decided they weren't too bad. Although she spent a lot of time just waiting for them to be over, she did occasionally hear something that made sense to her, or that made her stop and think.

On Saturday Jillian found herself humming as she worked. Even cleaning the house gave her great satisfaction. At supper Emma set down her fork and announced, "I'm going to church tomorrow. Listening to the carols on TV is nice, but it's not enough. I want to be in the same room with the singers and join in, too."

Luke looked concerned. "Are you sure you feel strong enough?"

"I'm up to it," she nodded. "Besides I want to take the sacrament again in the ward with my friends."

Luke glanced at Jillian. "We'll need to leave here about ten."

"Sure. Do you want me to go along?" She'd felt so safe in this house that she hated to leave. Would the bishop expect a report? How would the ward members treat her?

Emma spoke right up. "Of course, we want you to go, darling girl. You're indispensable." She beamed at Jillian, who returned her smile.

Each time she'd helped Emma bathe, Jillian had gotten a little better at it. She didn't always come out looking like a drowned rat, but this morning she took no chances. She bathed Emma first and helped her put on a red dress before seating her in her wheelchair and wheeling her out to the living room. She returned a short time later wearing her black dress, a dazzling array of pearls, crystals, and gold chains around her neck and throat. Her hair was twisted elegantly on top of her head.

Emma's mouth fell open. "Oh, Jillian, you're beautiful!" she cried. "You look exactly like a model should look. I especially love your pearls." Self-consciously Emma touched the strands around her neck. "They make mine seem insignificant."

Touched, Jillian leaned forward and embraced her friend. "There's nothing insignificant about you, Emma, I promise."

The older woman laughed. "You're just prejudiced, my dear, and I'm glad."

Jillian wrapped Emma's coat around her and then slid into her own red cashmere one. When Luke came in, they bundled Emma into the warm car. Jillian didn't imagine that the temperature could be much above freezing; just walking the few steps between the house and the car left her face tingling.

They parked in front of the church, and Luke helped Emma out. Organ strains of "Oh, Little Town of Bethlehem" filled the foyer as they entered. Once inside everyone hurried over to greet Emma, including Mrs. Prescott and Randy. One after another the ward members hugged her, saying, "We're glad you're here today. We've missed you." Then they smiled at Jillian and moved inside the chapel.

Jillian's throat tightened as she watched. How wonderful it would feel to be part of the community the way Emma was. She doubted that any of her own friends missed her or even gave her a second thought. She found she could barely breathe past the lump of pain that seemed to be growing in her chest. She'd made some stupid choices, she knew now, and she had to live with them. She had no one to blame but herself.

Emma clung to Jillian's arm as Luke marshaled them into the chapel and halfway down the aisle. Emma insisted on entering the row first, which left Jillian sitting between her and Luke. For the first few minutes, the only thing she was aware of was Luke's shoulder touching hers, but after a while she became absorbed in the prelude music as a sense of peace washed over her. What was different about this church that she would feel this way? Over the years she'd attended many churches, more to see and be seen than to worship, but in none of them had she experienced this remarkable serenity. Why here? In a country church with unsophisticated people, many of whom hadn't even left the state, let alone the country.

A smile lighting his face, the bishop moved to the podium and the music stopped. "Good morning, brothers and sisters. What a beautiful day to worship on. The air is clean and crisp." At the mention of crisp a shiver ran through Jillian. Frigid was more like it. "The skies are clear, and we are where we should be on the Lord's day, in His house with our brothers and sisters."

His gaze rested on Emma. "We are so blessed to have Sister Emma with us today and to feel of her spirit. And Sister Taylor, we welcome you, too. We will sing Hymn 271, 'Oh, Come, All Ye Faithful.'"

The organist played an introduction, and the most enthusiastic chorister Jillian had ever seen stood up to direct them. She couldn't help but join in—in fact, everyone did—and the chapel rang with their voices. Jillian was sure the Tabernacle Choir had never sounded any better. She glanced at Emma, who sang along, obviously and joyfully enthralled with the music. The congregation seemed to sing the next song just as fervently.

She closed her eyes during the passing of the sacrament, remembering how as a girl, she had taken it automatically each week, without a second thought. So much had changed since then. Though she did not feel she could take it now, with the life she'd been leading, she listened intently to the prayers and a soothing spirit filled her.

When the sacrament was over, the bishop stood again. "You might have noticed in the program that the Primary is presenting the Christmas service today. Sister Jackson, Sister Olsen, the teachers, and the children have been working very hard on it." He turned and beamed at them. "We want you to know how much we appreciate all your efforts."

Jillian felt a pang as she counted twenty-six children filing up to the choir seats. They had excited, expectant expressions on their faces, and for a moment she wished one of them belonged to her. They sat down, squirming to make themselves comfortable. She glanced at Luke to see how this scene affected him. He appeared to enjoy watching them, but she didn't discern any sense of longing on his face. She wondered how he felt about having a family. He'd certainly waited long enough to marry. She'd bet he was the only man in the room who had reached the age of thirty without marrying.

She forced her attention away from Luke and back to the program. Then he stretched his arm along the back of the bench, accidentally touching her shoulder and sending a shiver of delight through her that lasted nearly to the end of the meeting. Several of the older boys read the Christmas story from the Bible, while the rest of the Primary sang Christmas carols.

The program proceeded smoothly until they came to "Away in a Manger." Then a small boy and girl dressed like Joseph and Mary came to the front. A doll lay in a large wicker basket, which Jillian thought must be the manger. Mary picked up the doll and in a very motherly fashion started rocking it in her arms. Joseph watched for a moment and then grabbed the doll away from her. Incensed, Mary yanked at the doll's head while Joseph hung onto the feet, and an energetic tug-of-war ensued. Jillian thought their loud shrieks were an interesting accompaniment to the children's choir.

By this time the entire congregation was chuckling. Now glad they weren't her children, Jillian watched with amusement as one woman hurried to the front, gathered her son up in her arms, handed the doll to Mary, and returned with a wriggling armful to her seat. Without missing a beat, the Primary sang on.

She glanced at Luke and he grinned back, as diverted as she had been. As they left after sacrament meeting, the bishop pulled Jillian aside into his office. "Emma looks happy. But how are you doing?"

Jillian hadn't had time to collect her thoughts and prepare an answer that would sound good, so she simply told him what she felt. "I'm not the best nurse or housekeeper she could have, but I love Emma. She's a lady in every sense of the word."

The bishop smiled. "I thought you two would get along. Any problems with Luke?"

Jillian felt his genuine interest in her well-being. She thought, too, that here was one person who didn't seem to think Luke was an answer to every maiden's prayer. "Actually no, much to my surprise. At least, none on my part anyway. I think everything is working out . . . pretty well." Although she thought things were quite a bit better than that, she didn't want to appear too confident. With Luke, she never really knew what to expect next.

He patted her shoulder. "I thought it would." He gazed at her for a moment. "You've been on my mind. Don't forget the Lord is mindful of you and what you're going through. Don't forget Him. He won't forget you."

Tears came to her eyes at the bishop's gentle words. She managed a whisper and a tremulous smile as she thanked him. The warmth and concern emanating from him enveloped her, and the burden around her heart lifted.

—⁂—

On the way home Emma displayed more energy and vitality than Jillian had ever seen. Obviously, going to church had been good for her. She guessed she could say the same for herself. She had found the story of the birth of the Savior moving and had enjoyed the unexpected humor and the wonderful music. What more could she ask for? Lately, she had begun to think a husband and children would be nice. She shook her head, smiling at her thoughts. Growing up, she'd dreamed of a modeling career, never of marriage and a family, and she doubted if ten days in Quail Creek could change anyone that much. Still, sitting next to Luke had been downright pleasant, and she'd more than enjoyed the way he helped her out into the aisle . . .

That was it! She took a deep breath to clear her head. Thoughts of children, a family, a husband like Luke—it was just a momentary mental aberration. It could never happen. A relationship with Luke could go no place, and she'd be a fool to forget that salient fact.

—⁂—

The day hadn't warmed up any and an icy wind howled around the house as Jillian prepared for bed. She shivered when the cool sheets touched her body. Tonight she was grateful for the luxury of a furnace. But a thought occurred to her and before she could talk herself out of it, she slipped out of bed, and for the first time since she'd been a teenager, Jillian knelt to pray before getting into bed.

"Heavenly Father, I thank you for having this job and for bringing Emma into my life. Please bless Luke and me that we'll continue to get along. Thanks also for the bishop. Please help me know what to do, I pray. Amen."

With a light heart she snuggled back under the quilt and reflected on her day. Each day seemed to get better and better. Maybe God had blessed her with this job, so she could know Emma. Remembering how Emma had raved about Jillian's necklace, she decided to give it to her for Christmas. She couldn't afford anything nicer and didn't know of anything Emma would enjoy as much.

And Luke? What would she give him? Why was she even thinking about getting him anything? Jillian knew why he was on her mind. The problem was that no matter how much she tried, Jillian couldn't forget how comfortable it had felt sitting beside him today.

"No!" she said aloud, shaking her head decisively against the pillow. "I absolutely refuse to be attracted to Luke Prescott!" He was her boss and although he'd started acting more pleasant towards her, nothing had really changed between them.

She'd already spent a week's salary at Ben's. She'd better save the rest of her money.

—m—

Luke relaxed against the back of the leather chair in his room and admired the work Jillian had done. His room was cleaner than it had been since Emma had had her last stroke. He'd felt certain that Jillian was capable of keeping Emma entertained, though he'd never believed she had any capacity or inclination toward housekeeping. The house glowed from the decorating she'd done, and most of all, so did Emma.

He'd been so aware of Jillian sitting next to him during sacrament meeting today, he could hardly concentrate on the program. He found himself envying the parents of the children and longing for some himself.

In the last few days, he'd begun to see a softer side of Jillian, which alarmed him. He'd never had any natural defenses against kindness, and he found that it had only made her even more attractive to him. Watching her tenderness towards Emma, he wondered how it would feel if Jillian felt that same concern for him.

But that was a thought he refused to dwell on. He thoroughly disliked the unsettled feeling she had awakened in him. He didn't believe for a moment that she would stay if a better opportunity presented itself.

In high school, he'd managed to quell any attraction he had for her—and for the first time, he could admit he had been attracted to her—by belittling her. Not that it had affected her one way or another. She always tossed her head and stared at him like he had two heads, which had irritated him even more.

Even though he had to admit she'd gone the extra mile in her work here, everything she did reminded him of his mother's last Christmas. Like his mother, Jillian was beautiful, but staying power and beauty didn't come in the same package.

Nevertheless, he knew this Christmas would be difficult for her and that her pain at losing her father was real. He'd suffered the same way when his own father had passed away, and he could recognize that sense of loss in others. If only there were some way he could help soften the hurt . . . He couldn't think how he could help . . . but then the picture came clearly to him.

Feeling better, he reached for the phone.

CHAPTER 13

Jillian's eyelashes fanned her cheeks several times before she was able to do more than squint. When she realized it was Christmas morning, her eyelids snapped open. The gleam of falling snow softly lit her dark room. It had started snowing about the time she went to bed last night and she'd wondered at the time if it would continue through the night. It had, turning the outdoors into a storybook setting for this day.

Happiness suffused her body. God had blessed her with Emma. And what an incredible blessing! Only from her parents had she ever felt this much love. She could probably be happy staying here forever, if only Luke trusted her. Although he'd been more friendly in the last day or so, she sensed that underneath he had no faith in her.

But she refused to let that dampen her spirits. Raising her hands over her head and stretching the full length of her body, she decided that it was going to be a marvelous day. Even Mrs. Prescott with her dour expression couldn't ruin it.

Underlying the warmth and happiness, a niggling of worry fluttered in Jillian's stomach with greater and greater frequency. She told herself to relax. She was prepared for this day—at least as well as a person could be prepared the first time she cooked a Christmas dinner. She'd read Emma's cookbooks thoroughly, and practically memorized the food section of *Today's Home*. If those editors knew anything she didn't, the information obviously hadn't been important enough to print in the magazine.

Jillian glanced at the clock and realized that she'd better not just dream about today; she needed to get up and get started. She'd made

Christmas stollen yesterday, and she couldn't wait to see Luke and Emma's faces. After a quick shower, she dressed and, for a festive look, she donned her new red plaid shirt.

Passing through the living room, she plugged in the tree lights. She savored the Christmas tree, which, with all its angels looked "simply heavenly," smiling at her own witticism. As the colored lights reflected off the glossy icing, they filled the corner with a rosy glow. Jillian wished she could sit down and enjoy the magical feeling, but she knew she had no time to dawdle.

Taking the covered bowl of stollen out of the refrigerator, she lifted the towel and peered at the rich batter studded with pieces of dried fruit. She kneaded it a few times, then placed it on a cookie sheet.

She wasn't brave enough to attempt an omelet, so she simply beat the eggs for plain scrambled eggs. She'd set the table the night before, so that was one thing she didn't have to bother with. A few days earlier Emma had sent her down to the basement to find her dishes, which she had packed away. It had meant more poking around, but this time Jillian was careful to only bring up the boxes with "good china" written on the top.

Emma's dishes turned out to be fine English bone china, which she'd inherited from her mother. Jillian loved the pattern of dainty pink roses interspersed with raised white cabbage leaves. Yesterday, she'd carefully washed the dishes, and now they sat at the end of the counter ready for dinner. Where had her own mother's good china ended up? She shook her head, saddened by its loss.

Luke entered the kitchen from the outdoors. "Anything I can do to help?" he asked, his voice sincere and helpful, a pleasant change from his more familiar tone of annoyance. What a difference from the old Luke, Jillian thought, smiling at him. It seemed that Christmas had the power to soften even Luke.

"I never refuse help. Are you sure you're not trying to prove how handy you are?" She shot him a teasing glance.

He pretended to be offended. "Me? Never!" Then he grinned at her, and Jillian felt a warm shiver in her midsection. She turned her back to him, not wanting give herself away.

"Would you peel these oranges while I check on Emma? I'll put the stollen in, and we'll be ready to eat when it comes out." She slid the pan into the oven.

Emma was just sitting up when Jillian peeked in her door. "Merry Christmas, Emma!" Jillian sang out. "Are you ready to get up?"

"Merry Christmas, yourself!" Emma said, admiring Jillian's festive appearance. "You look very cheery in that red shirt. I think today's the day for me to wear red, too."

"Every day's an excuse for you to wear red," Jillian laughed and Emma joined her.

"You're right, of course," she said, lifting her arms for Jillian to help her into her wheelchair.

Emma showered, then Jillian wheeled her over to her dressing table. "Here. You put on the basics while I get some of my special Christmas glamour."

Emma's eyes lit up, and when Jillian returned, she deftly applied some blush to the pale cheeks. "A lot of eye shadow and a touch of liner." Using the brushes, she stroked on metallic beige shadow and a thin line of eyeliner.

"Now for some rosy lips." Jillian painted Emma's mouth a soft pink. "Then a sprinkling of fairy dust, and we're all finished." With her long-handled brush, she added gold highlights to Emma's expectant face.

"That's more like it," Emma said, peering into the mirror. She reached for her pearls and gold beads, which spilled over one side of the dressing table. Only when Jillian had them fastened did Emma brush her silver hair back. "Now I'm ready for Christmas."

In the living room, they found Luke stretched out in a chair, gazing at the Christmas tree, lost in thought. When he caught sight of Emma, he sat up and whistled. "Wow! Where are you going? You look too exotic for the Prescott ranch."

Emma responded to his whistle with a satisfied smile. "Thanks to my angel here." She patted Jillian's hand. "What would I ever do without you?"

"The question is—what would I ever do without *you?*" Jillian returned lightly, trying to keep the emotion from her voice. Self-consciously clearing her throat, she excused herself, "I'll finish getting breakfast now." She left Emma beside the table and returned to the kitchen, pleased to note that the air was filled with the mouth-watering aroma of baking bread.

In between stirring the eggs to keep them from burning, she measured cocoa into a large ceramic teapot she'd discovered in the cupboard and sliced the oranges, sprinkling powdered sugar on top. The buzzer went off, and she ran the hot water for the chocolate, before taking out the stollen. When that was finished, she started carrying everything to the table. "Breakfast is served!" she announced proudly.

Luke joined them at the table, and after the blessing, he said to Jillian, "This looks delicious! Even homemade stollen!"

"This is my first time for making bread," she admitted, "but it does look good." Picking up the bread knife, she was startled to find that she could not cut into the loaf. No matter how she applied the knife, the stollen lay there rigid and unyielding. Her heart sank. The bread looked so perfect and smelled so good.

"What could possibly have gone wrong?" She turned anxious eyes toward Emma.

"Did you forget the yeast?" Her voice was kind.

"No." Jillian knew she hadn't forgotten it.

"Did you let it double in size before you baked it?" was Emma's next question.

Jillian grimaced and shook her head. "I didn't. I took the dough right from the refrigerator and put it in the oven."

"It doesn't matter," Emma laughed, who, as usual, had a practical solution. "Get a sharper knife, my dear. This stollen is perfect for dunking in our cocoa."

Bringing back a butcher knife, Jillian managed to hack off three pieces of the stollen. After beginning the day with one disaster, she felt a knot of apprehension in her stomach about the dinner still to come.

Emma stirred her cocoa with her stollen and daintily bit into it. "This is much better than biscotti," she reassured Jillian. "Good flavor, size, everything!" She dipped the rest of it into her cup and appeared to relish every bite.

What a sweetheart Emma is, Jillian thought gratefully. With Emma to boost her confidence, she felt as if she could cope with whatever happened the rest of the day.

Luke on the other hand looked noncommittal as he dunked his stollen. But after his first bite, he nodded his head in agreement with Emma. "Not too bad," he complimented her.

When they'd finished eating, Luke suggested they exchange their presents before the others arrived. Jillian had checked the packages under the tree the night before and was relieved to find that only Emma had given her anything. She was glad she hadn't given Luke anything. It would have been embarrassing to give him a present when he hadn't given her one.

Luke helped Emma to the sofa near the tree, then went outside, probably to get his gift for Emma, Jillian thought as she cleared the table. The first thing she did was plunk the stollen into the garbage, making sure the paper napkins and towels were on top. She didn't want to leave any sign of her failure around for Mrs. Prescott to see.

Joining Emma on the couch, Jillian took the elderly lady's frail hand in her own. She gave it an affectionate squeeze, then spontaneously lifted it to her lips and kissed the back of her hand, then pressed it against her cheek.

Emma's eyes glistened with tears. "Heavenly Father blessed me with exactly what I needed by giving you to me. The first time I heard your name, I knew you were meant to come here. I didn't know how it would be accomplished, but Heavenly Father did." She smiled tenderly at Jillian. "If I had a daughter, I'd want her to be just like you."

What a beautiful thought, Jillian sighed as she gave Emma's hand another gentle squeeze and closed her eyes against the tears that came to her eyes. *But if she only knew all the stupid things I've done, she'd never want any daughter of hers to be like me.*

Feeling Emma's warm gaze upon her, Jillian blinked away the tears and looked hesitantly at her friend. *She knows,* Jillian thought. *Somehow she knows and she loves me anyway.* The love that flowed from Emma seemed nearly tangible as it surrounded her. In a voice husky with tears, Jillian whispered, "I'm the one who is blessed. God must have known how much I needed you."

They sat quietly together, enjoying the glow from the tree and from their friendship. When Luke returned, he handed a large package to Emma. She read the card. "To Emma from Luke." She eagerly tore off the wrapping and lifted the lid. "Oh, my! Red velvet." She held up a beautiful cranberry-colored top and cuddled it against her face. "This feels like a cloud against my skin." Handing it to Jillian, she reached for the matching pants. "I love it! Luke, you always know just exactly what to get me. I can't wait to wear this. It's so soft and cuddly." She looked at him, her face beaming. "Red *and* velvet. Come here so I can hug you." She held out her arms, and Luke stood and gave her a hug. "I'll need to change clothes, Jillian. Luke's gift is too wonderful not to wear it today."

"I agree." Jillian placed the clothes back in the box and moved it to the other side of the couch.

"Here's one for you, Jillian—from Emma." Luke handed her a small box that surprisingly turned out to be rather heavy.

"I can't wait," Jillian said, glancing at Emma's expectant face. Unfastening the tape, she carefully unwrapped the present. Beneath the red foil wrapping, she found a gold box with "Holy Bible" and "The Book of Mormon" written on it. Removing the lid, she found a set of burgundy leather books with her name engraved on them. Opening the first one, she found Emma had written, "For my darling Jillian—May the Lord bless you with an understanding of the gospel and with the righteous desires of your heart. Love, Emma."

Scriptures were the last thing she'd expected, but Emma's words left her heart brimming with gratitude. "Oh, Emma, these are wonderful. Thank you." Jillian reached over to hug her and as she did she glimpsed Luke's face. His lips were curled in a skeptical smile, as if thinking her too superficial to appreciate such a gift.

"This next package is to me." His eyes twinkled as his loving gaze rested on Emma. "Surprise, surprise."

When he opened it, his face *was* surprised. "How did you know I'd ordered a new handmade bridle for Lady?" He took it out and admired the leather work on the reins.

"I ordered mine first." Emma's love for Luke lit up her face.

"I thought it was strange when Jake told me he couldn't have it ready for a month. Now I know why. He knew I was already getting one from you. Thanks, Emma. You've made my day. This calls for another hug."

Hearing footsteps on the back porch, Jillian looked up, startled. It couldn't be Randy and his mother yet. It was too early. Besides she hadn't heard anyone drive up the lane. When she rose to answer the door, Luke said, "I'll get it." A moment later she heard him say, "Hi, come on in."

Jillian's eyes widened as Luke led two men in who were carrying a large box that looked like a casket. When they placed it in the center of the room, she recognized it and jumped up from the couch. Her mother's cedar chest! "Luke! What a . . . Where did you . . . How did you . . . ?" Incoherent thoughts rushed through her mind. She knelt before the chest, and her hands trembled as she lovingly touched the surface.

Overcome with emotion, she flew to Luke and hugged him. "How can I ever thank you?" She felt her earlier tears spill over once again. "I'm—I'm so thrilled. At last I have something of my parents. Thank you, thank you, thank you. You are so wonderful!" Looking up at him, she found his expression unreadable, but she didn't care how he reacted to her hugging him. The bishop and Nancy had been right—Luke was terrific.

"I can't believe it," she said for about the tenth time. "How did you track it down?"

Luke gently disengaged himself from her arms and stepped back. "The auctioneer kept good records. But for now I think we'd better move it out of the living room. You can look at the contents later." He motioned to the men and led them to her room.

Jillian ran to Emma's side next and wrapped her arms around her. "Emma, can you believe this?" She couldn't wait until the day was over, and she had time to reflect on her mother's treasures.

Emma just smiled at her. "Of course I can. It's just exactly the type of thing Luke would do."

These people evidently knew Luke better than she did. Never in her wildest dreams did she think he would do something like this and especially not for her!

The men left and Luke rejoined them. "We have one present left, and it's for you, Emma." He handed the package to her.

Guilt flooded Jillian. She hadn't gotten Luke anything! How awful! What could she possibly do for him on the spur of the moment? Her mind was a blank. He'd been so wonderful to her, and she'd even congratulated herself on not doing anything for him because he hadn't gotten her anything. Now he'd given her the best present she could have ever received! What a thoughtless person she'd been! But she vowed to make up for it. She'd question Emma later, so she could get something as meaningful for him.

"Jillian, my dear, you shouldn't have given me your jewelry, but I love it," Emma said, handing the strands to Jillian. "Fasten it on me, please, then bring me my mirror off the dresser. I can't wait to see how this looks."

Looking in the mirror, she smiled at her reflection. "Now I feel like a jet setter myself. What do you think, Jillian?"

"You'd put them all to shame, that's what I think," Jillian declared. When she remembered how miserable she'd felt two weeks ago, she couldn't believe the happiness of today. Her heart was so full she didn't know if she could make it through the day without collapsing on her bed. If only she could hold onto the joy of this moment forever.

Looking at the clock, Jillian realized she'd better get started with dinner if she wanted to be ready when Helen and Randy arrived. "Emma, my love, do you want to change into your new clothes now, before I start dinner, or after I get it in the oven?"

"Right now!" Emma said. "Why waste time? Besides, I don't want our company to arrive before I'm ready."

After Emma had changed her clothes, Jillian wheeled her to the dining room, where she could supervise the cooking and the setting of the table. During the week, Emma had told Jillian where to find the linen tablecloths, and Jillian had pressed the wrinkles out and now spread the snowy-white cloth along the table.

When Jillian finished setting the table, pride filled Emma's voice. "The bone china, the silver, and the crystal give the table such an elegant appearance. It announces that we're having a formal dinner, and will Helen ever be surprised! No ordinary turkey and trimmings for us!"

Jillian felt the pressure of Emma's expectations and feared that the dinner would flop and Helen wouldn't be surprised. "Sh-h, don't say anything," she warned Emma. "We don't want to jinx the dinner."

But Emma only smiled. "Don't worry. This dinner will be perfect."

Jillian hoped so, but she crossed her fingers just in case. She'd scrubbed the potatoes yesterday, and now she removed them from the refrigerator. The menu called for twice-baked potatoes, string beans almondine, tossed salad, and the *pièce de résistance,* the Beef

Wellington. She considered the menu poor planning on someone's part because every dish in this meal had to be prepared at the same time, which was the last minute. She shook her head, hoping she was up to the job.

Her first task was to roast the fillet of beef exactly twenty-five minutes. Then she would let it "rest" while she started the other dishes. She'd just gotten everything organized when Luke came into the kitchen. "How's it going?" he asked cordially, which gave Jillian a fresh infusion of confidence.

Brushing back the wisps of loosened hair with the back of her hand, she smiled as she declared, "Everything's under control." Then she looked at all the food still waiting to be prepared. "I think."

"I haven't a doubt," he said firmly and Emma added her vote of confidence as she looked around the kitchen. Warmed by their confidence in her, Jillian thought she might just pull it off after all. They heard the steps on the porch, and Luke opened the door to find Randy and his mother standing there.

"Merry Christmas, everybody," Randy greeted them exuberantly, a wide smile on his face as he unloaded an armful of boxes onto the counter.

"Where's Marci?" Jillian asked him. She had expected him to bring his fiancée.

Helen Prescott gave Jillian a wintery look. "She went home to Boise."

Jillian wondered what was going on between Randy and Marci. Surely an engaged couple would spend Christmas together. She would ask Randy later about it.

Mrs. Prescott embraced Emma enthusiastically, ignoring Jillian. "Go bring in the rest of the food, Randy," she directed in a no-nonsense tone. Randy shrugged at Jillian, then went to do his mother's bidding.

Ever the gracious hostess, Emma returned Helen's embrace with a cheerful welcome. "I'm so glad you came here for dinner. Jillian has prepared a wonderful feast for us." Her eyes gleamed. "Beef Wellington."

"*Beef Wellington?!*" Helen looked appalled and glared at Jillian. "Have you any idea how much fillet of beef costs?"

Jillian stepped back, stunned at Mrs. Prescott's vehemence. "N-no," she stammered.

"I thought not," she sniffed. "That little piece of meat probably cost close to forty dollars. You don't seem to realize we're just simple country folks. We eat ham and turkey on Christmas."

Jillian felt caught between two torrents. She was just the cook here, nothing more. Heavens! She hadn't a clue how much fillet of beef cost. Emma had concocted the menu, but she could hardly say so in the face of Helen Prescott's rude accusations.

"I'm s-sorry. I had no idea the beef was so expensive. Luke, why didn't you mention it?" she asked, hoping for some refuge from this unexpected attack. The pulse at her temple beat a rapid tattoo, and she breathed deeply, hoping to calm down.

"Because this time price didn't matter. We decided on something different, and we just went for it!" Luke smilingly reassured his aunt.

"I'm the one who insisted on Beef Wellington." Emma patted Helen's arm. "Have you ever tasted it?"

"Well, no." Helen looked somewhat mollified as she spoke to Emma. "It was always out of my price range."

"Same here." Emma nodded her head. "But this year I said, let's throw caution to the winds and have it!"

"So we did. Jillian graciously consented to fix it," Luke added.

Obviously discomforted by this new information, Helen changed the subject. "Emma, I've made your favorite pie, chocolate pecan. Luke, I brought apple for you and pumpkin for Randy."

Jillian hid a smile, observing that Mrs. Prescott hadn't gone out of her way to fix anything special for her! Not that it mattered. Randy entered with a covered pan. "Here are the rolls. Ready for the oven."

Oh, great, Jillian muttered to herself. *One more thing to bake at the last minute.* She had managed to stay calm up to now, but her head had begun to ache and she had started to feel shaky. "Emma, why don't you and Mrs. Prescott go into the living room so you can visit." she suggested. *And I won't have to put up with any more putdowns!*

Emma caught her eye and Jillian knew she understood. "That's a wonderful idea, dear."

Helen Prescott looked at her son. "Come with us, Randy. I'm sure Jillian can manage on her own."

Jillian was sure Mrs. Prescott thought no such thing, and nothing would make her happier than for Jillian to fail miserably. But she'd show her! Now if nothing turned out as tough and hard as the stollen, she'd be all right.

Luke, leaning against the counter, didn't follow them. "I'll stay and be the chef's assistant. Just tell me what to do."

Jillian looked around her, trying to get her bearings. "Will you check and see if the potatoes are done? If they are, cut them in two and scrape out the inside of the potato and put it in that bowl." She pointed to a large yellow ceramic bowl. "I've got to arrange all these mushrooms on the meat and then wrap it in puff pastry."

Working with the puff pastry was harder than it had sounded. It was an effort to keep the mushrooms on the beef.

Luke glanced over at her handiwork, looking impressed. "The magazine says to put an egg wash over all of this and then cut out pastry leaves to decorate it with," she told him, rolling her eyes. "Egg wash, yes. Cutesy decorations, no! Angel cookies were enough of a stretch for me." With that she slid the pan into the oven.

"You're doing admirably," he complimented her with a heart-stopping grin.

And her heart did just that—stopped. How in the world, she wondered, could someone as annoying as Luke Prescott had always been make her pulse race now? She had no idea, and with all the things to prepare for dinner and her desire to show Mrs. Prescott, she didn't have time to think about it. But for a startling moment, a wave of emotion engulfed her before she quickly brushed it aside.

Finally everything was on the table, and they all sat down to eat. Luke gave the blessing, thanking Heavenly Father for the birth of His Son.

By this time Jillian felt so flustered she barely remembered why they celebrated Christmas, and her mother's cedar chest was only a distant memory. She held her breath while Luke served the Beef Wellington. She hated to be sitting across from Mrs. Prescott, who would be sure to gloat if the main course turned out to be a disaster.

"I'm glad we decided to have Beef Wellington," Emma said, winking at Jillian. "You've done a superb job with it, don't you all agree?" She looked around the table.

"Fantastic!" As usual Randy exuded enthusiasm.

"Not too bad." Luke glanced at Jillian.

"No ringing endorsement?" she teased him, trying to hide her embarrassment at Emma practically demanding compliments on her behalf.

Luke grinned at her. "I'm convinced. You really did go to the Cordon Bleu."

Mrs. Prescott smiled insincerely. "I think it's delicious—although the bottom crust is a bit soggy. With practice, you'll improve." She arched her eyebrows. "Of course, dashing around the world on rich people's yachts, you won't have any need to cook, will you?"

Looking around the table, Jillian saw three frowning faces all looking as if they were ready to jump to her defense. She was determined to remain pleasant, however. "Before I do any more dashing, I'll be here practicing on Luke and Emma, if you two think you can stand it."

"We're honored to be your guinea pigs." Emma waved her arm dramatically. "Aren't we, Luke?"

Luke was still chewing, and it took him a few moments to swallow. "So far, so good," he said, appearing to enjoy his meal. "So count me in."

When it was time for dessert, Mrs. Prescott served her pie, making sure the others knew she'd made their particular favorite. When all but Jillian had been served, she addressed Jillian directly, "I don't suppose you eat pie, do you, Jillian? Too many calories, I'm sure."

"I love pie and bring on the calories!" Jillian tried to speak lightly. "I need to gain weight. Emma and I have a deal about that."

Randy's mother gave her chocolate pecan, which turned out to be fantastic. "No wonder Luke wanted you to bring the pies. I've never tasted crust this flaky or such sumptuous filling," Jillian sighed, having eaten more than she could ever remember eating.

Now Mrs. Prescott appeared to doubt Jillian's sincerity. "Thank you," she said uncertainly.

"You're really a good cook, Jillian," Randy said, not for the first time. "This meal was wonderful. The best ever."

"Especially your mother's rolls," Jillian said, glaring at him. For the life of her, she couldn't imagine why, if Randy valued his life or hers, he kept complimenting her. His mother appeared more irritated by the moment.

When everyone had finished his pie, Randy looked around the table, an eager expression on his face. "Why don't you all go in the living room and relax? Jillian and I will clean up."

Mrs. Prescott shot Luke a look of pure terror.

"We can't leave this mess of dirty dishes to you two. I'll help." Luke rose quickly and took Emma to the living room, then returned.

He and Randy cleared the table while Jillian put things away in the kitchen. Then she washed the dishes and the two men dried. Randy seemed put out by Luke's presence, declaring several times that he and Jillian could handle the dishes by themselves, but Luke ignored him. Jillian had little to say. The dinner over at last, she could hardly wait until she could go to her room and relax.

They finished the dishes, then joined Emma and Helen in the living room. Jillian made herself comfortable in an overstuffed chair; she was more than ready to relax for a few minutes. Luke and Randy sat on the sofa.

After going over one more time how good the food had been, how much everyone in the ward missed Emma, and how Quail Creek's basketball team would do in the state tournament, the room became silent. It had been a busy morning, and now after a good meal, everyone seemed tired and ready for a nap.

"I need to get something out of my car. Why don't you come out with me, Jillian, and get some fresh air?" Randy stood up and reached out his hand to her.

The snow had stopped and the day looked pure and crisp. Maybe this was what she needed to clear her head. Jillian let him take her hand and pull her from the chair.

Mrs. Prescott glared at Luke, who rose after a moment and followed Randy and Jillian from a safe distance.

At the back door, Randy stopped and gazed at Jillian as if he couldn't get enough of her. Then without warning he drew her into his arms. "I've been waiting all day for this moment, Jillian. You must know I love you. I've never stopped."

CHAPTER 14

Stunned by his declaration, Jillian froze, her arms still at her sides. What did she do now? She stared at him, horrified. "Randy," she began, not knowing what to say but only that she had to stop him before he said anymore.

"Listen." Randy raised his finger to her lips. He had apparently been preparing this speech for some time and would not be stopped. "You have no idea what it's like to pray every day for ten years that the only girl you've ever loved will return," he said. "These last three weeks have been horrible. I'm ready to explode. I love you, Jillian. You must know that."

Jillian knew that she didn't love Randy, and after all this time, she didn't think what Randy felt for her was love.

"You're engaged," she reminded him, pulling away. "You must care something about Marci."

Randy stared at her for a moment. "I do. She's a wonderful person. She's pretty, she's smart, she's fun, she's religious, but the bottom line is I don't *love* her, Jillian. I *love* you."

"Then why get engaged to her?" Jillian asked steadily.

His answer was simple. "Proximity. That's all it was," he said earnestly. "I'd given up on your ever coming home, although I hadn't quit praying about it. I even thought if you ever did come home, you'd be married to one of those guys I saw you with in those different magazines."

Not hardly, Jillian was tempted to laugh. Appearing in the tabloids didn't mean you were about to marry anyone you were seen with or that you were even on a first-name basis with them.

"So tell me how you met her," Jillian said. She leaned back against the door, putting some distance between them.

He shrugged as he began. "I finished college two years ago, and when I came back all the people our age had either married or had moved away. You can only go to so many high school ball games and watch so much TV. Life gets pretty boring after a while."

Jillian nodded her head. She could understand what he was saying.

"A year ago Marci came here to teach first grade. It was a relief to have someone my age to do things with. We sort of drifted into an engagement. I doubt she cared for me any more than I cared for her. We were just good friends. Of course, my mother was all for it."

Jillian could imagine that was an understatement, if ever there was one. Mrs. Prescott had probably been thrilled to death. And Marci? Jillian wanted to shake some sense into Randy. Men could be so dense at times like this. Marci seemed like a girl definitely in love with Randy, and Jillian felt sure Randy loved Marci. He just hadn't let go of Jillian and all the idealism of that first love she represented to him. She was almost ready to say this when he spoke up.

"She was the one who thought we ought to break our engagement," he said, "because she knew I was still in love with you."

What a magnanimous fiancée, Jillian thought wryly. But a foolish one. She should have hung on. Randy would come to his senses.

He looked at her pleadingly. "Don't you see, Jillian? Your coming back was a sign that we should be together."

She looked at him sharply. "You mean, my father died so I would come back and we could be together?" She expected he would realize how ridiculous that sounded and let go of this fantasy.

Hearing the irritation in her voice, he stepped toward her and tried to explain himself better. "No, I don't mean that. I mean, the way Frank Ross hunted and hunted and finally found you at the last moment, and you got here in time for the funeral. You don't think the Lord had a hand in that? I sure do. What if Frank hadn't found you until after the funeral was over? You probably wouldn't have come back."

Jillian didn't know what she would have done, and it didn't really matter now. "I think it was just luck." *Or dogged determination on Frank's part,* she thought silently. "But God? I don't think so."

Randy reached out and grasped Jillian's shoulders as if to wake her up. "It *was* a sign. You've got to realize that!"

Jillian shook his hands off her shoulders. "Randy, you listen," she said. "For the last ten years you've done everything that everyone expected you to do; you've gone to college, served a mission, came home to take care of the farm. My life has taken a completely different path."

A flash of bewilderment crossed Randy's face. "That doesn't matter. I still love you. I always will."

Jillian shook her head and said forcefully, "Listen to me, Randy. I am not the same girl you used to love. Part of me yearns to be that person again, when life was so much simpler. But the rest of me doesn't know who I am or what I want. I just know I haven't accomplished anything my parents hoped I would." She caught her breath and her heart filled with pain. "I don't even know what I believe about the Church any more."

He looked at her, not sure what she was saying. "You'll regain your testimony," he reassured her. "I'll help you. It'll be okay."

At Randy's eagerness, the knot of anguish exploded in Jillian's chest. When she spoke, it was barely a whisper. "It isn't that easy. My life . . . I hardly know what . . ."

"I'll wait for you to work things out."

"No, you can't! I don't know what tomorrow will bring." She tried to make him understand. "I could never promise to stay here, and when it comes right down to it, you could never be sure of me. You don't know me," she said again. "You really don't."

Silenced at last, Randy just looked at her, and Jillian could see tears in his eyes and feel them in her own. "You're my first boyfriend, and what we had between us will always be priceless to me," Jillian said softly. "I know you don't want to hear this right now, but I'm going to tell you anyway. Marci is the girl for you. She's active in the Church, she'll make a good farm wife, and most of all, she's crazy about you. Don't let her get away because of some long-ago memories that are best set aside to make room for some fantastic new ones."

Jillian hoped he'd agree, but all she could see was a face filled with sadness. He walked away abruptly, slamming the door behind him. Jillian took several deep breaths, trying to restore her composure.

Then she followed Randy outside. She did need some fresh air, and she dreaded raising eyebrows—especially Mrs. Prescott's—by not coming back shivering from the cold. She walked up and down and back up the porch stairs, then chilled, but still unsettled, she returned to the living room.

Emma's face lit up when she saw her. "I'm glad you're back inside. I was worried when you didn't take your coat." Emma's friendly concern was deeply satisfying and Jillian perched on the arm of the love seat beside her. When she glanced at Luke and Mrs. Prescott, she found only irritation on their faces. Why? They should both be thrilled she was here and Randy wasn't. She turned back to Emma, who was looking a bit worn out. "Are you ready to rest for a while?"

"That sounds splendid, my dear, thank you." She excused herself to Luke and Mrs. Prescott, who both nodded.

"Heavens, don't let us keep you from resting. We need to be leaving soon anyway. I wonder where Randy is?" Mrs. Prescott looked pointedly at Jillian, but Jillian merely shrugged as she moved the wheelchair beside Emma and helped her into it. Once in the bedroom, Emma yawned. "I'm so tired. Why don't you help me into my nightgown? I'd like to get ready for bed right now."

"Now? It's only five o'clock." A sudden knot of worry tightened Jillian's chest.

"I just need to rest, dear, and you know a person can't completely relax fully clothed," she pointed out reasonably.

After Jillian had tucked her in, Emma reached up and took Jillian's hands. "Thanks for the wonderful day. You're such a darling." She held Jillian's hands to her lips and kissed them. "I think that was the best Christmas dinner I've ever had. Even Helen admitted she liked the Beef Wellington. Now that's something! Next year we're going to have to find a main course equally as exotic. In fact, why wait until next Christmas? Let's start with Sunday dinner." She laughed, releasing Jillian's hands. "But maybe we'd better find something cheaper than ten dollars a pound!"

"If we can't, let's go for it anyway," Jillian suggested. Emma's excitement served to alleviate some of Jillian's concerns about her.

Closing her eyes, Emma smiled. "A girl after my own heart!" She sighed with satisfaction.

Jillian adjusted the drapes so the room would be darker and kissed Emma lightly on the forehead before leaving the room. Closing the door softly behind her, she crossed the hall to her own room. Luke and Helen Prescott could certainly manage for themselves, and there was no need for her to play the gracious hostess.

Inside her bedroom she slipped off her shoes then knelt beside her mother's cedar chest, anxious to explore her family treasures. She pressed the lock on the chest and lifted up the lid, almost afraid to breathe. Right on top lay the tiny dainty satin and lace dress she'd been blessed in. She held it up to examine it more closely and found two little satin shoes beneath it. Her great-grandmother had made this dress for her by hand, sewing tiny tucks down the front with an embroidered rosebud on each one. Jillian hugged it to her, thrilled to have this special dress once again. She wondered if she would ever have a baby girl who would wear it on her blessing day.

Under some piles of embroidered dishtowels, she found her mother's wedding dress. The satin was becoming yellowed, but Jillian decided if she ever married, this was the dress she wanted to wear. Her mother had been shorter than Jillian, and she measured the dress against her body. It could easily be lengthened a few inches with some lace.

Jillian looked at her mother's wedding picture, comparing the dress in her hand with the one in the old photograph. Lifting her eyes from the dress, she studied her mother's face, thinking how young and innocent she had looked, in comparison to her daughter, who at almost the same age appeared world-weary and worn down. Jillian glanced in the mirror and was surprised to see that her haggard look was disappearing and she had gained a little weight, both no doubt the result of keeping regular hours instead of racketing around. Equally important, she knew, had been Emma's love and acceptance, which had nourished and comforted her.

Turning back to the chest, Jillian found some doilies and dresser scarves her grandmother had crocheted. She thought she might frame them one day when she settled permanently somewhere.

Closing the lid on the chest, she whispered a heavensent "thank you" for Luke's thoughtfulness and for the willingness of the buyer who had given it up. Each day Jillian would take a few more things from the chest, stretching out her pleasure as long as she could. Putting the baby dress in her drawer, she wrapped her mother's wedding dress in white towels and put it on the closet shelf. The dish-towels she left on the arm of the sofa.

Plumping up the pillows, she lay down on the bed, grateful at last to rest after her labors of the day. But pangs of guilt marred the satisfaction she'd expected to feel. What was she going to do about Randy? She had no control over what he did, but she felt burdened by his confession. Although she still cared about Randy, he was her past. When she thought of the future, she thought of Luke.

Luke? What game was her mind playing, putting Luke in her future? He was the last person who would ever be there. But, she suddenly realized, she did want Luke to be her future. He was a good person, and she had grown to admire him and enjoy his company. There was a time once when she would have scoffed at using the word "good" to describe a man, but now it seemed the highest compliment she could pay. But even though he had all the attributes she admired, she didn't know what she had to offer him. She imagined he'd scorn the very idea of marriage to someone like her.

A troubled sigh escaped her lips. She had to forget Luke. Instead, she would keep her mind on all the good things happening in her life, and there were many.

—m—

She woke with a start. She'd never meant to fall asleep. What time was it anyway? The room was completely dark. She strained to see the clock. Eight o'clock! Had she slept for the past two hours? She didn't think Emma had called her, but decided she'd better check. Emma lay on her back and every once in a while snored delicately. Leave it to Emma, Jillian chuckled softly. Even her snores were ladylike!

Tiptoeing out of Emma's room, she returned to her room, where she slipped on her shoes before going to the living room. Everything was quiet and deserted. Wandering into the kitchen, she discovered that Randy's mother had left the pies, which had been very gracious of her, Jillian had to admit. She cut herself a sliver from each of them and went back to the living room. Curling up in a chair, she ate her pie as she watched the snow fall against the windows. The day had been an unexpectedly emotional one, leaving her drained.

She heard Emma call her name and quickly stood and hurried to Emma's room. She flipped on the hall lights but left the bedroom dim. "Are you ready to get up?" she asked softly.

Emma's voice was thin and weak. "I don't think so. Would you help me into the bathroom and then bring me some ice water? I'm awfully thirsty."

"Do you want some pie with your water, or some leftovers," Jillian asked. "I'm sure a little Beef Wellington would be delicious."

"Just the water," Emma said faintly. "Then I'll go back to bed."

As Jillian helped Emma into the bathroom, then returned later with some ice water for her, she tried not to worry. It had been a busier day than usual and she hoped Emma was simply feeling the effects of the extra excitement.

After Emma was settled in bed again, Jillian returned to the living room to finish her pie. A few minutes later, she heard Luke come downstairs, and to her surprise, he eased into the chair across from her with a friendly smile. "Tired?" he asked.

Jillian felt a start of pleasure at his concern. "Not any more," she said, "but I'm worried about Emma. She wanted to go to bed at five and just now she woke up, asked for a drink, then went back to sleep. Do you think she's all right?" Seeking reassurance, she looked up at Luke.

"She's probably just tired from today." Although he said it with confidence, he added, "But why don't you call me if she wakes up during the night?"

Jillian thought she saw him eyeing her pie so she asked if he wanted some.

"I can fix it," he said, but he didn't move and she found the somber way he watched her unsettling. She wondered why he was staring at her. Was something wrong?

Although she had already thanked Luke earlier for her Christmas present, she felt she owed him more than that. "I can't thank you enough for finding my mother's chest for me. Getting it today was the best present I've ever received." She hesitated, then admitted, "I've never given you credit for being the generous person you are."

He held up his hand with an embarrassed smile. "Don't get too complimentary, I won't recognize you. But I have to say, I've never given you credit either. I appreciate all you've done for Emma. The

Christmas decorations—" he waved around the room at the various things, "—your willingness to go out of your way to make her happy, just everything you've done. I hoped the chest would ease some of the pain of losing your parents and say thanks for all the work you do around here."

Jillian wanted to apologize for not getting him a gift, but she couldn't think of any adequate words. She was determined, however, to find something later that would be a meaningful present. When she stood up to take her plate back to the kitchen, she asked Luke a second time, "Sure I can't bring you a snack from the kitchen?"

This time he accepted her offer. "Well, if you're determined. Is there any ham for a sandwich?" She nodded. "And some pecan pie, please."

She put her plate and fork in the dishwasher, then found the ham and rolls and made Luke a sandwich. She also poured him a glass of milk and cut him a large slice of pie.

"Thanks to Mrs. Prescott, we have lots of good things to eat," she said as she handed the plate to him.

"She's an excellent cook, but you did a good job of the meal," he complimented her.

Jillian didn't know if she could stand all this praise from Luke or not. "I'm glad you didn't mention the stollen."

He grinned wickedly. "I was waiting for just the right time to rub it in."

She and Luke were truly having a civil dialogue, including his actually teasing her. Would wonders never cease? She pinched herself to make sure she wasn't dreaming. She lounged against the sofa pillows, feeling perfectly comfortable with the silence. This was a Luke she liked. And if she examined her feelings very deeply, one she longed for. She wished things could be different. She wished they could start over. But as her grandmother always said, "If wishes were horses . . ." Why couldn't she be worthy of someone like him?

Luke stood to return his plate to the kitchen. "Want to watch some television for a while? I think 'Christmas from the White House' is on."

"Sure. That sounds like the perfect way to end this day." She sat up straighter and reached for the remote. "Any idea what channel it's on?"

"No. I haven't a clue." He made himself comfortable in the chair while she flipped through the channels.

"Here it is. Perfect timing." The White House and the national Christmas tree had just come on the screen. The camera took them on a tour through the White House while the First Lady described the decorations. Then came the music: The Harlem Boy's Choir, Kathleen Battle, Pavarotti, and Charlotte Church. After that Ossie Davis read the Christmas story from Luke. At the end they all joined together and sang "Silent Night."

Jillian turned to Luke. "What a magnificent program."

"A very nice way to end Christmas Day."

"Yes," she said thoughtfully. Her Christmas season had begun and ended with the words ". . . peace on earth, good will to men." And her heart seemed ready to burst from the peace and good will that radiated from it.

Luke stood. "Ranch work never ends. I need to be up early tomorrow so I'll call it a day." Then he said softly, "Merry Christmas, Jillian," and went up the stairs.

—⚬—

Going up to his room Luke was loathe to break the spell of the last couple of hours, but he knew he had to fight his attraction to Jillian. He had enjoyed watching television with her; at least for a while, they'd had an easy camaraderie. He'd even been able to forget her words to Randy. Why did life have to be so complicated? All he'd wanted was someone to care for Emma and who turned up? Jillian Taylor, just as grand and self-assured as she'd been years ago even if now she was broke and down to her last few dollars Then there was Randy, hanging over Jillian like he was back in high school. Luke's lips tightened. If Jillian hadn't come back, Randy would have married Marci and lived happily ever after. Now he'd broken the engagement. Luke was pretty sure that as long as Jillian was around, Randy wouldn't even consider Marci. But then if Jillian hadn't come back, he wouldn't have had anyone to care for Emma.

What a mess! Randy's actions had upset his mother, who didn't hesitate to manipulate him, Luke, into becoming involved. At her bidding, he'd followed Randy and Jillian out and heard his cousin announce that he loved Jillian.

Still, Jillian had shown more sense than he'd given her credit for. She didn't see Randy as an easy way out and agree to marry him, which a woman in her position might easily do. Of course, with Helen as a mother-in-law, she'd probably have had a rough time of it.

If he hadn't found himself attracted to Jillian in the first place, it wouldn't have mattered how much she was like his mother. But it was one thing in high school; for her to have the same effect on him twelve years later was absurd. He wished he trusted her. But how could he. He now had the hard evidence of her own words that she'd be off when something better came along. Her words to Randy had shown that even she didn't consider herself reliable.

There was no getting around the fact that he found her attractive, but he knew she had spoken the truth to Randy. She never commit herself to staying in Quail Creek. He didn't just imagine it; he'd heard her say it himself. For that reason alone, he'd never let himself love Jillian—which had been difficult enough when he'd thought her shallow and self-centered. Now, having seen the compassion and tenderness she had to offer, it was nearly impossible. But if he wanted to be safe, he'd have to avoid her as much as possible. At this thought, the ache in his heart intensified.

—⚏—

The next day Jillian peeked into Emma's room to see if she were all right. It was nearly nine and Emma never stayed in bed this late. Through the faint light, she could see Emma's chest moving as she breathed and relief flooded Jillian's body. Pulling the door closed, she went into her own room. She opened the chest and had just removed a pair of leather baby shoes when she heard Emma calling.

Quickly Jillian moved to the other room and smiled as she entered the door. "Are you awake, sleeping beauty?" She went over to the bed.

"Yes, but I don't think I'm going to be worth anything today." Emma just lay there, making no move to get up. The huskiness of fatigue in Emma's voice worried Jillian, but she didn't let on to her.

"Yesterday was an exciting day—I felt it myself—but you'll probably feel better as the day goes on. Do you want breakfast before your bath?" She kept her voice nonchalant.

"I'll just wash my face and hands and put on a robe." After Emma had tidied herself up, the two went to the dining room. "Just Instant Breakfast and toast for me," she said as Jillian helped her out of the wheelchair. "I ate so much yesterday, I'm still not hungry."

True, Emma had eaten more than she usually did, but it still hadn't been very much. Jillian didn't comment, but worry nagged at her again. She fixed breakfast and took it to the table. "Here we are. I'll pour as soon as you say the blessing."

Emma looked at her. "You ask it this morning, I haven't been giving you a chance."

Jillian didn't want a chance to pray out loud in front of Emma, but she couldn't think of any reason not to. Her words came slowly. "Our Father in Heaven, We're thankful for this food and ask you to bless it. Please bless Emma so she'll feel stronger. Amen."

"A lovely prayer, my dear, thank you." Emma dunked a corner of her toast in the Instant Breakfast and ate it leisurely. But after only a few sips of her drink, she pushed her food away. "That's enough for me. I'm full."

"Emma! You worry me." She'd never get any stronger this way. "Can't you eat a couple more bites of toast?"

Emma shook her head. "Would you get some of my pillows and just settle me on the love seat? I won't get dressed yet, and I'll take my bath tonight. For now I just want to relax out here."

Jillian made the older woman comfortable and then cleared away the dishes. Returning to the living room, she sat in the overstuffed chair at the foot of the love seat. Emma's appearance did concern her. This listless woman bore no resemblance to the lively lady Jillian had seen yesterday. "Still tired?"

"Just a little bit, but don't worry, darling. I'll just take it easy today, and I'll be fine tomorrow," she reassured her.

Jillian hoped so.

Before she could say anything else, Luke came in. "How's my best girl?" he smiled at Emma.

Emma gave him a quizzical look. "What are you doing in here in the middle of the morning?"

"Just needed a break and decided this was the best place to take it." He made himself comfortable in one of the chairs. "Thought I could use a little religion."

Jillian rolled her eyes at that statement. He caught her expression, and to her surprise, grinned at her.

After the BYU devotional assembly concluded, Luke made no effort to move from his chair. Emma, still reclining against the pillows, said, "Jillian, tell me more about living in New York. What did you like best?"

Jillian tried to think. "Oh, there's always so much going on in the city. There's Broadway. The Village. Concerts in the park. Fantastic shopping. Everything! You can feel the energy. Show business is a big part of that excitement, and I was lucky enough to know a lot of actors and musicians. I found front row seats at openings intoxicating." She grinned. "In the best possible way, of course."

Luke added, "And Quail Creek's own Jillian Taylor was the hottest model in town."

His voice was so matter-of-fact that Jillian couldn't tell if he was giving her a little dig or not. She found it hard to believe he'd react with equanimity towards anything having to do with her modeling career.

Jillian shook her head in regret. "It didn't take me long to get caught up in that world. In fact, it was so fast my head swam. Have either of you been there?"

Luke was silent, but his expression said he'd rather be killing snakes.

"No. I always wanted to but I never made it. I'm jealous of you." Emma's wistfulness saddened Jillian.

"Don't be. Remember the last line of that old song, 'We stayed too long at the fair'? Well, I stayed too long in New York." The wave of desolation that came over her at the realization startled her.

"I hope you'll stay here forever. It's been only three weeks, and yet it's like I've always known you. I can't imagine life here without you," Emma said lovingly.

Luke watched Jillian as she nodded her head in agreement with Emma. To his horror, he found himself feeling the same way. But what good would it do? Jillian was not a stayer. Her own words to

Randy had convinced Luke she had no idea what she wanted or where she wanted to be. When something better came along, she'd be gone. If her love for Emma wouldn't keep Jillian here, nothing he could do or say would. Besides, how could anyone who was a celebrity and loved New York City be expected to trade it all for ranch life in Quail Creek?

"I feel the same way. I can't imagine life without you." She gazed at Emma for a few minutes and then asked, "Why didn't you ever get to New York?"

Emma looked pensive. "A lot of reasons. I wanted to be a writer and live in the Village or on the Left Bank in Paris—and become rich and famous. But it was the thirties. I'd grown up on a ranch at Three Creek in the southwestern part of the state. My parents were grounded in the "here and now," and my dreams were simply preposterous to them. So I put them aside and found a job. What I ended up becoming was the youngest chief telephone operator in the state of Idaho. I was nineteen." She smiled. "My one claim to fame."

Jillian looked thoughtful, hearing of Emma's lost dreams. "Did you ever write?"

"Oh yes. I continued to write and to dream. Then I met a handsome sheriff named John Gillette. The rest is history. We got married." Her words had a calm acceptance to them. This was news to Luke; he couldn't visualize Emma as a writer let alone living a bohemian life in the Village. She didn't seem grounded in the "here and now" like her parents but rather in the gospel.

"Couldn't you and your husband have gone to New York?" Jillian spoke up.

"It was during the Depression. Times were too hard, and by the time they weren't, John had no desire to travel. So we stayed put."

Jillian sighed. "It makes me feel bad that you've never had an opportunity to travel. You would have loved New York, and I just know you would have been a famous writer."

"We're the lucky ones." Luke regarded Emma fondly. "Where would we be if she'd become a famous writer? It's because of you, dear Sister Gillette, that I've had a wonderful life. You gave me a mother's love that I would never have experienced if you'd been the toast of the New York literary circles."

"That's pretty selfish to think of yourself instead of Emma," Jillian scolded Luke, then turned to Emma. "But I have to admit I'm glad you're here."

Luke glanced at his watch, then rose and gave Emma a hug. "I can't repeat it too often—so am I. Now I better get back to work. See you later."

As he left, Jillian wondered, not for the first time, why Luke had assumed responsibility for her. "Do you have any children?" she asked Emma.

"No. I had two little boys who both died in infancy. I came here when Luke was ten, and he's been like a son to me. My husband was the ranch manager, and when Luke's mother left, I became the house-keeper. He's been everything a mother could want in a son." Emma seemed reconciled and content at the turns her life had taken.

A few days ago Jillian would have scoffed at the idea that Luke could be the ideal anything, but now she didn't. His love for Emma was obvious, and he treated her as if she were, in fact, his mother. His thoughtfulness in giving Jillian her mother's chest just added to her increasingly positive opinion of him.

"His father was a good man," Emma shook her head, "but at times he could be hard and unyielding, consumed by the ranch. Luke takes after him. He does two things: church work and ranch work. I want him to get married, but there are simply no single women around here." Her eyes gleamed and she smiled slyly. "Except you!"

Jillian shook her head. "I don't think so."

She turned the conversation back to Emma's writing. "Did you ever have anything published?"

"A few things. I've got a scrapbook filled in my closet. And I had a poem included in an anthology. The book is in there too, if you'd like to read it."

Jillian was touched by Emma's eagerness to have her read her writing. She quickly retrieved the books from the closet and returned to Emma's side. They poured over the books until every page had been read and remarked on. Seeing Emma's delight in sharing her writing, Jillian felt a sweet tenderness well up inside of her.

Finally, noticing how late it was getting, Jillian suggested lunch. Again Emma ate very little and as Jillian helped her down for a nap, her heart was heavy at Emma's growing weakness.

CHAPTER 15

"Luke, I am not taking no for an answer!" Nancy's voice brooked no argument. "You and Jillian both need a break. I'll be glad to come over and stay with Emma. I want a chance to visit with her anyway. There's no reason you two can't go cross-country skiing. She can borrow my skis. After all the snow these last few days, the conditions are perfect."

"Let me check with Jillian," he said reluctantly and lay the phone down, wishing he could think of a good reason not to go. He didn't want to spend the afternoon alone with Jillian, but he could hardly tell Nancy that.

He found Jillian cleaning the kitchen. "Nancy wants us to go cross-country skiing while she stays with Emma. She has a pair of skis you can use. Want to?" He hoped she'd have an excuse not to go.

But she looked up and smiled, a smile that sent his heart beating erratically. "Sure. I haven't cross-country skied in ages. It'll be fun." She hung the dishcloth over the drainer. "What time are you planning on going?"

"About one." He was stuck. She wanted to go.

Her face was radiant. "I can't think of a better way to spend New Year's Day."

He wished he couldn't. Spending the day with Jillian was no way to lessen her hold on his heart or free his mind of longing for her. Picking up the kitchen phone, he told Nancy they would be ready.

Promptly at one Jillian answered the door to find Nancy loaded down. "I didn't know what you needed, so I brought my gloves, ski jacket, boots, and some thermal underwear. Plus, of course, the skis."

Jillian leaned out and saw the skis leaning against the pickup. "This is going to be so much fun. I can't wait." She didn't say that she couldn't wait to be with Luke, although that was uppermost in her mind. Taking the clothes from Nancy, she followed her into the living room.

"Emma, you look mighty perky sitting there in your red velvet outfit," Nancy complimented her, giving her a hug. "How're you feeling?"

"Not as good as I did on Christmas, but I'm getting there." Emma patted the seat next to her. "Sit here and tell me what you've been up to."

Jillian went into her bedroom, where she quickly dressed in Nancy's ski clothes. The boots were a little snug, but she thought she could manage. Putting on her dark glasses, she walked into the living room and struck a pose. "Ta-da! What do you think?"

"You look fabulous," Emma said. "Ski clothes are very becoming on you."

"I thought I looked good in that pink jacket, but to use Emma's words, you look fabulous." Nancy grinned back at her and Jillian smiled her thanks.

"See you later," she said, going outside.

Nancy had parked next to the house, and Luke stood leaning against her pickup, his skis already on. "Ready to go?"

The warmth in his voice startled her, and she willed her heart to beat normally. She certainly didn't want him to know how much being with him mattered to her. "As soon as I get my skis on." She took a few steps toward him.

"Here, let me." Before she could touch the skis, Luke laid them on the ground in front of her.

Jillian laughed. "I'd forgotten how narrow Nordic skis are. Nancy must really be good. Hers don't even have edges on them."

"She is." Kneeling next to her skis, Luke looked up. "But skiing is like riding a bike, you never forget how."

"I don't know about that. I haven't gone in several years, and I don't want to embarrass myself too badly." She brightened up. Most winters had been spent skiing with friends; summers she swam, water skied, played beach volleyball. Any sport anyone suggested, she was game to try. She'd always considered herself naturally athletic, and it felt good to be on skis again. "I refuse to let anything dampen my spirits. Let's be off."

Digging her pole into the snow, she flew past Luke then fell down. So much for natural athleticism! Luke leaned over to help her out of the awkward position and she clambered up. "How humiliating. We aren't even off the lawn yet and I crash."

Luke laughed. "I like the way you set the standard. Now I won't have much to live up to."

"Thanks a lot!" Although she was up on her skis, her stance felt tenuous. Did she really want to do this? She looked at Luke again. Definitely! He brought out her competitive spirit.

This time she clumped along slowly and carefully, her eyes focused on the ground in front of her. About six inches of snow had fallen on the lawn, so they were able to make their way easily to the pasture gate. After traversing the forty feet, Jillian stopped and sighed in relief.

Luke opened the gate for them. Then they were off across the wide, downy valley. Ahead she could see dark splotches of trees interrupting the white expanse that stretched for miles. When Luke stopped, Jillian pulled up beside him. "Are we skiing as far as the trees?"

"They're still a mile or so away, so it depends on our stamina. This is the first time I've been skiing all season, and I'm winded already." His eyes narrowed, seeming to measure the distance. "We've still got two-thirds of the way to go."

He didn't look as if he were winded to her. In fact, he looked in superb condition. He wasn't even breathing heavily and here she was panting. She tried to regulate her breathing, but it was impossible.

"I'm game to keep going, but if you want to go back, just say so," Jillian said. She didn't mean it as a challenge, but Luke stared at her.

"For someone who's fallen down, you're awfully cocky." Her "I can do anything" look always irritated him, which was probably a good thing. This way he could concentrate on her annoying traits instead of how beautiful she was with her blond hair flying, or how kind she could be to Emma, or . . . He groaned silently. Just the things he didn't want to think about, or he'd find himself succumbing to her.

"Come on."

He watched her push off ahead of him, attempt a stenmark, and trip over her ski. "So much for showing off!" He skied up beside her. "Need any help?"

She reached for his hands and pulled herself up. "I can see trees, not dark splotches, so we must be pretty close to our goal."

He tilted his head and looked at her quizzically. "Our goal? I didn't realize we'd set one."

"Of course, we did!" She pointed with her pole. "Those trees." She started off, leaving him standing there. She turned back. "Coming?"

And fell down again.

Luke burst out laughing. She had a lack of self-consciousness that he admired. She had fallen. So what?

"Hold back this time. Don't pretend this is the Olympics, and I'm an opponent." He skied over to her. "Take it easy."

The meadow angled up gradually, and so it was easier to ski without falling down. They reached the stand of trees at the same time. Just as if it had purposely been placed there, a tree had fallen and the sun shone on its black bark. "Now we can relax."

Jillian eyed the tree as she unfastened her bindings and stepped out of the skis. "Did you put this here for a resting spot?"

"No, nature took care of it for us." Luke put their skis against the log and then sat down himself.

"The skiing isn't what's so hard. It's the getting up from falling down that wears me out. I don't know whether I'd compare it to jumping jacks or sit-ups, but I've definitely had my exercise for the day. Make that two days."

Her blond hair glinted in the sun as she flashed him a marvelous smile. Her entire face glowed as if she were having the time of her life and with the most important man in her life. For a moment he found himself enveloped in her magic. He caught his breath. No wonder she had succeeded as a model. Her entire persona appeared real, heart-breakingly real, but he had to remember that bewitching the onlooker was her stock in trade.

"The trip back should be good for two more days, so all in all you can forget exercise for at least four days. Happy?" He wanted to keep everything light, but with the grip she had on his emotions all he could manage was a half smile.

"Are you all right?" Jillian's expression showed concern. "Your face looked like you were in pain."

Now he had to laugh. His attempt to keep things light had been misinterpreted as discomfort! "I'm fine," he said.

"Good." His hand rested on the log between them and she patted it briskly. When she looked into his eyes, he could feel the tension mount between them. What should he do next? He wanted to kiss her, but that was insane.

He broke off his gaze and stood slowly. "Ready?"

"Sure." She stood up, giving him a smile so wondrous that a sharp pain knifed through his midsection. No. Absolutely not! He wasn't getting tangled up with Jillian Taylor.

He helped her on with her skis, then fastened his own, and they took off. Everything went well for a hundred feet or so, until they came to the steepest part of the slope. It wasn't really all that steep, but Jillian fell again, face forward, her skis sprawled out to either side behind her.

"Are you all right?" The severity of her spill worried Luke. Whereas the others had been tumbles, this had been a hard fall, leaving her face buried in snow. She lay there without responding.

"Jillian!" He quickly unfastened his skis and knelt beside her. "Are you okay?" What if she'd broken something?

Finally, she lifted her face and brushed the snow off. "My face is wet, my knee hurts, and I really whacked my forehead. No, I am not okay. However," she said, her face determined, "I'll survive. Unless a medevac helicopter discovers us, I see no way out but to get up and go on."

Luke unfastened her skis so she could maneuver herself up. When she stood, he held out his hand to help her onto the skis. She stepped into the first one, but when she lifted her foot to put on the second ski, her feet slipped out from under her on the slick snow, and she went down, pulling Luke down, too, and knocking off her glasses in the process.

They both laughed and tears ran down Jillian's face. Their eyes met, and they stopped laughing. Without conscious thought, he rolled to his side, and his eyes never leaving hers, he took her face in his hands. He felt as if he were drowning in the remarkable green depths of her eyes. With no thought to repercussions, he kissed her.

His lips lingered on hers for a minute or so, then sanity struck him. What on earth was he doing kissing Jillian? He wrenched himself away and abruptly stood up. Still lying in the snow, Jillian appeared to be watching him. He couldn't read her expression, which made him uncomfortable. She boosted herself up and carefully fastened her skis once again. He followed suit, neither of them saying a word.

Luke picked up his poles and stabbed at the snow, grateful he had something physical to do. To say that the last few minutes had disturbed him would be putting it mildly. He fought to keep his face impassive. He couldn't let on to Jillian what great pleasure he'd found in that one kiss. Oh, for heaven sakes, now he was as moonstruck as Randy. Over Jillian. Never in his wildest dreams had he thought he'd be on Randy's level, but he was! How did she do it? His cousin had been sappy about her since high school, so it was natural Randy would fall under her spell. But for Luke to do the same? How could a level-headed man find himself in love with someone as unsuitable as Jillian? In love? How could he even let that word invade his mind? No.

He admired the way she could be loving and caring to Emma, willing to help in any way she could, going all-out for a Christmas to fulfill Emma's dreams. But the bottom line was he didn't even like her. She'd neglected her parents. What kind of person did that to her own family? She might have good reasons for that, but the bottom line was she refused to commit to staying in Quail Creek. When she had enough money to get to New York, she'd leave. Loving Emma wouldn't hold her here, and he knew from experience that a husband and child certainly weren't enough to keep a woman on the ranch.

As stupid as it sounded, he could feel his heart breaking. There was no way he could marry Jillian, if she agreed to, without a life of grief and heartache in the bargain. No, he'd been through that once with his mother. Once was enough. When Jillian got ready to leave, he'd do nothing to stop her.

Why did the right decision have to hurt so much?

—⧓—

Glasses on, skis fastened, Jillian stood up, stabbed the snow emphatically with her poles, and pushed off. She knew she absolutely couldn't stand to ski next to Luke. She couldn't even bear the thought of looking at him again. She'd wanted him to kiss her, and she'd fervently kissed him back. Then he'd torn himself away so fast he'd nearly fallen. She'd thought things were better between them, but from his response to one short kiss, it seemed to her he didn't even like her.

Embarrassment flooded over her. Although she kept smiling, tears blinded her. She blinked furiously to clear her vision. From the time that she'd been a freshman in high school, he'd made it plain he didn't like her, and it was ridiculous to think the intervening years would have changed his feelings. Seeing his devotion to Emma, she had felt a change in her own feelings toward him as they had begun to soften. But his gift to her had completed the reversal of her opinion of him. Her mother's chest wasn't something he could pick up at the store. It had taken thought and effort to track the chest down and bring it to the ranch. Now that she'd seen this compassionate side to him, she realized how she'd misjudged him. He did have a loving heart.

But he didn't love her, obviously. The pain of his rejection simply crushed her. She tried to shake off her heartache. Why was she making such an earth-shattering deal out of this? But she knew. She was starting to care for Luke. She couldn't say, "A kiss is a kiss is a kiss." This kiss had been too important. She skied onward, aware that Luke was somewhere behind her, but she concentrated on putting some distance between them.

At last the ranch became more than just a speck on the landscape, and she flew even faster over the snow, willing herself to keep her balance. She'd suffered enough humiliation today.

She stopped in front of the house to remove her skis, putting them in the back of Nancy's pickup. By that time, Luke had caught up with her, but she hurried into the house, not giving him a chance to say anything.

Nancy and Emma both looked up as she came through the living room. "Have a good time?" Jillian could see the mischievous sparkle in Emma's eyes.

"The best," Jillian said briefly. Not wanting to go into more detail, she added, "Being out in this beautiful weather was wonderful. Give me just a minute and I'll change clothes and give you back your gear." She vanished into her bedroom.

When Jillian rejoined them, Nancy gathered up her belongings and left, promising to come back so Jillian could have more time off.

Jillian agreed halfheartedly. The last thing she wanted or needed was more free time. She certainly didn't want to spend it with Luke, and she already had more than enough time to herself. Most of all, she'd pass on another ski trip.

During supper, Luke was unusually upbeat, which Jillian found extremely galling. From the way he acted, one would have thought nothing remarkable had happened to him today. He obviously didn't feel the same way she did about their kiss, and Jillian could not think of a single word to say to him.

Emma watched them, her eyes gleaming with curiosity. "My dear, this stew is wonderful, but if I eat any more, I won't have room for cake and ice cream." She put her fork on her plate and pushed it away.

Jillian smiled at Emma as she handed her the dessert. "The crunchy things in the icing are vitamins, not nuts." She wished they were. A steady diet of chocolate cake and praline ice cream was not going to make Emma stronger.

"That's good to know. So between the cake and ice cream, which is made from cream and whole eggs, I'm eating quite a nutritious meal." Emma's smile lit up her face, but Jillian thought she appeared tired.

Looking concerned, Luke studied Emma as well. "Has today been too much for you? You seem tired."

Emma shrugged it off. "Not at all, but I do think I'll go to bed when we finish eating and just watch television in my room."

He nodded in agreement. "Sounds like a winner."

Jillian helped Emma to bed, and Luke went upstairs, thinking what an ordeal the last hour had been. Thank goodness, he'd made it through. Emma had looked at him a little strangely, as if she suspected something. Maybe he'd been too nonchalant, but there was no way he was going to let Jillian know how she affected him. Lambing started in a few weeks, and he needed to focus all his energy on that.

CHAPTER 16

Two weeks had passed since he and Jillian had gone skiing, and as he entered the house, Luke congratulated himself. It hadn't been easy, but he had managed to act detached towards Jillian, as if nothing had ever happened. Right now he was glad to hear her vacuuming upstairs; he wanted to visit with Emma alone. He had tried to spend as much time as possible with her although it hadn't been easy. They were gearing up for lambing season, the busiest time of the year on the ranch.

His heart lifted when he saw her sitting in her favorite place, the love seat in the living room. She always appeared the same. Her face was carefully made up and she wore her favorite strands of pearls and gold chains. But he thought she looked thinner and ever so much frailer. "How about a snack?"

"Thanks, but I don't feel like eating right now." Emma gave him a wan smile.

"I can't tempt you with cake and ice cream?" he asked in disbelief, knowing that if anything would get her to eat, chocolate cake and pecan praline ice cream would be it.

She shook her head. "I just never feel hungry these days." Motioning to the chair across from her, she said, "If you've got time, why don't you pull up that chair? I've been thinking about some things, and I need to talk to you."

Luke pulled the chair close to where she sat on the couch. Making himself comfortable, he smiled and picked up her hand. "What dainty hands you have."

"You should have seen them when I was a girl. They were beautiful." She pulled them away from his grasp and sadly examined them. "Now look—age spots everywhere." She laid them in her lap.

"Age spots or not, your hands are still beautiful, and I don't want to hear otherwise." Luke didn't fear death, but he feared life without Emma. *How bleak and empty it would be,* he thought. Why did she have to become old and fragile? He wanted the vigorous, take-charge Emma he'd always known.

He wondered if her lack of energy had brought on thoughts of dying, and she had plans she wanted him to know about. He hoped not. This was something he didn't even want to discuss. "Now what have you been thinking about that I need to know?"

Her voice became stronger. "Jillian."

Jillian? That was the last topic he expected, and his heart sank hearing the name. Wariness shaded his voice. "What about her?"

"I've known from the beginning that she was the special person meant for you to marry."

"You've what?" Luke was astonished.

She gave him a placid smile. "Calm down."

"Calm down? When you spring something this ridiculous on me?" How had Emma come to this thought? It was almost as if she could sense the battle he was waging over his feelings. But there was nothing to discuss. "She's not my type."

Emma didn't blink an eye. "Really? I thought she was just your type—kind, caring, a hard worker, independent, and as beautiful on the inside as she is on the outside."

If he hadn't spent most of his time since New Year's thinking about Jillian, he'd have been able to shrug off Emma's remarks more easily. Instead, he said, "I have to admit she's been all that while she's been here, but you're naive, Emma, if you think that's all her life has been about."

Emma gave him a steady gaze. "I know she's run with the fast crowd, but she's home now. She's different."

"No, she's not. You're only seeing the surface. Underneath she's the same old Jillian." He leaned forward towards Emma. "Do you want me to be abandoned again? Look at the way her father died alone." He shook his head to emphasize his next words. "I'm sorry, Emma, but that's a risk I'm not willing to take."

"We don't know the whole story about her and her father's relationship. There's undoubtedly much more to it," Emma pointed out.

"I don't want to get sanctimonious, Luke, but remember the commandment: 'Judge not that ye be not judged.'

"I think you're also judging your mother too harshly. I know her abrupt leaving was tragic for you, and I certainly don't condone her actions. But while your father was a good man, he saw everything in absolutes. The ranch was important. The Church was important. You were very important. Your mother was a poor fourth. His own parents never spent time on entertainment, so he saw no need for the two of them to go dancing or into Idaho Falls for a movie or dinner.

"I know Sandra loved your father, and I believe she just left to get his attention. She got his attention all right, and I don't know if he was too proud or what, but he let her go. She felt unloved, and if he'd shown her he loved her, she'd have come back in an instant."

Luke couldn't believe what he was hearing. He'd never viewed his mother in that light. He'd only known that his father had been a hard worker and had devoted his entire life to ranching. Luke had carried an image of a caring father with him his entire life, but what had he known as a twelve-year-old boy? His father had never expressed any regrets to Luke before his death five years ago, but now that Luke thought about it, he realized they'd never spoken of his mother after that fateful New Year's Day.

Luke's gaze, when he looked at Emma, was troubled. "That may be. But I want to marry someone with a strong testimony of the gospel."

"You're not paying attention to Jillian or you'd see how she's changing. She doesn't recognize her feelings, but can't you tell she's hungry for a family and the gospel?" Emma gave Luke a stern look. "You're usually more perceptive."

"Maybe I am, but this is different." His heart was involved this time. "I would only tell this to you, Emma. I overheard her tell Randy she was definitely going to leave here, and she couldn't commit herself to staying here or to believing in the Church."

Emma laughed. "No wonder you've been acting so grumpy lately." She sighed as if she were explaining something to a small child. "Of course, she doesn't want to marry Randy. What else would she tell him? She certainly wouldn't lead him on. Remember, he's not you." She emphasized the last three words.

The vacuum stopped and they both glanced up. For a moment he panicked. He'd become so accustomed to the noise of the vacuum that he'd forgotten it was even on, or that Jillian was even in the house.

"You think about what I've said." Her words were definite. "I'm right!"

Luke shook his head again, and his words were firm. He seldom crossed Emma, but on this subject he was determined. "I won't try to stop her when she leaves."

Emma gave him a disgusted look then watched as Jillian dragged the vacuum downstairs and announced, "Well, I got that finished, just in time for the BYU devotional assembly." Then she went into the kitchen to put the cleaning equipment away. At the mention of the devotional assembly, Emma smiled knowingly at Luke.

"She's only doing it for you," he protested.

"We'll see." Emma's voice didn't have even a hint of doubt, and giving him a little wave of dismissal, she picked up the remote and turned the TV on.

Luke put on his sunglasses as he left the house. Seeing the sun reflecting so brightly off the snow, he found it hard to believe it was the middle of January.

He couldn't keep his mind from going over Emma's words. What was she thinking of? Besides, if the Lord wanted him to marry Jillian, surely He would have told him, not Emma. He couldn't help but believe that Emma just wanted her own way. She loved Jillian, and she wanted to tie up the package neatly. But he wasn't buying. Whether Emma loved her or not, and regardless of his own feelings, Jillian wasn't the girl for him.

—⚟—

"Let me plump up your pillows and get you situated so you can see the TV better." Jillian scooted the television around so it was in Emma's line of vision. "Now we're all set." When she snapped the set on, Emma's face lit up. This was the highlight of her day. She always insisted Jillian watch the program with her. Mostly Jillian used the time to relax, but she'd actually learned quite a bit about the Church.

The speakers, who were usually Church general authorities, had a spirit about them that Jillian liked.

During the program, she glanced over to find Emma's eyes closed and glanced at her chest to see if she were breathing. She was, thank goodness. She hadn't let age slow her down a bit; the stroke might have limited her physical ability, but mentally she still had a vital interest in everything. They'd discussed modeling until she was sure Emma knew as much about the field as she herself did. She'd wanted to know every place Jillian had gone on location, the famous people she'd met, what her New York apartment had been like, what she'd seen at the Metropolitan Museum of Art, what were the best restaurants, had she ever eaten at The Four Seasons, and on and on and on. Emma had spent a lifetime reading about New York City, and she'd been excited to talk to someone who had actually been there. She wanted to know all the tiniest details firsthand and Jillian had been happy to oblige her.

"Jillian, darling . . ." Although her voice was weak, it startled Jillian. "Would you help me to the bedroom? I think I'd like to rest in bed for a while."

Jillian glanced at her watch. "The program still has a half hour to go. Sure you want to go now?"

Emma nodded her head yes slowly. "I've heard this talk before."

"Do you want to eat first?" She knew the answer before she asked.

"No, later. Right now I'm too tired." Her voice dropped off as if she had already fallen asleep.

Jillian was scared to see Emma so lifeless. She wished Luke were there to share her fears. Pushing the wheelchair to the sofa, she helped Emma into it and took her to her bedroom, where Emma asked for Jillian's help putting on her nightgown so she could relax. About two o'clock, Emma thought she was ready to get up, but after only a half an hour, she was tired and wanted to go back to bed. For lunch Jillian could only coax Emma into eating a little ice cream.

When Emma was back in bed, Jillian dropped into the nearest chair, wondering what was going to happen next. Jillian had come to love Emma so much and now she had a sick feeling in her stomach. Would Emma get well? What would Jillian do if she didn't? How could she stand it? Emma had been like a second mother to her. She was her best friend.

If anything happened to Emma, Jillian also had to face the fact that she would no longer be needed here. The thousand dollars she'd saved would get her out of town, but even if she were careful, she knew it wouldn't last more than a few months.

And there was Luke. How could she manage without him? Her feelings towards him deepened each day, even though he continued to act as though the kiss had never happened. He was friendly enough, but at the same time remote. She guessed she was making too much of a kiss, but his ability to shrug it off was disheartening.

Lifting her chin, she resolved not to give him another thought. Emma was enough to worry about.

—⁂—

A week later Emma's raspy breathing frightened Jillian so badly that she dashed outside to find Luke. He was in the shed talking to some men.

"Emma can't breathe!" she shouted.

Without another word, he rushed past her and into the house. He outdistanced her so quickly that by the time she reached the house, he was already on the phone with the doctor. "Our sheds have tin roofs with Prescott Ranch written on them. The helicopter will have landing room in the yard. We'll be ready," he was saying.

Helicopter? Jillian's heart quickened its pace.

Returning the receiver to the hook, Luke looked at her. "Dr. Neilson thinks Emma has pneumonia. The drive into Idaho Falls would be too hard on her, so he's sending the medevac helicopter. It should be here within thirty minutes. Right now we need to get her bundled up. Do you think you can bring the car to the hospital? Dr. Neilson will meet us there. I want to ride with Emma."

Emma didn't protest as they put her coat on her and wrapped her warmly in some quilts. It seemed like only minutes later that the frighteningly loud whir of the helicopter rotors hovered over them as the medevac set down on the front lawn. Unable to stop her chin from trembling, Jillian hugged Emma good-bye. As soon as the helicopter had lifted off, she hurried to the car and left for the hospital.

She had difficulty keeping her mind on anything but Emma, and the drive seemed interminable. Finally she was in the emergency room, where she was directed to room 416. She entered the room and saw that Emma was on oxygen and an IV had been inserted. Her eyes were closed and her breathing seem erratic. Luke hovered nearby. His pale drawn look shocked her.

"You made good time," he said simply.

"At the speed I was going, I should have. How is she?" Moving closer to the bed, she looked down at the small ethereal figure.

"Right now it's touch and go. They should know in a little while whether or not she'll make it. They're giving her a massive dose of antibiotics in the IV, and they're also replenishing her fluids. Did you realize she was dehydrated?"

"No." Guilt flooded her. "I should have known she wasn't getting enough water. I guess I only focused on getting her to eat more."

"You did your best." He put a comforting arm around her, though he continued to watch Emma carefully.

Jillian's worry increased. She loved this lady who'd been her only lifeline the last few months, and she couldn't endure the thought of losing Emma. But she knew Luke would be devastated. She and Luke clung to each other in silence, watching Emma as she slept.

Once she opened her eyes and looked at Jillian. "You're here," she whispered. "Good." Her eyelids closed again. After a while Luke pulled up chairs and they continued their vigil at Emma's side.

Several hours later, Luke glanced at his watch. "I think you'd better get something to eat. You'll be as weak as Emma is, and that's the last thing we need right now."

She shook her head. "I can't leave this room until the doctor comes, and we know what is happening to Emma."

Luke stood. "I need to stretch my legs, so I'll go to the cafeteria and bring us some sandwiches. If there's any change, page me."

She nodded. "Okay." While he was gone, the nurse came in and checked Emma's vital signs.

Luke brought her a sandwich, but she couldn't force any of it down. Her throat felt as knotted up with fear and worry as the rest of her.

At seven o'clock, Dr. Neilson came in. He checked Emma and looked at her chart, then said, "Her vital signs are good. If she makes it through the night, her chances will be a lot better. I'll be honest with you. It's hard for someone her age to throw off pneumonia, especially someone as frail as Emma. She has no reserves to draw on. I suggest you two leave and get some rest. Come back in the morning. There's not a thing you can do here."

Jillian and Luke looked at each other.

"I can't leave her now." Luke's anxiety showed in his voice.

"No. I'd rather be here than home pacing the floor." Her eyes met Luke's, and she saw a welcome response in them.

Dr. Neilson shrugged. "The nurses will call me if she gets any worse. Otherwise, I'll see you in the morning," he said, then left them alone.

"I'm glad you're staying." Luke's words were strained.

"I just have to be here with Emma. I wouldn't get any rest away from here, so there's no reason to go." Worry etched his face, and she knew she couldn't let him face this crisis alone. His vulnerability brought her feelings for him to the surface, and she reached over and clasped his hand. "I'm glad we're in this together." He tightened his grip on her hand and looked at her gratefully.

The intensity of his gaze brought the blood to her face and her heart yearned for a tender word from him. He remained silent, but he didn't relinquish his hold on her as they sank back into their chairs and resumed their watch.

—⁂—

Three weeks had passed since Emma had been airlifted to the hospital. She'd stayed just three days before demanding to be taken home.

Down on her hands and knees, Jillian furiously scrubbed the kitchen floor. A mop wouldn't satisfy her need for physical exertion. She gave the floor next to the sink a vicious swab. Who made the black marks? Probably Luke. Why couldn't he be more careful? She reached for the cleanser and scrubbed even harder. Finally satisfied that this part of the floor would be clean enough to eat on, she got fresh water in her bucket and moved to the far corners of the room. No one ever walked here, so usually she just gave it a light going over, but not today. She scoured the floor as if it were filthy instead of only dusty.

Finally, she stood up and surveyed her work. The kitchen was spotless, as was the rest of the house. She'd spent the last few days scrubbing, dusting, and vacuuming the entire place.

She looked at her skinned knuckles and red hands. Scrubbing had taken its toll. Going to her bedroom, she wearily sank into the chair. She'd involved herself in a fierce round of activity to keep her mind off Emma and her deteriorating health. The last three weeks had been difficult.

Once Emma was conscious, she had refused to stay in the hospital another minute, insisting that Jillian could do everything a nurse could do. She'd rather be home because she wanted to die in her own bed.

Jillian had protested that she needed to be in the hospital, that she wasn't going to die. Emma had only smiled weakly, saying she wanted to go home, and the doctor had agreed to it. So three days later they'd returned home.

The doctor had given Jillian explicit directions, and in her nervousness, every time Emma breathed a little differently, Jillian had been on the phone to him. She'd sat with Emma day and night until finally Luke had called the Relief Society president and several of the sisters had come over to give Jillian a break.

Every time she thought life couldn't become any harder it did. First her mother, then her career, her father, and now Emma. Always hovering in the back of her mind was her love for Luke, and the hopelessness of it all only compounded the pain.

Fear clutched at her and for a moment she felt as if she were strangling. She couldn't lose Emma.

"Jillian," a voice called weakly.

Even in the next room with the door open, she could barely hear Emma's voice. Steeling herself not to show her sadness, Jillian went into the bedroom. "What can I do for you, my dearest dear."

"Help me up," Emma directed her. "I've been spending too much time in this bed." Jillian was heartened to see that Emma, though weak, was her usual upbeat self—not content to lie around all day.

Jillian turned back the covers and swung the frail little body into the wheelchair. She helped Emma into her robe and they went to the living room. "Do you want on the couch or in a chair?"

"Would you bring out my pillows, darling girl, and prop me up against them on the sofa? I've got some serious talking to do to you."

Jillian propped her up, wondering what she wanted to talk about. *Serious talking?* What was going on? Fluffing the pillows, Jillian moved the overstuffed chair next to Emma. "All right. I'm ready for the lecture."

Emma gave a little laugh. "Not a lecture. Just a good old-fashioned heart-to-heart talk."

The elderly lady's feeble voice barely reached her, so Jillian leaned closer.

"I've done a lot of thinking and praying about this, and I know the Lord wants you to marry Luke."

"What?" Jillian's heart rose in her throat. She didn't believe those words for a moment. Marrying Luke might be her dream, but it was an impossible one. She was certain neither the Lord nor Luke felt the same way. "What are you talking about?"

"It's really very simple. I've known from the beginning that the reason you were here was to marry Luke." Emma's face was calm and her words were matter-of-fact as she looked at Jillian.

"I think not," Jillian said, shaking her head. "I've always considered you wise, Emma. How could you even think something as crazy as this? Listen to me. Luke has disliked me from the first moment he became aware that I existed. He's made no bones about it. Nothing's changed."

"What about you? How do you feel?"

"He's always intimidated me," Jillian sighed. Even to her dearest friend she could not admit she loved him. "I've seen a different side to Luke while I've been here, but that's all. No, the two of us are not marriage material."

"Yes, you are," Emma said with an assurance that thoroughly exasperated Jillian. She'd thought that Emma could never do anything that would aggravate her, but she'd been wrong.

"I don't know what the future will bring, but one thing I'm sure of is—it won't be marriage to Luke," she told Emma. "He would never marry someone like me."

Emma gave her a patient "you poor soul" look, which only served to irritate Jillian more.

"Randy's mother was good enough to point out my numerous shortcomings to me," Jillian added, "and if there's one thing I know now, it's that I'm not good enough for a Prescott."

"Phooey." Emma brushed away Helen Prescott's opinion with a wave of her hand.

At one time Jillian might have shared Emma's opinion, but now her expression was earnest. "Emma, in this case, she's right. I never went into detail about my life to you, but I know I'm not good enough for either Luke or Randy." The sad truth of this statement engulfed her, and Jillian felt as if she couldn't say another word. She sagged back against the chair cushion and lay there motionless.

"I don't know what you've done and I don't care to," Emma said briskly, "but your sweet spirit radiates from you. Why do you think the Lord gave us repentance?" She didn't wait for an answer. "So we could overcome our sins and weaknesses and enter into His kingdom. That's what the Atonement is. Christ paid for our sins, so we can be forgiven when we make mistakes.

"You are a beautiful daughter of God. He loves you and He wants you with Him again." She gave Jillian her usual beatific smile. "You will be."

Jillian gave a wry look. "I don't know if I believe that."

Emma ignored her protests. "You will." She held out her arms to Jillian.

Jillian moved into them and Emma hugged her. "You've been one of the greatest blessings in my life. Do you think I could enjoy heaven, or that your wonderful parents could, if you weren't there? No, to both questions," Emma answered for Jillian.

The tears that streamed from Jillian's eyes dampened Emma's cheeks as well. "You're so good to me," Jillian said in a choked voice. "I don't know what I would do without you." A few moments later, she drew away and met Emma's eyes. Her voice was quiet and definite. "But Luke isn't for me."

Emma simply smiled.

The next day it snowed all afternoon and by late evening the wind had picked up. Jillian couldn't remember when she'd ever witnessed such a blizzard. They were in the middle of lambing season, when about four hundred lambs were born a day. It seemed an incredibly high number to Jillian, who thought she might ask Luke where he kept them all. The sheds didn't look that big. What an awful night for anything except sitting around a fireplace. She continued pacing. Things must be bad if Luke hadn't even taken time to come in and eat.

Jillian looked in on Emma and found her sleeping. Checking her watch, she found it was midnight. Lately, Luke spent most of his nights outside, but none so far had been as raw and cold as tonight. She stared out her bedroom windows, and all she could see was a white blur.

She glanced at her watch again. If she hadn't heard from him in ten minutes, she was going out to check. Surely nothing had happened to him, or else one of the men would have informed her. But she needed to know for herself. Meanwhile she'd make some hot chocolate to take with her. She vaguely remembered seeing a thermos during her cleaning rampage, and once she got the water in the microwave, she started looking for it.

Fifteen minutes later she bundled up in her fur jacket, woolen mittens, and a heavy scarf. Thermos in hand, she started out. The fierceness of the wind blew the snow against her face with what felt like the force of a jackhammer as it ferociously bit her face. She knew the yard lights were on, but when she stepped down from the porch, the snowy night was impenetrable. Once she'd found the first shed wall, she'd be fine. She kept on moving towards her left. The snow clung to her coat and pants. She kept going, but she still hadn't found the shed. This had been a harebrained idea. Luke was probably tucked safely away in some corner, while she, the intrepid would-be rescuer, was lost in the blizzard.

At last she bumped into the wall of the shed. Now all she had to do was follow the wall to the first opening. That ought to be easy enough. With one hand touching the wall, she continued on her way. Then it stopped. She'd thought the sheds continued for a good quarter of a mile. Where on earth was she? Should she go back? She felt the corner. The wall went on in another direction, but she wouldn't. Now was certainly not the time to explore further. She turned around to retrace her steps. Somewhere behind her had to be a door, and if nothing else, the house. She was so cold she didn't think she could move her facial muscles, let alone blink her eyelids.

When she didn't think she could lift her feet one more time, she stumbled into an opening with a burlap bag hanging down to cover it. Pushing the bag aside, she found herself in a large shed with what looked like a million sheep, more or less. The lambing shed had a roof over it, so even though it was cold, at least she didn't have to fight the snow hurtling against her face. Relief at not having to fight the storm any longer flooded her entire being.

Now to find Luke. There were a number of men all working, either helping ewes give birth or separating the sheep, which were bunching in the corners. The first person she asked shrugged; the next one pointed vaguely to an uncovered corner of the yard where it was snowing heavily. She made her way over to the man, only to find it wasn't Luke.

She turned around and there he was. When he grabbed her arms to keep her from falling, Jillian's pulse raced even through the nearly dozen layers of clothing that separated them.

"I thought I recognized the jacket, snow and all. What on earth are you doing out here? Is Emma all right?" he demanded, as if her appearance meant something had gone wrong.

"She's okay," she hurriedly reassured him.

At those words, his frozen white brows lost their worried scowl, and his anxious voice turned warm and welcoming, which started a slow melt through her body.

She held up the thermos. "I brought you some cocoa. I don't think I'd ever have recognized you. I can tell you've been out in the blizzard. You look like an iceman. Are those eyebrows or icicles?" She tried to smile, but her muscles wouldn't move.

"Speak for yourself. You look like a giant white panda." Putting his arm around her, he guided her over to a wood-burning stove. "Stand here and warm up. What made you decide to come out in a blizzard with hot chocolate? You could have gotten lost just coming a few yards."

"Believe me, it felt like more than just a few yards. Miles is more like it. But I was concerned when you didn't come back to the house.

The weather was so bad, I thought something must have happened. Here, drink your hot cocoa." She handed the thermos to him.

He smiled at her, his special, heartbreaking smile, as he took the thermos from her hands. As he pulled the cork out, steam rose up. "From the looks of it, this should warm me all right." He poured himself some.

The bond between them at that moment jolted her. Her senses were alive to an awareness of him, not an adversary, not a kind bene-factor, but an attractive man. Emma's comments earlier made her even more aware of his appeal than usual. Darn that Emma!

She glanced at Luke's face, at the tender curve of his mouth, at the warmth of his eyes and knew that he experienced it too. She found herself unable to say or do anything beyond staring at his face.

Luke's eyes didn't leave hers either as he brought the cup of cocoa to his lips. "Good" was the only word he uttered until he'd finished. It was almost as if he were afraid of breaking the spell between them.

He screwed the cup back on the thermos and handed it back to her. "I wish I could take you back to the house, but I've got to get back to work. With this storm the sheep keep bunching, and I'm afraid we might lose some." He pulled a bale of straw over for her to sit on and she caught sight of the door that she'd been looking for to begin with.

"Let me help you." Forgetting everything else, she only knew she wanted desperately to stay out here and be with Luke.

"Thanks for the offer, but the best way you can help me is to stay inside with Emma tonight."

Jillian cringed, mortified that in her eagerness to be with Luke, for a moment she'd forgotten all about Emma.

"But thank you." His words were soft, almost a caress, and he leaned over and kissed her lips. Just a light, butterfly kiss, but she felt herself respond. He stepped back and touched her cheek. "Stay here until the storm lets up." Then he turned and walked away.

Her body tingling, Jillian watched him until he disappeared in the snow. Yes, she loved Luke, she knew it now. But Emma was wrong. Luke would never want to marry her; she wasn't good enough for him. Emma could talk all she wanted about repentance, but she doubted it could change her enough that Luke would be interested in her.

In her self-centered, youthful carelessness, she'd thrown away eternal happiness for momentary fame. She huddled against the straw while grief filled her soul. She wasn't good enough for Luke. And she'd never be.

Finally the wind stopped rattling the shed, and she made her escape back to the house. Although it was two A.M. by the time Jillian crawled into bed, sleep did not come easy. The inconceivable loneliness of loving Luke kept her awake.

CHAPTER 17

When she got out of bed the next day, Jillian found that the blizzard had moved out and left a chilly, snowy world behind. When Luke came in for a couple of hours of sleep about ten o'clock before returning to the sheep sheds, Jillian felt especially grateful to be warm and cozy inside the house. But her worry about Emma increased and she found it impossible to concentrate on anything, even the devotional assembly. Finally she clicked off the television and just sat in Emma's room with her.

When the phone rang unexpectedly, she jumped, startled by the abrupt sound breaking through the silence. Hurrying into the kitchen, she answered it. "Hello."

"Jillian?" It was Randy. Jillian groaned to herself. What did he want? She had no desire whatsoever to see him any time soon, especially not after their last conversation.

"I know you're busy taking care of Emma, but could I come over? I won't stay long, but I need to talk to you." He sounded determined.

"Couldn't you tell me on the phone and save a trip?" She couldn't keep the impatience out of her voice and she was sorry for that, but she wanted to prevent another scene. "The snow's pretty deep, and the roads are bound to be messy."

"I've got snow tires and I'll be fine." His voice was firm. "This has to be said in person."

"Come over then. But I can only spare a few minutes." She didn't want to appear ungracious, but she didn't look forward to another discussion with him. She'd been honest with him on Christmas. It was now the 6th of March; surely he didn't still believe that things

would work out between the two of them. Although she was barely
cordial to Jillian, his mother did call every day to check on Emma,
but she hadn't expected to hear from Randy. Right now Emma's
condition consumed her thoughts. She didn't have time to worry
about anything else.

Emma's life had completely turned around. When Jillian had first
come to care for her, Emma had spent very little time in her
bedroom; now she only left her room for thirty minutes or so a
couple of times a day. The rest of the time she spent in bed, not both-
ering to dress anymore. Except for lipstick, she also didn't bother with
makeup though she still wanted to wear her pearls. What little she
ate, Jillian brought to her on a tray. She was afraid that Emma had
just given up and was ready to die. Jillian couldn't stand the thought.
She wasn't ready to let her go.

Today she hadn't planned to do anything except sit by Emma's
side. Luke would be in soon, which always relieved her mind. She felt
like she could depend on him to know what to do. Caring for Emma
through the last month had brought the two of them closer together.
She dared not hope for anything more. When this crisis was past, she
was afraid the fragile ties between them would not last.

Jillian had pulled the overstuffed chair closer to the bed earlier.
Now she just relaxed in it and watched Emma sleep. Even with her
dark furniture, this room was light and airy. Emma wanted the blinds
left open so she could look at the snow-covered mountains. The peaks
of the mountains disappeared into the mists, and there were smudged
streaks of purple where the snow had melted. The gray overcast sky
made the day as dismal as her thoughts.

When Randy drove in, Jillian met him at the back porch, leaving
Emma's bedroom door open only a crack so she wouldn't be
disturbed.

"Hi, come on in." She held the door for him, still leery of what he
might say. "If you don't mind, let's sit at the table, so we don't wake
Emma."

He nodded, thoughtful as usual. "That's all right with me. I
certainly don't want to cause Emma any distress." He waited while
Jillian closed the door quietly, and then followed her to the dining
room.

When they were seated at one end of the long table, Randy gave her a deliberate look. "How's it going? How's Emma?"

"Not too good. I don't think she's going to get well." Jillian made no effort to blink back the sudden rush of tears.

His concern was obvious. "I know how much you care for her. It's got to be hard to watch her fade away." He reached for her hand and squeezed it. "How are you holding up?"

She let him take her hand, appreciating his sympathy. "I'll make it." She had to because there was nothing else she could do.

He shook his head. "I wouldn't have believed it, but despite nursing Emma, you look better than you did at Christmas."

She smiled at him. "I've gained a few pounds, so I'm not as haggard. That's probably the difference."

Randy kept his eyes focused on her as if judging the accuracy of her words, and then said, "There are a few things about our last conversation that I want to clear up, and I wanted to do it in person. Your comments cut deep. They were things I didn't want to hear, especially from you." He smiled slightly. "I thought about them, and then I thought about them some more. When I got over being hurt and angry, I knew you were right.

"Until then, all I could see were my teenage dreams being fulfilled. I kept thinking everything was the same as it had been ten years ago. I didn't dare think about what all had happened to us both during those ten years and how we'd both changed. For a few weeks there, I admit I acted like an adolescent."

He shook his head ruefully. "I can hardly believe I was stupid enough to throw over Marci for you—"

Jillian laughed. "Thanks a lot!" But it was one load off her shoulders, and she hoped his next words would even lift more.

He looked sheepish. "You know what I mean. Your life has been different, but, my gosh, my life hasn't just been spent here in Quail Creek. I've been places, done things, and here I was sounding like I'd just fallen off a turnip truck.

"Anyway, the important point to all this is that I realized how much I love Marci. We might have started out as the only two people our age in town, but that's not what we have now. As trite as it sounds, I realize that she is the one for me. We really do fit together, and I lost sight of that for a while. After some long hard talking, I finally convinced her that she's the only one I've ever *truly* loved. It took me years, as you well know, to see the difference between love and infatuation.

"We've made plans to be married in the Idaho Falls Temple at Easter time and spend a week in Mexico for our honeymoon. By fall we should have our own house built, and until then we'll live in Marci's apartment." He grinned. "Not with my mother!"

Jillian leaned across the table and clasped his hands, smiling into his eyes. "I can't imagine any news that would have made me happier."

"I knew you'd be happy for me, and you're the first person I've told." He studied her face for a moment. "Jillian, I don't know what the future holds for you, but I hope it's a testimony of the gospel. When we were kids, I know you knew the Church was true, I didn't. I want you to have that feeling again."

"So do I," she said softly. She wanted so deeply to know that the Church was true. She knew the most wonderful gift she could give Emma would be to tell her she knew the gospel was true, but she couldn't. She wanted to know, but she didn't. Randy, Emma, and Luke meant too much to her for her to be anything less than honest about her beliefs.

"Well, I'd better run along." He stood up and pushed his chair back under the table.

Jillian walked him to the door and they hugged. Jillian watched until he'd driven away. She kept shaking her head. She couldn't believe Randy's news. What a fantastic surprise!

Returning to Emma's room, Jillian found her awake. She helped her to the bathroom and made sure she drank some water before tucking her in again. Other than to faintly shake or nod her head at Jillian's questions, Emma made no comments. Each day she had become more and more quiet. In her heart Jillian knew that couldn't be a good sign. She was definitely getting worse.

She smoothed back Emma's hair from her forehead and straightened her pearls. "Now that you're all set, I've just heard some exciting news."

Emma smiled slightly, but she still didn't say anything.

"Randy came over, and he and Marci are getting married at Easter." Jillian made her voice especially enthusiastic, hoping that Emma would respond.

Emma's eyes gleamed and she smiled a little. Then she glanced out the window at the mountains and the next thing Jillian knew, Emma had fallen asleep.

Jillian sank into the chair, afraid of what might happen next. "Heavenly Father, don't take her. I'm not ready to let her go. I don't know what I'll do without her love and encouragement. Please let her stay with us longer. Amen."

The bishop and his counselors had come out several times since her hospital stay to administer to Emma. If God didn't hear their prayers, she knew He wouldn't hear hers. She was so afraid she was going to lose Emma.

—m—

When Luke came in, he found Jillian in Emma's room weeping. He looked over at his beloved Emma and frowned. "What's happening?"

Jillian got out of the chair and brushed back her tears. "She doesn't say a word. Just smiles occasionally. I don't think she can last much longer."

He could have wept at this point himself, but he steeled himself against the pain. "I'll call the doctor and see what he suggests. I don't know if he would want to airlift her to Idaho Falls again or not."

He went to the kitchen and called. But Dr. Neilson had already left for the day. The nurse offered to find the doctor and have him call Luke, but there was nothing more she could do. Luke hung up, feeling helpless and hating it. Right now there was absolutely nothing he could do but wait for the doctor's call back. Going back to Emma's bedroom, Luke slumped into the other chair, his hopelessness apparent in every line of his body. Jillian waited, not speaking.

"He's gone for the day. I explained to his nurse, so she's going to locate him and have him call." In frustration, he slammed his fist once against the palm of his other hand, then fell silent. He didn't want talk; he just wanted Emma well. But he knew it wasn't to be.

Although neither he nor Jillian said anything as the room grew darker and darker, he was glad she was there. He found her presence comforting, and he realized that regardless of what he had said to Emma, he couldn't let Jillian leave. He was not only grateful for how she'd cared for Emma and him; he admired her. The house had never been cleaner, and he knew that wasn't easy for someone who was used to being waited on, rather than doing the waiting on herself. And to his surprise, she'd managed to do a credible job of the cooking. He couldn't conceive of the Jillian he knew now abandoning Quail Creek for the bright lights of New York City.

When the phone finally rang, they both jumped. He hurried into the kitchen to answer, anxious to talk to the doctor.

"Luke? Is that you? I can't hear you. Speak up."

His heart sank. Aunt Helen. "Sorry." He raised his voice. "How are you doing?" If she rattled on, he would end the conversation. He was taking no chances on missing the doctor's call.

"I'm wonderful, but how's Emma?" Her voice was chipper.

She must have some other reason for calling because a report on Emma's condition wouldn't make her happy. "Not doing too well. We're waiting for the doctor's call."

"That's too bad, but you know she's ready to die,"she said briskly.

Luke cringed at her crisp, abrupt words. "No, I don't know that she is, and I don't want her to."

"Now, Luke, you know all about the plan of salvation," she continued as if he hadn't protested her last statement at all.

He gritted his teeth. He couldn't take any more. But before he could hang up, she said, "I won't tie up the line any longer, but I have wonderful news. Randy and Marci are getting married at Easter."

"What?" She couldn't have said anything that would have shocked him more.

"Randy and Marci are getting married at Easter," she repeated. "Isn't it wonderful?"

"It is. Give them both my regards. I've got to hang up. Talk to you tomorrow," he said abruptly. He'd just put the phone down when it rang again. This time it was Dr. Neilson, who asked how Emma was doing.

"She's been sleeping nearly all day," Luke told him. "She's eating and drinking very little. She barely says anything."

The doctor's voice was gentle. "Her system is shutting down. It probably won't be long now. All you can do is make sure she's comfortable. I don't see much point in bringing her back to the hospital just to keep her alive on machines. She wants to go. Let her."

Luke could barely speak, but he finally managed an almost inaudible, "All right."

Back in the bedroom he stood looking down at Emma. Her tiny little body lay there quietly, her ankles neatly crossed. She'd enriched his life with her understanding of what a boy and then a man needed, and seeing her go was as difficult as letting go of his father.

"What did the doctor say?" Jillian asked, rising from her seat to stand beside him.

"Just make her comfortable."

"Just make her comfortable? We have to do more than that. I won't let her go!"she said stubbornly.

Luke put his arms around her. "I know." He smoothed her hair back from her face. "I know. I feel the same way. But it isn't up to us."

"I've pleaded and pleaded with Heavenly Father. Why doesn't He hear our prayers?" she asked him, her eyes glistening with tears.

"He does. His answer to us is 'no.' His answer to her is 'Come home.'"

Jillian's grief amazed Luke. He'd never given her credit for having the ability to feel deeply about anything other than herself, but her desolation at losing Emma was genuine. He looked down at her beautiful tear-stained face. Even with her reddened eyes, Jillian was lovely.

She pulled away and he let her.

"I need to put some cold water on my eyes. Maybe that'll stop the tears." When she returned, she brought a damp washcloth and gently wiped Emma's face and hands. Emma's lips curled in a smile at the coolness of the cloth, and she looked happy.

—∞—

After a few hours of waiting, Luke felt himself start to doze in his chair, so he stood up. This was one night when he didn't want to sleep. In the glow of the night light, he could see Jillian watching

Emma. He went to her, took her hands, and pulled her to her feet, putting his arms around her.

The soft fleece of her sweatshirt cushioned his arms. "It's hard to see someone you love pass away. Aunt Helen reminded me today that we're fortunate to know about the plan of salvation, although I admit I wasn't ready to hear her say that Emma's death is all part of God's plan. I know we'll see each other again, but it's so hard to let her go now."

"It is." She leaned her head against his chest. "I will always regret that I wasn't here when Daddy died, but I remember feeling just like this watching my mother pass away. I felt such an awful emptiness, and I thought I would feel it the rest of my life. It's strange but Emma's love has filled the hole I've felt since my mother's death."

"I know what you mean," Luke said quietly. "She did the same for me when I lost my mother and then later when my father died." They stood there together, feeling the comfort of their shared love for the woman who had affected their lives so deeply.

Emma murmured something and opened her eyes, looking up at Jillian and Luke, though she didn't seem to see them. Then her eyes seemed to light on something across the room and she suddenly sat up in bed, startling them.

"John! Oh, John!" Emma cried out as she reached upward. Her voice sounded youthful, happy, even excited, as in the days when Jillian had first meet Emma and been nourished by her gift of her loving, joyful spirit.

Luke and Jillian rushed to Emma's side, but she had already fallen back against the pillows. Luke took Emma's hand, feeling for a pulse. There wasn't one. She was gone. In the moonlight shining through the window, Luke saw that her face was smooth and her skin glowed like porcelain.

Jillian lifted her gaze to the window.

"Did you feel that?" Her voice filled with wonder. "I could feel her presence leave." She moved closer to Luke and looked down at Emma. "She looks so beautiful and at peace."

Luke glanced at his watch, two A.M., then pulled the sheet carefully up to Emma's chin. He couldn't bring himself to cover her face.

"What does it mean?" Jillian moved closer to Luke, who put his arm around her shoulder as naturally as if he'd been doing it all of his life. Drawing her against him, he rested his cheek against the top of her head, feeling the silky texture of her hair and breathing in the sweet fragrance of her perfume.

"I believe that our loved ones come to meet us when we're ready to pass through the veil."

Jillian's forehead furrowed, as if she didn't quite know what to make of Luke's words, and she looked doubtful. "Do you really believe that?"

"Yes," he said distantly. "I do." He had a palpable sense of grief, and at this moment, holding Jillian seemed to alleviate it. He needed a few minutes to absorb what had transpired.

It was nearly four-thirty A.M. when Luke finally crawled into bed. He felt utterly drained. Jillian had looked just as worn out when she had left him to go to her room. The men from the mortuary had come and gone, and now there was the funeral to arrange, Emma's nieces and nephews to notify, and the bishop to tell. Luke also needed to write the obituary for the newspaper and find her temple clothes. He thought Jillian ought to be able to help him there.

After what they'd shared, especially this evening, he believed that Jillian would stay, and he felt great consolation in this thought. Emma's death grieved him, but with Jillian at his side, he could manage.

—⁂—

Jillian sat in the second row of the chapel, once again dressed in black as she studied the program for Emma's services. She nodded at several acquaintances, then resumed reading the program. She saw that Luke was speaking, followed by the bishop. She was anxious for the funeral to begin so it would be over. It had been almost three months to the day since she had attended her father's funeral and now she was attending another. For someone she dearly loved, though she hadn't even known her then. Someone who had changed her life.

Jillian wished she were more like Emma, that she had her friend's zest for life and her faith in the gospel. But she didn't. And even though she loved Luke, she couldn't stay here. What good would it do? She wasn't good enough for him, she knew that.

These last few days had been filled with painful reminders of her darling Emma. Neighbors brought in food and then sat and reminisced about her—her personality, her testimony, her love for life, her love for chocolate.

The organ prelude ended and the funeral began. As Luke approached the pulpit, Jillian could see that the devastation so apparent in his face at Emma's death was now softening, and that he was coming to terms with her death. He spoke of Emma and what she had meant to him over the years. She had been witty and funny, and the congregation laughed at many of Luke's remembrances of her.

A woman with a lovely soprano voice sang, "A Wintry Day." Jillian couldn't remember ever having heard this song before. She listened intently to the reassuring words, which brought comfort to her grieving soul. Then the bishop stood up to speak.

"This afternoon we have come to remember a valiant sister in our ward, Emma Gillette. We all have good memories of her, and we could spend the hour sharing how the things she did changed our lives, but that's not what she wanted. She asked me if I would speak on what we need to do to return to our Heavenly Father. I am pleased to do as she wished.

"Alma, a prophet from the Book of Mormon, asks us several important questions. He begins, 'Have you spiritually been born of God? Have you received his image in your countenances? Have you experienced this mighty change in your heart?'

"Can you answer yes to these questions?" He paused as if to let the gravity of each question and the importance of the answer sink in. "And if not, what do we need to do so that we can? First, we have to have faith. Faith in the redemption of him who created you."

Jillian sat quietly, absorbing the bishop's words. Did she have faith that God had redeemed everyone? Was that the essence of the gospel? That they could all live with Him again? She did believe that.

"Have you been stripped of your pride?"

Pride. Even when she'd hit rock bottom, she'd been too proud to humble herself. Not until she'd gone to the bishop as a last resort, had she been able to admit her failures. She didn't know if she'd humbled herself, or if she'd just been so desperate to get help she was willing to divulge her problems. But was that humility? But while the bishop and

Luke knew of her wrecked career, and of course God, she didn't know if she could let anyone else know that she was no longer a popular model.

"Can you stand blameless before God if you have not repented?"

At the picture these words created, Jillian squeezed her eyes shut, feeling as if her heart would break. She had so much to repent of, and yet she lacked the faith to believe Heavenly Father would forgive her. Where did she even start?

"Remember to pray unto God continually by day and give thanks unto his holy name by night. Let your hearts rejoice because of his greatness, his grace, his mercy, and his love."

Though she kept her eyes tightly shut, she felt the tears slip down her cheeks. *The bishop believes what he is saying. I know Emma believed this, too. Oh, Heavenly Father, please let me know it's true also. I know I'm not worthy now, but I want to become worthy so that Your image is in my countenance. I beg You, Father, please help me. Please.*

"Our sister Emma had a strong testimony of these words and of this plan. I ask the Lord to bless us that we might all experience this burning in our bosom, experience this knowledge of the plan of salvation, experience this love our Savior has for each one of us." The bishop concluded and returned to his seat while Jillian sat with her head bowed, seeking to find comfort.

—⁂—

The return home was silent, with both Luke and Jillian lost in their own thoughts. It was after six o'clock and the sun had set, leaving the night as dark and dreary as Jillian felt. Luke stopped at the door to let her out, then took the car around to the garage. Once inside the house, Jillian could feel Emma's absence as if it were an enormous gaping hole. The visit to the cemetery had only intensified the painful memories of losing her parents, and with Emma gone, Jillian felt cut adrift, without an anchor or a port. For the last several weeks she had been needed and she had made herself useful, which were both new and different feelings for her. Now, with Emma gone, Jillian knew she was no longer needed. She wondered how soon Luke would want her to leave. Taking off her coat, she sank back in the leather chair to wait for him.

She heard Luke's footsteps as he walked slowly through the house and started for the stairs. "Good night, Jillian," he called softly. "See you in the morning."

She didn't want to wait. She needed to know now so she could start thinking about what to do next. She forced herself to respond, "I think we have some things to discuss."

She stood as he came towards her, and his face softened as he gazed at her. "You're right, we do, but it's nothing that can't wait. After this long day, I don't think either one of us is up to it tonight. I know I'm not. Tomorrow or even the next day is soon enough." He smiled and patted her shoulder. "Now get some rest." He turned back towards the stairs and she didn't try to stop him.

Jillian dropped back into the chair. Luke's touch disarmed her as did his smile, which held a promise of safekeeping. They'd shared so much these last days that she believed he felt something towards her. He couldn't have put his arm around her and treated her with such warmth if he didn't. But a nagging voice said, *Oh yes he could. He's just lost the most important person in his life.* Maybe he had been only seeking solace from her. Nothing more. She didn't know for sure and her uncertainty made her hesitate to read anything into his words or the expressions in his face.

She didn't want to leave him, but if he didn't want to marry her, she knew she had no other alternative. She certainly couldn't stay here if they weren't married. And that thought brought up an entirely different problem. She wasn't worthy enough for him. She sighed deeply. Completely spent from the events of the last few days, she didn't think she had enough strength to even stand up. After a few moments she pulled herself up out of the chair, picked up her coat, and stumbled down the hall to her room.

Once there she tossed her coat over the back of the sofa. Her Book of Mormon was in its usual place on her nightstand. Even as tired as she was, she couldn't rest until she'd looked up "spiritually born of God" in the index. She read the entire fifth chapter of Alma. She was so sorry for the mistakes she'd made and the sins she'd committed. How could she have forsaken the gospel? Nothing in her life had been worth what she'd thrown away.

She laid the book down and knelt by the side of the bed. *Dear*

Father in Heaven, I want to say how much I love You. I am terribly sorry for the mistakes I've made, for neglecting my father. I am sorry for the life I've led, and I'd give anything if I'd been true to what I've been taught. But I haven't. Please, please forgive me.

I want to be worthy to be with You again. I want to hear Your voice saying, "Come unto me." I want my hands to be clean and pure. Please help me overcome my sins and be forgiven. I am grateful for the blessing of returning to Quail Creek, and of knowing Emma , and of receiving her wonderful influence. Thank You.

Please help me know what direction I should go now. Thank You again. Amen.

Slowly Jillian rose to her feet and undressed. She needed Heavenly Father's help in order to get through the next few days. She felt weighed down with concerns, and she needed to know she wasn't alone.

Limp with fatigue, she turned off the light and glanced at the night stand. It came to her at that moment that she loved the Book of Mormon. The words were like poetry, and since she started reading it each day, she had felt closer to Heavenly Father. In the last five years she hadn't prayed once; now she found it difficult to get through the day without praying.

She sighed as she wondered what tomorrow would bring.

CHAPTER 18

Although the sun shone the next day, a dark cloud seemed to be hovering over Jillian as she tried to decide where to go if Luke didn't want her here. Plane fare for New York would take half her savings and wouldn't leave enough to live on. Besides, Simon had made it clear that there weren't any modeling jobs for her. Any other employment, like selling clothes or merchandising, she could do as easily in Idaho Falls or Salt Lake City. The cost of living around here had to be less than that of New York, and she wouldn't have to spend everything she had getting there. But then, three months had passed, and she hadn't heard from any of the places where she'd applied. Of course, someone might have tried to reach her at the Prescotts', and who knew if Mrs. Prescott would pass on any messages.

First thing tomorrow morning she would call the stores in Idaho Falls where she'd already applied and see if they had any openings. If anyone was still interested in her, she'd move into town for a while; if not, she'd go on to Salt Lake City. Her heart ached at the thought of leaving, but she had to face her losses and get on with her life. *Get on with her life.* What a callous phrase that was. Her heart was breaking; how was she supposed to think about "getting on with her life"?

At sixteen, she had waved good-bye to Quail Creek, eager to leave, confident she was going to be rich and famous. How times had changed! Now she didn't want to leave here. She loved Luke. And she was scared to death.

Now New York City wasn't even an option for her. She'd miss the excitement of life in the big city, but without a big paycheck, New York was just too expensive. She had lived that dream, and never,

never, never did she want to go back to the life she'd led there. To resume her existence as a professional house guest was a sickening thought. Now was the time to center her life around the gospel. She desperately wanted to know for herself the truthfulness of it, and she couldn't accomplish that without more study and prayer.

With her newly discovered love for Luke, she couldn't stay here if he didn't ask her. It would be too painful. But she knew in her heart he wouldn't ask. Even though it was true that he seemed to feel differently about her, she'd been on the receiving end of his sharp retorts too often to even think of telling him what her feelings were before she knew how he felt.

She knew it would be a long time, if ever, that her heart didn't leap every time she saw a tall, dark-haired man. While her heart ached at leaving Luke, she felt a sense of relief just knowing she'd made some definite plans.

She'd been in her bedroom packing for an hour when she heard the phone. Luke, who was in his office, called from the top of the stairs for her to pick up.

"Jillian? This is Bonnie from Simon Grant's." Jillian would have known that aloof, elegant voice anywhere. "He wants to speak to you. Will you hold please?"

Simon? What could he possibly want? The last time she spoke to him he had essentially told her that she was completely washed up. She was. She admitted it. So what did he want now?

"Jillian, darling!" His exuberant, phony greeting nauseated her. How had she ever put up with him so many years?

"Yes," she said politely, if a trifle coolly. She absolutely refused to buy into whatever he was selling.

"How is our little country girl? Ready for the city again?" His voice was patronizing.

"Oh, I don't know." Jillian intentionally made her tone disdainful. "I *love* living in the country. It's so peaceful. I have time to think and to reflect and to . . . " She deliberately allowed her voice to trail off, leaving Simon to wonder what else she would have said.

"You? Think and reflect?" His voice was aghast. "Am I really speaking to Jillian Taylor, the number one all-time party girl? Come on! I don't believe it!"

She couldn't stand to hear his cynical description of her and her life. Nausea rose in her throat. She closed her eyes, willing herself not to throw up. "What do you want, Simon?"

"Darling, don't be like that. I have fantastic news. *Vogue* magazine is doing a retrospective on models: 'Where are they now?' They want you for it. Isn't that marvelous? They'd like to come out to Idaho to photograph you at home and—"

"No." She spoke sharply, but she absolutely refused to let the blasé people of the fashion industry intrude on her world here.

"What? You'd refuse this job?" Shock waves rolled through his voice.

"No. I'd like the job, but they can't come here."

"Oh." Simon sounded relieved. "We'll work something out. Listen, they're also shooting in Palm Beach. Four days on the Florida beaches. Isn't that fantastic?"

"When is this fantastic job?" Her queasiness had subsided, but she couldn't keep the sarcasm out of her voice.

"In two weeks, darling. We'll make hotel arrangements here and airline reservations for you. I'll be in touch."

Before he could hang up, Jillian said, "Make the reservations for tomorrow." Despite the fact that she and Luke hadn't talked yet, she could see no reason to hang around here any longer torturing herself.

"Fine, darling! Ciao."

Jillian slowly put down the receiver. Amazement washed over her. She was going back to New York after all. Then to Palm Beach. How had all this happened? She had to believe the Lord had a hand in it. No one would automatically think of Jillian Taylor for a job assignment any more. Once it was over, however, she was heading west again, unless the Lord had something else in mind for her.

What would Luke's response be? Undoubtedly he'd be glad everything had worked out so she could leave. If only he'd ask her to stay . . . but she knew he wouldn't. She'd better put on her "happy face" so she could tell him. That way he'd never know the truth: that she really didn't want to go.

Jillian slowly ascended the stairs to Luke's office. "Guess what?" she said from the doorway. "My agent called and *Vogue* wants me for a fashion shoot." She stared at him, willing the smile on her face to stay put, so Luke wouldn't see that underneath she was broken-hearted. "I can't get over the timing of this job. I couldn't hang around here any longer. I didn't have enough money to go back to New York and live, and this job comes along—all expenses paid. I consider the whole thing a blessing. I'll never say the word 'luck' again."

Luke seemed thoughtful. "When do you leave?"

"Tomorrow. Isn't that great? I'll be gone and you won't have to put up with me any longer." Jillian smiled again although she really didn't see anything pleasant about it.

"That's one good thing, I guess." His words were matter-of-fact.

Forcing herself to be the old Jillian, she wrinkled her nose at him and left before he could see through her facade. It might be a relief to have a job, expenses paid, but all it really did was force her to leave Luke. She could intellectualize all she wanted about what was the right thing to do, but her heart begged to stay here. She closed her eyes. *Please let him want me to stay.*

At the top of the stairs she paused. She knew right now she wasn't good enough for him, but she wanted to be. She knew it would take time. She hoped God could forgive her. But whether or not anything between Luke and her ever worked out, her goal was to be right with her Heavenly Father.

———

When Jillian waltzed out of his office, apparently just as light-hearted as she had entered, Luke wadded up the piece of paper he was writing on and forcibly threw it across the room. He scowled. It had arrived. The day he'd known all along would come. Jillian going back to the big time. After that, he couldn't imagine ever seeing her again since there was nothing in Quail Creek for her. Just as well. He'd had enough pain to last him a lifetime, and Jillian only meant more pain. He hoped she'd be successful. Only this time he prayed she'd be wiser.

Luke slowly shook his head. "Emma, you were wrong. Obviously Jillian and I weren't meant for each other." But, oh, how he wished they had been.

If Jillian hadn't been so excited about getting the job and going back to New York City, he would have said something. He'd been convinced Jillian felt something for him, and he knew he loved her. But he'd been right all along. Jillian didn't belong here, and she'd grabbed at the first opportunity to leave. *Better to suffer now than later.*

Luke stood up abruptly. *What a stupid thought,* he told himself. He wasn't like his father, who had done nothing to stop the woman he loved from leaving. Jillian wasn't going anywhere until she knew that he loved her, and he had at least heard it from her own lips that she didn't love him. He knew she'd changed, and no matter how frivolous she'd appeared a few minutes ago, he didn't believe for one minute she wanted to go back to her old life. He'd been arrogant and self-righteous, but he'd changed. Now if Jillian could forgive his former judgmental attitude and accept him, flaws and all, he would be happy.

—⁓—

With no further need to hide her true feelings, Jillian clung to the railing for support as she made her way down the stairs. She found the very word "modeling" abhorrent. Even if she could regain her popularity and make pots of money, she'd pass it all up to stay in Quail Creek. She wandered into Emma's room and sank into her rocking chair.

Oh, Father, I need Your help. I feel devastated at leaving Luke and my life here. Do You really want me to go? Is returning to modeling even for a short time the right thing to do? Please, please help me. I want my life centered around the gospel. I believe the gospel is true and I want to keep it in my life.

With these words, a strong burning filled her bosom and tears flowed down her cheeks. A peacefulness enveloped her body, and she knew without a doubt that no matter the outcome with Luke, all would be well.

She rocked a few more times and then stood. She couldn't sit still any longer; she needed to do something. Jillian didn't know what Heavenly Father's answer would be, but she would be ready when it came. And she'd clean the house for Luke from top to bottom before she left.

Suddenly Luke appeared in the doorway. He looked like the Luke of old—a scowl on his face, a determined gleam in his eyes, and an unyielding stance.

She caught her breath. "Is something wrong?"

"Yes, there's something wrong. You might think the Lord blessed you with a modeling job, but I consider it more of a test by the Lord to see if you would choose to be here or with your old crowd. I don't intend to let you fail. You are not leaving." His words were uncompromising.

Jillian stared at him. His whole attitude puzzled her. "Why?"

"Because I'm in love with you, and I won't let you go."

His blue eyes burned into hers and seemed to penetrate her soul. Behind his brusque facade, she saw his fear of losing her. He wanted her to stay. He loved her. Luke loved her!

"I—"

"I'm not taking no for an answer." His fierce words rushed out.

"I—"

"I'm not my father. I will not let you leave. I—"

He had stepped closer to her, and Jillian reached out and shook him. "Will you listen to me? I love you, too." Her words were every bit as fierce as his.

He stared intensely at her then grasped her shoulders, as if to physically keep her in the room. "So why are you leaving?"

Jillian's voice softened. "You never asked me to stay."

He shook his head, his gaze never wavering from her face. "How could I? You told Randy you didn't know if you could live in Quail Creek."

"I couldn't with *him,* but I'm crazy about staying with *you!*" Her eyes sparkled. She wanted him to get the facts straight.

A smile lit his face, and he hugged her close, his mouth gentle against hers. The kiss deepened, and Jillian melted against him.

"I love you, Luke Prescott," she murmured.

"Will you be my bride, Jillian Taylor?" His words tender on her cheek. "I want to be with you for eternity."

She stiffened at his words and drew back to search his face. "Luke, I'm not worthy to go to the temple. Not yet."

"You will be. Let's talk to the bishop. He'll know what we need to do. Now you listen to me, you're not getting away." His last words were firm, but he smiled. "Emma told me you were meant for me, and she was right."

"She told you that?" Jillian looked at him in amazement. "She told me the same thing. I didn't believe her, but—" she shook her head, smiling, "—she was right."

"So, Jillian, will you marry me?" His eyes were tender, but the look in them demanded an affirmative answer.

"Yes, Luke. Yes, yes, yes!" It would take time, but she'd do whatever she needed to do to be ready to go to the temple with Luke. She knew he would help her, and more important, she knew Heavenly Father would help her, as He had already. Her heart swelled with joy. She was home to stay and—best of all—she was with Luke.

He drew her back into his arms, and once again his lips met hers.

ABOUT THE AUTHOR

A native Idahoan, Beverly King currently resides in Salt Lake City and has retired from teaching to follow her dream of writing.

Bev naturally enjoys reading, particularly mysteries and legal thrillers. She also loves reading cookbooks and making cookies, and she is a compulsive collector.

A self-acknowledged "news junkie," she says, "I also never miss a do-it-yourself program or magazine. Bob Vila and Norm Abrams are my heroes!" She loves designer clothes, fur coats, expensive shoes, and XK-type Jaguars, but says, "a lack of funds and 2 Nephi 9:51 keep me grounded."

She loves the gospel and at the present time is a Relief Society teacher.

She is the author of *Christmas by the Book,* published by Covenant Communications.

Forgotten Notes

BY SIAN ANN BESSEY

15 May 1881

Dear Father,

I have only a few precious moments to write to you before our ship casts off for America. I could not leave without putting your mind at rest regarding my welfare. The thought of your distress over my sudden, secret departure has been the only thing marring my happiness. For I am happy, Father! And safe and well.

I hope you can find it in your heart to forgive me for leaving with no word of good-bye. It was perhaps the hardest thing I have ever done.

Glyn and I are married. We have loved each other since the first day we met. Our lives would have been forced to follow separate paths had we stayed in Pen-y-Bryn. I could not have born such a lonely, loveless life.

I have followed my heart, but I grieve for those I've hurt—especially you, Father, and Joseph Lewis. He is a good, kind man. I will always admire him and be flattered that he showed interest in me—but I could not love him as a wife should love her husband. And he, of all people, deserves that.
I have taken the small oval portrait of you and Mother. I will treasure it always. I have also taken the pearls that Mother gave me. It was all I had of my own to help augment Glyn's hard-earned savings. We will manage. We love one another dearly and look forward to our lives together in a new land.

I must go. My thoughts are with you.
Your loving daughter,
Mary

ᚥ ᚥ ᚥ

Sarah Lewis sighed and tucked a stray wisp of long, chestnut-colored hair behind her ear. She sat up straight, stretched her aching shoulders and glanced longingly at the beam of bright sunlight pouring in through the small casement window above her head. After days of gray, wet weather the warm sunshine felt like a healing balm. She sighed again, and wished she could enjoy the beautiful summer day outside. But until inventory was complete, she was relegated to sitting in the chilly, uninviting back room of the shop, surrounded by dusty boxes and shelves of cans.

Sarah had been tempted to find a reason for doing inventory at another time. But then she would have had to face Aunty Lil. That was one of the disadvantages of working with family members—they knew you so well. Although she probably wouldn't have let on, Aunty Lil would have seen through any excuse she could have mustered. Then feeling guilty all day would have ruined Sarah's time off anyway. And so she found herself perched on the top of a rather ancient step stool alternately glaring at the rows of cans before her and the stack of papers on her knee.

It had been different when her dad was alive. She had always helped him do inventory. Perhaps that was why it fell to her lot now. Her father had made Sarah feel as though her assistance was invaluable, even as a young child. They had worked as a team. Sometimes she counted items and her father acted as scribe; sometimes they reversed roles. There were still pages in the old books on the office shelves with Sarah's large childish numbers meticulously listed in columns.

The shop had been in the family for almost three generations now. It was called "the shop" by everyone in the small Welsh village of Pen-y-Bryn quite simply because it was the only shop. Sarah's grandfather, Joseph Lewis, had been the first shopkeeper. Her father and aunt had taken over a few years before her grandfather's death. Now her aunt ran it alone with part-time help from Sarah and her mother.

The problem with being the sole retail establishment for the village was that it meant you had to stock everything from three-inch nails to cauliflower; pipe-cleaners to milk. As a child Sarah had always thought the back room of the shop was her very own

Aladdin's grotto. If you dug deep enough you could find almost anything. But now, as she sat chewing on her pencil and surveying the crowded shelves, it looked more like a lot of tedious work.

She heard the doorbell chime in the distance and the heavy tread of footsteps entering the shop. But Sarah didn't pay any heed to it until she heard her aunt's voice from behind the front counter.

"Can I help you sir?"

Sarah stopped tabulating numbers midstream, and raised her head with interest. A stranger? Having lived here all her life, Aunty Lil knew everybody in the community by name. They didn't get many visitors to Pen-y-Bryn. It was sufficiently off the beaten path to preclude the tourist traffic that frequented many of the other villages in mid-Wales.

"Sure! I'll take two of these candy bars please." He had a deep voice with a very distinct accent. Sarah heard the objects being placed on the counter and money exchanging hands. As the cash register rang out, the man's voice continued "I was also wondering if you could recommend somewhere my mother and I could stay near here? A guest house or bed and breakfast maybe?"

Sarah held her breath. There was only one bed and breakfast in the village. It was her house.

After her father's death two years before, she and her mother had been the only ones left at home. Her two brothers were already married. Kevin and his wife Mair lived on a farm about five miles away. John and Eileen were in south Wales for the time being. John was a banker and was transferred to a different branch of the bank every few years.

Since her sons were out on their own, Sarah's mother had decided to renovate their bedrooms. With some help from Kevin they added a small but serviceable bathroom to that part of the house, and listed the home as a 'bed and breakfast' establishment. Aunty Lil had clucked her tongue disapprovingly throughout the venture, but it had given her mother a much-needed diversion after the loss of her husband and, although the opportunities were infrequent, allowed her to use her abundant homemaking skills in making guests feel comfortable.

Sarah knew that if Aunty Lil had any hesitations about the character of the American in the shop, she would direct him to stay at the Black Swan Hotel in Llansilyn, six or seven miles away. The fact that he was American was not in question. Even if she had not heard his obvious accent she would have known. No one in Wales called chocolate a "candy bar"!

She heard footsteps again, this time her aunt's measured tread along with the man's. They were talking but Sarah couldn't make out what was being said. Overcome with curiosity, she inched her way down the step stool and quietly placed her papers on the floor. Quickly she tried to brush the dust off her pink T-shirt and faded jeans. The hair that had worked loose from her ponytail fell forward again. She brushed it back impatiently. She wasn't very presentable, so she would just peek.

She walked softly to the connecting doorway and was just in time to hear Aunty Lil say, ". . . and I'm sure you would find it suitable. If you follow this road just around the corner there . . . ."

They were walking towards the outer door and Aunty Lil was pointing down the lane that passed the shop and led to Sarah's home.

To her frustration, Sarah could see her aunt well, but her view of the visitor was obscured by shelves. She got an impression of blonde hair, long legs in blue jeans, and what appeared to be a tan, light-weight jacket covering broad shoulders.

". . . It's not more than a few hundred yards. A gray stone house with a navy-blue door. You'll see the sign in the front garden."

To Lil's obvious surprise, the man then grasped her aunt's hand and shook it. "Thank you so much. You've been very helpful."

Aunty Lil colored with pleasure. "Well, you're very welcome, I'm sure." The doorbell rang again and he was gone.

Sarah stepped into the shop. "Aunty Lil, who was that?"

"Well I never!" Aunty Lil was still slightly pink cheeked and looking a little bemused. "Umm, what was that dear?"

"Who was that man? You sent him on to our house didn't you?"

Aunty Lil ran her work-worn hands down her serviceable but faded floral apron, seemed to collect her thoughts, and finally focused on Sarah.

"Why yes dear, I did. He seemed to be a very nice young man. Yes indeed. Very polite too, and handsome. Didn't quite catch the name . . . Peterson, Pedersen, or something like that." She absentmindedly began rearranging the apples sitting in a box next to the counter. "Do you know, he reminds me of someone . . . perhaps . . . yes, y'know, I'm sure I've seen him on that *Dallas* program on the telly."

Sarah burst into laughter. "Aunty Lil, the only Americans you've ever seen are the actors on *Dallas* and the President when he's on the news."

Aunty Lil looked a bit sheepish. "Well, I dare say you're right dear. And he did look a bit young to be President."

Sarah grinned. "Oh well, if anyone can find out who he is and what he's doing in Pen-y-Bryn, Mam will!"

"You can be sure of that bach. The whole village will know within the hour." Aunty Lil gave a sniff that was intended to mean that she didn't approve one bit of her sister-in-law's tendency to chatter. Sarah hid a smile at the intentionally subtle reproof. She knew that beneath that prickly exterior beat the kind heart of someone who loved Sarah and her mother dearly. After all, they were almost all the family Aunty Lil had left.

Lillian Lewis was her father's only sister. She had never married and had lived in the flat above the shop ever since she was a young girl. She had co-owned the shop with her brother, Edward Lewis, and they had worked together daily. But each evening Edward, Sarah's father, had walked a short quarter of a mile down the lane from the shop to his own home, where his wife Annie and three children, Kevin, John, and Sarah were waiting with his dinner.

Mindful of his sister's single status, Edward and his wife had always tried to involve Lillian (or Lil as she was known by) in their family activities. She spent a great deal of time with Edward's family, and there could be no doubt that each of Edward's children held a special place in her heart. But she always found pleasure in returning to her own quiet haven above the shop. She was, by nature, fiercely independent and had capably taken control of the reins, running the shop quite successfully after her brother's death.

There was no question that she missed her brother. But in her mind, by continuing to operate the shop, she was showing her love for him, and doing what he would have wanted. She even felt it her duty to try and guide his widow against some of her more frivolous schemes (such as opening a bed and breakfast.) But to Lil's chagrin, Annie didn't give much heed to Lil's opinions unless they coincided with her own. Annie, it seemed, had her own share of the independent streak.

"How are you getting along?" Lil's question brought Sarah's thoughts back to the job at hand.

She groaned. "Oh, it's coming. But it's painfully slow."

Lil gave her a sympathetic nod and went back to rearranging apples. Her nonverbal message was clear. Time for pleasantries was over. It was back to work. Reluctantly, Sarah returned to the lists, ladder, and boxes.

ह ह ह

By Sarah's small wristwatch it was precisely forty-two minutes later when the front door bell rang again and Mabel Jones trotted in. Sarah stifled a giggle. The grapevine was really humming today. This must truly be news of note! Well worth setting aside her paperwork, she reasoned, and she stepped into the shop front just as Mabel set her wicker basket on the counter and launched into her gossip. Big news indeed. There was none of the usual opening small talk. She got right down to business.

"Well Lil, you'll never believe who's staying at Annie's place. Not in a million years." Mabel paused for effect, then continued. "No, you'll never guess so I'll have to tell you."

Leaning forward on the counter as though about to impart something top secret Mabel whispered, "Glyn and Mary Jones' granddaughter!" Despite her somewhat dramatic overture, Mabel Jones could hardly have asked for a better reaction from her audience. She leaned back and nodded slowly as fright, surprise, questioning disbelief, then reluctant curiosity flitted across Lil's face in turn.

Before Lil could say a word, Mabel continued. "Her name's Iris Pearson. She's here with her son. I didn't catch his name. Came to see where her grandparents came from. Can you imagine that? All the way from America just to see where Glyn and Mary used to live. And then to end up at Annie's. Well I never!"

Sarah sensed immediately that there was something underlying this conversation that she didn't understand. It wasn't so much what was being said as much as what was not being said.

"Who are Glyn and Mary Jones?" she asked.

Both ladies looked up startled. Neither had been aware of her silent entrance. A quick look passed between them.

"Oh for goodness sake Lil, Sarah's all of twenty-two," Mabel exclaimed.

"Twenty-three" Sarah corrected her.

"Are you really, bach? My how time flies! Well, I think you're old enough to hear the story. Besides it was long ago. Only us old ones even remember." She looked at Lil, as though awaiting approval.

Aunty Lil pursed her lips and frowned slightly. "Well the whole village will be buzzing with it before the sun sets" she sighed. "She's going to hear it anyway, more's the pity. I suppose it's best that she hears it here. Then I can correct any embellishments that may find their way into the story." She gave Mabel Jones a pointed look.

Mabel responded with a wry smile. "All right, all right. But Lil, you know as well as I do, there's hardly any facts to this story. The wonder of it was all the guessing people did. People had all sorts of grand ideas. Some of them were right romantic too. Mind you, there were some that weren't an' all."

"Mrs. Jones, why don't you tell me what you can?" Sarah was beginning to get a bit impatient with all the piecemeal information being bandied about.

"Right you are. And quite a story it is too. You see, Glyn Jones lived with his mam and dad up on Mynydd Mawr in the small farm house Tom and Cerys Roberts redid a few years back." Sarah nodded. She knew the old farm house. She delivered groceries there often. Cerys was a sweet girl, not much older than Sarah. She and her husband Tom had worked hard renovating the rather dilapidated main building to create their now cosy home.

"'Course in those days there weren't as many roads as there are now and that old house was pretty isolated and by all accounts quite primitive. Glyn's dad was a shepherd working for the Bixtons from Deniol Manor. Poor as church mice they were. Shepherding didn't pay well. Why they'd have even been without a roof over their heads if it wasn't for Squire Bixton letting them use the old farmhouse up there. Glyn's mam helped out a bit by taking in needlework. Quite a seamstress she was. People used to say her stitches were about invisible.

"When Glyn was old enough he went to work for the Squire too. Doing odd jobs around the manor. He was a nice boy they say. Always willin' to work and cheerful too.

"Anyway, it was at the manor that Glyn first saw Mary. Mary Williams, as she was then, was the daughter of the minister. Reverend William Williams took care of the preaching for the four chapels in the area. His church work kept him traveling quite a bit, but he checked in at Deniol Manor regularly. I think the Squire thought it would be good to be seen with the Methodist minister every once in a while even though he was Church of England himself. They were on quite friendly terms by all accounts.

"Young Mary often accompanied her father to the manor. Her Mam had passed away when she was a baby. She was a lot like her Mam I think. Yes indeed, a pretty little thing and quite the apple of her father's eye. I think he had high hopes for her—marrying well you know. And she might 'ave too if she hadn't gone an' fallen in love with Glyn."

Mabel Jones paused for a second, glanced over at Lil, then continued.

"Love at first sight, they said it was. For both of them. They didn't see each other much at first. Just at the manor. But they must have started seeing each other at other times too. Though no one knew it at the time of course. A big secret it was. They both knew her father would not 'ave approved at all. Not with all his high hopes for Mary. Glyn, for all his handsome looks and cheery disposition, just wasn't good enough.

"Well now, this is where the story gets a bit mysterious. No one really knows what happened for sure. One day everything was normal; the next day Glyn Jones and Mary Williams were gone. And no one ever saw either of them again. Reverend Williams was transferred to another diocese. Glyn's mam and dad moved away too. Some say the Squire made them go because of Glyn. But nobody seems to know for sure. Some of the other servants at the manor said that Glyn had talked about going to America. But they'd never really taken him seriously. Where would he come up with that kind of money?"

Mabel got a faraway look in her eye. "My, but there were all sorts of stories going round." She paused and glanced at Aunty Lil again, then added lamely, "but none of them were ever proven of course."

Sarah could well imagine the types of stories that were being spread about the couple. She had lived all her life aware of the village grapevine and the distortion caused by gossip. Truth and hearsay often had fuzzy edges. She felt instinctively sorry for Glyn and Mary who had probably been the fuel for all sorts of fabrications.

Aunty Lil cleared her throat, as if in an attempt to return the conversation to the here and now. "Well I dare say we'll all find out what happened soon enough. If this Mrs. Pearson is who she says she is, then she'll know more than the rest of us put together."

Mabel Jones wasn't quite ready for Lil's pragmatic return to reality. "But Lil," she said, "just think, after all these years, to suddenly turn up like this. And at Annie's of all places"!

"Well that's my fault and no one else's," retorted Lil. "The young man came into the shop and asked about a place to stay. He seemed a nice enough boy. I told him about Annie's bed and breakfast.

Sarah could tell by Aunty Lil's defensive answer, that there was still more to this story than she'd been told. But Mabel had not seemed to notice. Instead she pounced on another jewel. "Lillian Lewis, you've seen him!" she gasped. "Why didn't you say something? What's he like?"

Lil, obviously anxious to end her part in the story as quickly as she could, responded brusquely, "He was tall, blonde, and very polite." Then she turned and went back to rearranging apples in their box.

"Well I never!" breathed Mabel Jones and shook her head wonderingly. "What a day for Pen-y-Bryn."

Sarah took one look at her aunt's face and knew that discussion of this topic was over for the time being. But her curiosity was roused. The story she'd just heard should not have created a strained atmosphere in the shop, but it was most definitely there nonetheless. Even impervious Mabel Jones seemed to sense Lil's guarded apprehension. She opened her mouth to say something more, then abruptly changed her mind.

Instead, it was Lil who spoke first, and immediately steered the conversation onto more mundane things. "What can I get for you today, Mabel?"

Mabel glanced vaguely around the shop, as if searching for something. Her gaze fell upon a box of shining, red tomatoes.

"Oh, those look nice. I'll take a quarter pound of the tomatoes please."

"Yes, they do look good don't they? They're fresh in today." Then as an afterthought, Lil called to Sarah over her shoulder. "Sarah, be sure to take some home to your mother this evening. They won't be this nice for long."

Sarah nodded, silently acknowledging her dismissal. As she turned towards the back room, Aunty Lil was ringing up the tomatoes on the cash register. She and Mabel Jones were talking about the rising price of eggs. Things were back to normal. On the surface anyway.